Slowly the door behind him opened. There was no sound. An immaculately clad arm with a carefully starched cuff at the end of the dark sleeve drew nearer to the figure standing in the doorway. A strong brown hand, its nails meticulously groomed, politely but firmly took hold of Mr. Owen and deftly withdrew him from public circulation.

To be unceremoniously snatched through a doorway is almost invariably a disconcerting experience for anyone ... Quite naturally he was surprised by the size and magnificence of the establishment in which he found himself. He thought at first, from its noble proportions, that he was standing in some celestial railway terminal. The vast space was diffused with a soft yellow radiance shot with currents of sheer elation.

Only gradually was it that he became aware of the fact that he was standing in what could be nothing in the world other than a spacious and admirably planned department store, but such a department as he had never ever seen before!

By Thorne Smith
*Published by Ballantine Books:*

TOPPER

TOPPER TAKES A TRIP

THE NIGHT LIFE OF THE GODS

THE STRAY LAMB

RAIN IN THE DOORWAY

*TURNABOUT

*Coming soon from Del Rey/Ballantine Books

THORNE  SMITH

# Rain in the Doorway

A Del Rey Book

BALLANTINE BOOKS   •   NEW YORK

A Del Rey Book
Published by Ballantine Books

Library of Congress Catalog Card Number: 79-55331

ISBN 0-345-28727-4

Manufactured in the United States of America

First Ballantine Books Edition: September 1980

Cover art by Norman Walker

*For*
HELEN, KATHLEEN, *and* LILLIAN,
*for whom Allah be praised*

# Contents

# CHAPTER I

## *Waiting*

THE RAIN FALLING NOT MORE THAN A FOOT AND A half from the geographical tip of the nose outjutting from the face in the doorway had in it a quality of falsely apologetic but, nevertheless, stubbornly persistent despair.

It seeped under one's nerves, that rain, and left them uncomfortably soggy.

"Like a hypocritical old woman selfishly enjoying her misery all over the confounded house," reflected the face in the doorway. "That last drop actually sighed quaveringly on my nose. It's quite wet, my nose."

The face produced a handkerchief which had withstood, not without scars of service, the onslaughts of numerous laundries, and the wet nose was solicitously patted back to a state of dryness.

And when the face itself was once more disclosed to view from behind its crumpled concealment, no pedestrian on that rain-simmering street paused to view it. Not one pedestrian gave it so much as a passing glance. This universal lack of interest was apparently accepted by the face without bitterness or regret. It seemed to appreciate the fact that it was the type of face at which few persons ever troubled to look, and even when they did look they found no difficulty in pursuing the even tenor of their thoughts, assuming they had any to pursue. The face was well accustomed to being not looked at. Of late it had much preferred being not looked at. It had felt rather retiring and undressed, as if uncertain of the expression that might be surprised on its unremarkable surface.

This face was the exclusive property of a Mr. Hector

Owen. At the moment its moody eyes were staring from lean, bleak features through a vista of rain-drenched twilight upon the untidy prospect of Sixth Avenue at Fourteenth Street. The rumble of the elevated trains on the tracks above formed a monotonous background to his thoughts. Without his realizing it, colored electric lights were flashing in his mind. Eva Le Gallienne's theater kept reminding him that it was still there. A little farther down the street the stones of the armory bunched themselves together in the wet gloom as if desirous of a blanket.

Mr. Hector Owen's chief occupation in life was that of a sort of urban bailiff for a wealthy estate, the owners of which, so far as he could gather, spent nearly all of their time either in jail, in bed, or intoxicated, or in any combination of the three, such as intoxicated in bed, intoxicated in jail, or just simply intoxicated somewhere in Europe, and always in trouble.

There had been times—usually when Mr. Owen was reading letters from the heirs in difficulties or depositing untoiled for funds to their accounts—when he had secretly wished he too were intoxicated in bed or in jail or even right there at his desk. Any one of these places of intoxication would have been a welcome relief to Mr. Hector Owen of the legal profession if not of the legal mind.

Recently there had been increasing agitation on the part of the heirs—probably the disgruntled result of an especially virulent hangover—to transfer the estate from the conscientious hands of Mr. Owen to the less human but more efficient management of a trust company. And this agitation had been augmented by the fact that he was unreasonably held accountable for the strange disappearance of one of the estate's most invaluable heirs, one who had mysteriously ceased to offend the public eye. The remaining drunken or bedridden or incarcerated heirs were considerably worked up over this. In the absence of anyone better to blame, they became indignant at Mr. Owen. They demanded that he return to them at once the missing heir. They desired this missing heir not because they had affectionate natures or felt in the least responsible or were in any way decent minded or public spirited. Probably they would have been gratified had Mr. Owen returned the missing heir to them quite dead. In lieu of a death certificate or a dead body, they earnestly desired the signature of the missing heir in order to dispose of enough real estate to enable them to pursue uncramped their lives of lavish debauchery.

Accordingly the shadow of the trust company lay across Hector Owen's business like a threat of suffocation. It lay across more than his business. It darkened his entire life, for without that estate to manage there would not be enough left of the Owen law practice upon which even the thinnest shadow could sprawl with any measure of comfort. That missing heir was essential to the man's continued existence. Also, in a lesser degree, it was essential to the happiness of Lulu Owen, his wife. Of course Lulu had money of her own, but of late Hector had rather begun to suspect that his wife regarded her money as entirely and exclusively her own while the money he made she considered in the light of a joint income in which he held the short end.

This was by no means the only thing he had begun to suspect of Lulu, and these suspicions served to intensify the steadily deepening shadow through which he had been laboring during the last six months of depression. Only this morning a tentative draft of the estate, or trust, transfer had been laid before him together with a covering letter signed somewhat shakily by all of the heirs but one, and that one was still missing.

Inwardly, as he stared misanthropically at the rain-dimpled surface of the street, Hector Owen cursed the missing heir. The fact that the missing heir was a girl, a girl, young and beautiful though no better than she should be, if as good, diminished neither the size nor sincerity of Mr. Owen's oaths. He cursed her sexlessly and selflessly like God berating the world. While the missing signature of this loose creature prevented him from carrying out the wishes of the other heirs to their entire satisfaction, it did not prevent them from carrying off their estate to some trust company to his utter and eternal undoing. Mr. Hector Owen was not temperamentally equipped to compete for business in the modern marts of law. The estate business upon which he depended had been a legacy from his father, who in turn had received it in the same convenient manner.

Standing there in that doorway, Hector Owen had much more than enough to think about. Any one of his thoughts would have been sufficient to send a heart far stouter than his down for the third time. Especially the one about Lulu and Mal Summers. That was a black thought indeed. A man could not very well walk up to his wife and say: "By the way, darling, yesterday you spent a pleasant but nevertheless highly adulterous afternoon with a dirty snake in the grass by the name of Mal Summers." His wife would promptly accuse him of having an evil mind, after which she would throw things at him and end up by packing her suitcase during a protective fit of hysteria.

Nothing could ever be settled that way. Nothing ever was. Although he was morally certain of his facts, he could confront her with no shred of actual proof. And even had he been in a position to say: "Yesterday, my dear, I enjoyed the somewhat doubtful privilege of being present though concealed while you and one of my alleged friends conducted yourselves in a manner which, to say the least, was disillusioning"—even had Mr. Owen been prepared to make this statement he would have balked at it like a nervous horse. In spite of his legal training his reticent nature, inhibited as it was by all sorts of gentlemanly instincts, would have pleaded with him to remain silent. Mr. Owen had one of those visual minds that beheld in graphic detail the things of which he spoke. Anyway, he was sufficiently well acquainted with his wife to forecast the nature of her reply. That good lady would indubitably have told him with bafflingly feminine sophistry: "In the first place, you wouldn't have been there if you hadn't an evil mind, and, in the second place, if you hadn't an evil mind I wouldn't have been there myself."

It never occurred to the less quick-witted Mr. Owen to admit quite frankly that he had an evil mind. For some strange and unexamined reason it is an admission few persons care to make, even those whose minds are a great deal more than evil. Yet, if the simple truth were known, everyone has an evil mind when it comes to such matters, and if they have not, they are extremely dumb, or indifferent to a fault.

Hector Owen was neither dumb nor indifferent. His face, such as it was, had looked out on the passing of thirty-eight neat, orderly, uneventful years. Although it was not a face to attract at first glance, it was one that amply justified a second. It was a keen face in a quiet way, keen, thoughtful, and sentient. A trifle long, with high cheek bones, and lips of a rather attractively unplanned pattern. It could look exceedingly mournful, as it did now, this face, and even when the lips arranged themselves in a smile, the blue eyes above responded slowly, as if skeptical of the levity taking place below. This gave to Mr. Owen's smile a sort of double emphasis, and made it something to be pleasantly remembered. It was such a slow, well considered smile that the observer found himself, or herself, in a position to get to know all of it. One felt that one had played a helpful part in this smile—participated at its birth, so to speak.

Among his various other incongruities was the studious dignity with which he moved his five feet eight inches of slim body from place to place. He was by nature a jointy sort of an animal whom God or evolution had designed to assume a lounging attitude towards life, yet Mr. Owen, for some stuffy reasons of his own, had seen fit to set these intentions aside by imposing on his person a bearing of austere restraint. This made it all the more alarming when Mr. Owen, unexpectedly seized by some lighter impulse, was discovered in the act of twirling experimentally on his toes or thoughtfully moving his feet to the rhythm of some secret melody. In spite of the rigorous restraint he placed upon his actions, he was occasionally subject to these seemingly frivolous seizures. Those who beheld them carried away the impression that they had witnessed something only a little short of a resurrection, and were for the rest of the day depressed by the instability of matter.

In private life Mr. Owen, with the tactful aid of his wife, had come to regard himself as one who danced uninspiredly, mixed even worse, and who understood the social amenities not at all.

However, he had his moments of rebellion—moments when he refused to accept his wife's valuations either of himself or of life, and when he gave inner voice to the opinion that Lulu's friends were for the most part common, coarse, uninteresting men and women who upon the loss of their sexual powers would have nothing else left in life. These moments were not so rare as they were self-contained. Leading so much as he did through his professional activities the lives of others, he had developed an elaborate private or secret life of his own. And this secret life was composed of many and various lives which fortunately for society, but unhappily for himself, he would never live in reality. Of course, it was nothing less than a system of escape set up to provide Mr. Hector Owen with the excitement and self-esteem his days so sorely lacked.

For example, there were mornings when he arose with the well considered opinion that had he the time and opportunity he could become a moving-picture actor of no mean ability. On other mornings he was content to be merely an inspired director. There were other moments when he quite modestly decided that if he only set his mind on it he could dance with the best of them and sleep with the worst. The detached manner in which he arrived at this last conclusion softened somewhat its lewd character. On occasions Hector's suppressed ego would be satisfied with the part of a victorious general leading his troops not only into battle, but also clean through the lines and out on the other side while even the enemy cheered. The safe arrival of himself and his troops on the other side pleased him a great deal more than the actual shedding of blood itself. The enemy cheering, he thought, was a nice touch. He had no desire to shed the blood of those brave and cheering soldiers.

As a matter of fact, he had no desire to shed any blood at all save that of the missing heir and Mr. Mal Summers, who had become such a humid friend of the family. Mal's blood he would have gladly extracted with an eye dropper. To have observed him seated solemnly at his desk earlier in the day, no one would have suspected that Mr. Hector Owen, the third in an honorable line of lawyers, was happily watching himself in his mind's eye as he busily went about the business of extracting drops of Mr. Mal Summers's blood, searching with diligent patience from vein to vein until not a drop of the unfortunate gentleman's blood remained to foul another nest

In his more serious moments Mr. Owen saw himself in the flattering rôle of a leader and liberator of men, swaying them by the sheer intellectual vigor of his reason and the measured eloquence of his winged words. That he was not and never would be even the least of the characters he felt himself so well qualified to become occasionally depressed him. However, owing to the fact that even while envying the good fortune of one of his creations he was already arranging for himself another career of equal honor and distinction, his moods of depression were of short duration. And inasmuch as no one suspected the man of entertaining such mad thoughts of self-aggrandizement in his seemingly sober mind, no harm was done to anyone, and Mr. Owen was better able to struggle through the day, scrutinizing bills and speculating idly as to the number and quality of the mistresses jointly maintained by the heirs. It faintly amused him to reflect that although he knew none of these women he could walk into their apartments at any time of the year and tell them where their underthings came from, how much they cost, and give each article its technical classification. Occasionally he toyed with the idea of calling one of them up and inquiring how she enjoyed her last selection of Naughties or if she was making out any better in the recent delivery of Speedies.

Yes, Hector Owen's life was extremely secret and, it is to be feared, not always nice, which is, of course, part of the fun in having a secret life. Good clean thoughts no doubt have their place in the scheme of things, but there is nothing so satisfactory as a good evil one unless it is the deed itself. And this is especially true when the evil thought can be hurled with crackling vigor into the innocuous ranks of a lot of neatly dressed clean ones.

Of Mrs. Lulu Owen it would be perhaps more charitable to say that she was merely a female member of the race, and let matters stand at that. In so far as she presented to the world in the form of an agreeable body those time-honored dips and elevations so commonly found diverting by members of the opposite sex Mrs. Lulu Owen was every inch a woman. True enough, the elevations were threatening to become immensities and the dips were gradually growing less alluringly pronounced. Still, with regular exercise and careful dieting, the charming creature had at least ten good years of sheer animalism ahead of her. After that she would probably become active in a movement whose aim was a constructive criticism of the morals and manners of the young.

Lulu was such a creature of sex that she never found time to stop to have a baby, which shows that the modern conception of the cave man and woman is a totally erroneous one. Cave people got busy about sex only by fits and starts, and these opportunities were much rarer than is commonly supposed. One cannot become very sexy in the presence of a frowning Ichthyosaurus, while one glance at an enraged Mammoth is quite sufficient to make the ruggedest voluptuary forget all about sex save perhaps has own, which, if he is in his right mind, he will remove from the scene of danger as speedily as possible.

Lulu was not at all like a cave woman. She was impurely a modern creation. There was nothing frank about her. Nor could it be said of Lulu Owen that she was lacking in mentality. She had a mind quite definitely her own. It was one of those small, unimaginative, competently dishonest compositions that can twist its owner out of all tight places while others are left stupidly holding the bag. It is an exceedingly valuable type of mind to have if one wants to live comfortably in the world as it is constituted today. Although adept in the art of registering all the nicer and more conventional emotions, she was capable of responding sincerely to only the most elementary, such as hunger, cold, heat, anger, greed, gratified vanity, fear, and, of course, all sorts of sex stimuli in little and large degree. In short, she was no better nor worse than thousands of other men and women who for lack of a more accurate name are loosely classified as human beings in contradistinction to their betters, the brute beasts.

And the irony of it was that Mr. Hector Owen had always considered her just about the finest woman, the most desirable creature and the loveliest spirit that had ever sacrificed herself to the coarse and selfish impulses of man. Thus it has always been.

As a lover his wife had always found Mr. Owen far from satisfactory. To her way of thinking the bed was no place for vaguely poetic fancies or idly philosophical discourses such as her husband habitually indulged in as he eased his various joints and members into what he fondly hoped would be both a pleasant and comfortable ensemble. It was all quite simple to the lady. One went to bed either to sleep or not to sleep.

It is to be feared that Lulu Owen was not much of a companion. Of recent months her husband had come to suspect as much. Although they carried on more or less as usual, their words ceased to have any special value or meaning. They were merely words dropped at random like so many scraps of paper about the room, then later collected and carelessly tossed away.

Hector was not the man to thrive under this sort of existence. His wife was indifferent to it. As long as men continued to inhabit the world she would have enough food for thought to occupy her mind. Hector was not so easily satisfied. He was growing afraid to think at all. He was still sufficiently old-fashioned to want his wife to be exactly that, to want her also to be a companion, an audience, admirer, and what not. He did not demand so much in the line of admiration—merely an occasional word or so, a small scrap to make a man feel a little less grim and alone.

When eventually it was borne in on his consciousness that in Lulu he could find none of these sources of comfort, he was surprised no less than distressed. He had married her under the impression that she was a

delicately complex creature of many charming moods
and fancies. Now he found her no better than a sleeping and eating partner. He might just as well have a
great big beautiful cat in the house. A cat would be an
improvement, in fact. Cats did not give utterance to
hateful, goading remarks and pack suitcases and slam
doors and hurl books and talk for hours of their sacri-
fices in life and the innumerable stitches of clothing
they did not have to their backs. Yes, taking everything
into consideration, a cat would most decidedly be a
welcome relief.

Yet, in spite of this knowledge, there he stood waiting in the rain for this very wife to whom he would
have preferred a cat. Certainly, he decided, he would
not have stood there waiting for all the cats in the
world. Why, then, should he wait for his wife, who was
not as good as any one of all these cats? It did not
seem reasonable. Why not tell her to go incontinently
and blithely to hell for all time, and then walk diago-
nally across Sixth Avenue to that speakeasy where he
could get himself as wet inside as most people seemed
to be outside? Better still, why not grab off some
wench and ply her with gin and improper proposals?
Why not make a night of it? It had been years since he
had made a night of it. And then it had not been a
whole night, nor had he made so much of it. He still
had money enough in his pocket to buy the companionship he lacked at home. Some of these Greenwich
Village speakeasy girls were good sports, he had been
told—rough and unreliable but good hearted and regular. They understood men and knew how to please
them. He would get himself one of those.

Strangely impelled by the fascination and the prospect of immediate release presented by this daring idea,
Hector Owen's secret life was about to merge for once
with his real one. He cast a swift, bright glance across
the street and was on the point of directing his feet to
follow the path taken by his eyes when a face peered in
at him through the curtain of the rain.

# CHAPTER II

## *In The Doorway*

EVER SINCE HE HAD ARISEN THAT MORNING HECTOR Owen had been increasingly aware of the presence of his head—unpleasantly aware of it. The roots of his fine, light, strailing hair seemed to be unduly sensitive today. Each root prickled ever so faintly. Taken collectively these insignificant individual manifestations formed an irritating whole. And the scalp in which Mr. Owen's various hairs were somewhat casually imbedded according to no plan or design hitherto devised by God or man showed a decided disposition to tightness. Farther back a dull buzzing like the far-away droning of bees, or more like a wasp in a hot attic, had been accompanying his thoughts with monotonous regularity. Taking it all in all, it was a peculiar sort of head for a man to be lugging about with him on his shoulders, Mr. Owen decided. There were too many thoughts in it beating against his skull in fruitless effort to escape. He heartily wished they could escape and give him a moment's peace—especially those thoughts associated with his wife and Mal Summers, the rebellious estate and the trust company, his automobile and its overdue payments, certain life insurance premiums, and, finally, a neat sheaf of bills for the various stitches of clothes that Lulu tragically told the world she never had to her smooth, well nourished back. Yes, there were far too many thoughts.

Also, there was another source of worry in Mr. Owen's mind. This last one was especially upsetting. So much so that Hector Owen almost feared to admit the truth of it even to himself. The fact is, all that day he had been mysteriously experiencing the most confounding difficulty in recognizing faces which from long years of familiarity he had come to know, if anything, too well. At breakfast that morning Lulu's face had presented itself to him as a confusing smear; which was not at all unusual for Lulu's face at breakfast on the rare occasions of its appearance there. What had worried Mr. Owen, however, was the fact that, so far as he was able to make out, there had been nothing reminiscently characteristic about this particular smear moving opposite him at the table. It might just as well have been made by a demon or an angel. There was nothing definitely Lulu about that smear. And even before breakfast his own face, as he had studied it in the bathroom mirror, had struck him as being only faintly familiar. There had been a dimness about its features and a strangely distressed expression round the eyes.

Disconcerted, he had glanced over his shoulder to ascertain if some perfect stranger had not by chance strayed into the room and become absorbed in watching Mr. Owen shave. Some men were like that, he knew—fascinated by anything pertaining to razors and their use. There was something in it. The sandy, crackling sound emitted by severed whiskers was not unpleasant to the ear. He had always enjoyed it himself. The thought had even occurred to him sardonically at the time that this strange person behind him might be one of the more daring of Lulu's many callers who, unable to wait longer, had preferred to risk the displeasure of the master of the house rather than to offend the laws of common decency. The situation had tickled some low chord in Mr. Owen's nature until he had discovered he was quite alone in the room. For the sake of his reason he would almost have welcomed the presence of a lover.

This difficulty about faces had continued with him throughout the day. At the office his clerks and stenographers, even old Bates, his comfort in times of storm, had displayed only the remotest semblance to their former selves. Then, too, why had he suddenly and amazingly asked himself, or rather his secret self, who for the moment seemed to be sitting unobserved beside him in the elevated train, what business had they on that untidy, jarring conveyance, and why were they worming their way downtown with a lot of damp, uninteresting people? Why had he unaccountably questioned the almost ritualistic routine of a lifetime? Was the world receding from him, or was his mind gradually growing dim, so that only faint traces of the past remained? Something was definitely wrong with his usually clear head.

Now, when this face unexpectedly thrust itself through the curtain of the rain, Mr. Owen was seized with the conviction that he was going a little mad.

Involuntarily he asked: "Do I look much like you?"

"Huh?" replied the face, startled, then added gloomily, "It's wet."

"What's wet?" asked Mr. Owen.

"Me," said the man in a husky voice. "Everything—the hull world."

"You're right there," Mr. Owen agreed. "The world's all wet."

The moist, unadmirable figure that had materialized out of the rain thrust forward a head from between shoulders hunched from sheer wet discomfort, and two gin-washed eyes studied Mr. Owen humbly.

"Yuss," said the man emphatically, but without much expectation. "And I want a nickel."

"What for?" Mr. Owen inquired, more for the purpose of holding his thoughts at bay than for the gratification he would derive from the information.

"Wanter go ter Weehawken," replied the man.

"You want to go to Weehawken." Mr. Owen was frankly incredulous. "Why do you want to go there?"

"I've a flop in Weehawken," said the man in the rain.

"I'd rather die on my feet," Mr. Owen observed, more to himself than to his companion. "As a matter of fact, if someone gave me a nickel, that would be the last place I'd think of going."

"Is that so!" replied the man, stung to a faint sneer. "Where do yer want me ter go?"

"Away," said Owen briefly.

"I will," answered the man, "if you'll slip me a piece of change."

"All right," agreed the other, "but tell me first, is

there any faint resemblance between my face and yours? I have an uneasy impression there is."

For a moment the man considered the face in the doorway.

"Maybe a little round the eyes there is," he admitted.

"Only round the eyes?" Mr. Owen pursued with rising hope.

The man nodded thoughtfully.

"Well, thank God for that," said Mr. Owen in a tone of relief. "Here's a whole quarter."

The man accepted the coin which he scrutinized in the dim light.

"It's a new one," he observed. "All bright and shiny, ain't it? One of them new Washington quarters."

"Do you like it?" asked Mr. Owen politely.

"Yuss," replied the man, still scanning the face on the coin. "That must be old George hisself—a fine American, he was."

"Sure," agreed Mr. Owen. "A splendid chap, George, but I've a sneaking feeling that if the father of his country came back thirsty he'd jolly well disinherit his child and start a private revolution of his own."

"How do yer mean, mister?" the man asked suspiciously.

"Simply this," Mr. Owen told him. "If you spend that quarter for a couple of shots of smoke, as your breath assures me you will, there is a strong possibility that you will go blind and won't be able to admire the face of the man who fought for your rights and mine."

The wet figure considered this a moment.

"You must be one of them reds," he voiced at last.

"If you mean one of those snotty little teacup radicals who mutilate horses with nails stuck in planks, I'll take that quarter back," Mr. Owen declared. "As a matter of fact," he added, "I'm feeling blue as hell."

Once more the soggy man studied the face in the doorway. When he spoke there was an altered quality in his voice.

"It's the eyes," he said slowly. "I can always tell by the eyes. Yours don't look so good—look like they might hurt yer even more than mine—inside."

It was an odd remark. Mr. Owen thought it over.

"You have little left to lose," he told the man. "I am still watching everything slide down the skids."

"When it's all gone," the man assured him, "it won't seem so bad. I stopped minding years ago. Didn't have much ter begin with. All gone and forgotten. Don't know where the hell she is or they are or——"

"Please don't," said Mr. Owen firmly. "If you don't mind, I'd rather you wouldn't today. Why don't you go to the Zoo with some of that quarter and see if you wouldn't rather exchange your liberty for the life of a caged beast? I envy the life of a yak myself."

"What's yak, mister?"

Hector Owen made an attempt, then abandoned the effort.

"It's too hard to describe in the rain," he said.

"Guess yer don't know yerself," allowed the man.

"Are you trying to irritate me into describing a yak for you?" Mr. Owen inquired. "That's childish."

"No," replied the man. "I was just wondering why, if yer so mad about yaks, yer didn't go and look at some yerself."

"I didn't say I was mad about yaks," Mr. Owen retorted. "And, anyway, I'm waiting."

"Yer mean, waiting for a better day ter look at yaks?" the man persisted.

"No," said Mr. Owen with dignity. "Let us not pursue yaks. Sorry I brought them up. I'm waiting for my wife."

"Are the skids under her, too?" asked the man.

"I'm not worrying so much about what's under her," replied Mr. Owen.

"Oh," said the other. "So it's like that. Guess I'll be shoving off."

"Wish I could," observed Mr. Owen moodily. "I object to waiting here like the very devil and all."

"That's all I seem ter be doing," said the other, merging once more with the rain until his voice came back only faintly. "Just hanging about waiting for something to happen, and nothing ever does. I'll drift along."

And the figure, looking strangely disembodied,

moved off wetly down the glistening street. Deprived of the conversational relief afforded by the soggy man, Mr. Owen turned to examine the door in which he was standing. He had examined it many times before, but always with an idly inattentive eye. Now, in order to occupy his mind, he looked about him with almost desperate concentration. He would think about that doorway and not about all those other old unhappy things. Inevitably they would return to claim his entire attention, but not now. He would look at things—at anything.

It was a deeply recessed doorway formed by two jutting plate-glass windows. The windows were filled with a discouraging array of uninspired looking commodities, so uninspired looking, in fact, that Mr. Owen would almost have preferred his thoughts. He found himself almost surrounded and borne down by an avalanche of men's clothes in the worst possible taste. They were cheap, they were false, they were fancy. Yet, strangely enough, amid those flamboyant ranks of sartorial futility would appear with puzzling incongruity a stout pair of overalls or a rugged group of roustabout shoes. A wasp-waisted dress suit would find its shoddy shoulders rubbing against those of an uncompromisingly honest union suit, a fancy shirt would be forced to endure the presence of one made of sailcloth or khaki. A display of dress studs and cuff links would have as a background a grim row of tin lunch boxes. It was as if the individual who had decorated those windows had endeavored to keep an impartial mind concerning the relative importance of the laboring man and that of his more frivolous brothers who habitually loafed along Fourteenth Street and infested its gaudy dance halls, burlesque shows, and Chinese restaurants.

For some reason the sounds in the street were growing dim in his ears. Gradually the familiar scene around him was becoming strangely altered in appearance. Mr. Owen was giving credence to the belief that he was standing in a new city, in a different doorway, and that nothing and no one in this city bore any relation to him. The buzzing in his head had increased to a torrential roar. He was tingling with a feeling that something not far off now was going to happen most amazingly. Whether it was going to be in the nature of a rescue or a disaster he did not know, nor did he greatly care. He was mortally tired of thinking about himself, his wife, and those confounded heirs.

A heavy-lidded woman sinfully trailing the scent of moist but dying camellias drifted up to the door. For a moment she raised her shadowed lids and looked up at Mr. Owen. Then she spoke to him in a low voice.

"Hello, sad eyes," she said. "What are you doing tonight?"

Mr. Owen was startled by the sound of his own voice no less than by the readiness of his reply.

"Nothing to you, sister," he answered. "I'm waiting for my wife."

"Just a home body, eh?" observed the woman. "A clean little home body."

"The body's clean," agreed Mr. Owen, "but it isn't so very little. And why shouldn't it have a home?"

The woman looked a little downcast.

"I was a home body myself," she said, "once upon a time, but now I just taxi about."

"Well," Mr. Owen told her, experiencing a sudden pang of fellow feeling for this creature out in the rain, "if it's any consolation, you're playing an open game, which is a damned sight cleaner than cheating."

"They're the worst kind," replied the woman wisely. "The only way to get the best of a cheater is to cheat her first yourself. Sure you won't give her a stand-up for once?"

"No," said Mr. Owen. "That's just the trouble. I'm not at all sure. Be a good girl and hurry away without looking back."

Mr. Owen's eyes, a study in conflicting impulses, gazed through the rain after the heavy-lidded woman as she disappeared down the street. Idly he wondered what sort of man she would meet up with that night and what sort of time they would have.

"She seemed to take to me rather," he mused to himself, not without a small glow of inner warmth. "If I stand here long enough I'll become a well known figure," he went on. "I've met almost everybody except my wife." He took out a cigarette and lighted it, his hands cupped against the rain. "The trouble with me is," he resumed to himself, "I let myself get drawn into things altogether too easily."

Slowly the door behind him opened. There was no sound. An immaculately clad arm with a carefully starched cuff at the end of the dark sleeve drew nearer to the figure standing in the doorway. A strong, brown hand, its nails meticulously groomed, politely but firmly took hold of Mr. Owen and deftly withdrew him from public circulation.

Ten minutes later when Lulu Owen arrived at the spot with her excuses already straining on the tip of her glib tongue she was greatly chagrined to discover that Mr. Owen was gone. And only the butt of his still smouldering cigarette gave evidence that he had once been there.

## CHAPTER III

### Snatched Through

To BE UNCEREMONIOUSLY SNATCHED THROUGH A doorway is almost invariably a disconcerting experience for anyone—especially when the person snatched has every reason to believe that the door was securely locked, with no living creature behind it of more sinister aspect than a cat, a large store cat whose business lay chiefly with mice. Now, the surprising feature of Mr. Hector Owen's experience was that he felt no sensation of disconcertion at all, or hardly any. His first reaction to the sudden change was one of profound relief. There was an immediate dropping away of anxiety and responsibility, a sort of spiritual sloughing off of all moral obligations. In their place flooded in a glorious feeling of newness, freedom, and rebirth, that buoyancy which comes when one awakens fresh on a fine morning with the knowledge that one has something especially agreeable to do that day. In his quiet, self-contained way Mr. Owen was convinced that he not only felt younger than he had for many a year but also that he was actually younger and looked it.

Quite naturally he was surprised by the size and magnificence of the establishment in which he found himself. He thought at first, from its noble proportions, that he was standing in some celestial railway terminal. The vast space was diffused with a soft yellow radiance shot with currents of sheer elation. There was a fascinating fragrance in the air about him, tantalizing in its diversity. The aroma of coffee, the scent of soaps, spice and perfumes, the vague, indefinable breath given off by new materials, rugs, and furniture, and the pleasing tang of leather goods drifted past his keenly alert nose like so many little unseen sails on a calm, invisible sea.

Only gradually was it that he became aware of the fact that he was standing in what could be nothing in the world other than a spacious and admirably planned department store, but such a department store as he had never been dragged through at the heels of a ruthlessly spendthrift Lulu in some dimly remembered reincarnation.

From a large central plaza broad aisles between handsome rows of counters radiated in all directions like spokes in a giant wheel. And Mr. Owen's roving and rejuvenated eyes noted with a thrill of gratification a number of remarkably good-looking salesgirls standing in happy profusion behind the counters. From any one of these young women Mr. Owen would have eagerly purchased practically anything he could have induced her to sell.

The roof of the store was lofty. Like the sky itself, it curved out from a dim central dome and seemed to run away into mysteriously shadowed infinity. Balcony upon balcony, with gay and graceful balustrades, circled round the huge hall and mounted dizzily skyward, each balcony presenting itself to Mr. Owen's fascinated eyes as a fresh plane of discovery in an altogether new universe. Through wide doorways opening on gracious vistas Mr. Owen caught glimpses of a broad boulevard spiritedly splashed with sidewalk cafés at which men and women were eating and drinking and reading the newspapers and making improper proposals to each other, as men and women will upon the slightest provocation and even without. And who would not make improper proposals in such a delightful atmosphere, Mr. Owen asked himself? He himself would like to make some perfectly terrific ones right there and then to any number of salesgirls. And surely improper proposals were the only proper ones to make when surrounded by so much beauty. Chivalry was taking a new lease on life in Mr. Owen's breast. He would bide his time, however, before risking any of the proposals he had at that moment in mind.

From the street scene his eyes were attracted by an unprecedented burst of activity taking place at one of the counters near which he was standing. As he watched this activity he decided to defer his proposals indefinitely. It was activity of a decidedly unpropitious nature. Mr. Owen was vaguely aware of the presence of a gentleman standing beside him. This gentleman seemed also to be absorbed in what was going on. His being exuded an atmosphere of pleasant anticipation. Mr. Owen could hardly understand the reason for this because what he saw going on struck him as being anything but pleasant. In fact, it was the very last thing he would have expected to witness in such an obviously fashionable and well regulated establishment.

What Mr. Owen saw was bad enough, but the sounds that accompanied it were even worse. A young and beautiful salesgirl had reached across the counter separating her from her customer and had angrily seized the customer's nose in a grip of eternal animosity. The customer, one of those large, officious, disagreeably arrogant ladies who infest department stores, was emitting a volley of objectionable and highly unladylike noises. But above her voice came the clear, crisp, furious words of the salesgirl.

"You mean-spirited, over-stuffed, blue-faced old baboon, you wicked-hearted old cow walrus," said the salesgirl, "take that and that and that."

The that and that and that designated three separate and distinct tweaks administered to the nose of the customer. Mr. Owen was faintly surprised and not a little relieved that the appendage did not come away in the salesgirl's fingers. He turned to his companion, and was even more surprised to find him murmuring delightedly to himself.

"Good!" the gentleman was ejaculating under his breath. "Oh, very, very good, in fact, capital. Titanic tweaks. By gad, sir, they fairly sizzle."

He smiled upon Mr. Owen, who stood regarding him with dazed eyes.

"Are we both seeing the same thing?" Mr. Owen asked somewhat timidly. "A lady being assaulted by one of your salesgirls?"

"The same thing, my dear sir," replied the man proudly in a voice of polished courtesy. "The same thing exactly. Isn't she doing splendidly?"

"Splendidly!" gasped Mr. Owen. "She's doing it brutally. Nearly murdering the woman."

The gentleman regarded the tweaking scene with an air of professional detachment.

"But not quite," he commented. "Do you see the woman whose nose is being tweaked? Well, she's a most pestiferous old bitch." Mr. Owen drew a sharp breath. "Yes, yes," the gentleman went on almost gayly, "most pestiferous old bitch describes her nicely—a regular she-dragon. And a bully. Attend a moment and you will see something amusing. Watch how she gets hers."

To the accompaniment of chuckles and muttered exclamations of encouragement from his strange companion, such as, "Boost the old bird in the bottom," and "I fancy that old fright will never show up here any more," Mr. Owen watched the she-dragon literally get hers. And he was forced to admit to himself that from the looks of the lady she was getting no more than she deserved. From all directions sales attendants were rushing down the aisles, converging *en masse* on the assaulted woman and showering her with a deluge of violent language. Everyone who could find space on her person to grab laid violent hands on it, whatever it chanced to be, and the lady was hurtled through the store and hurled out upon the street. Upon the completion of this apparently popular task the group of attendants broke up into individual units and returned quietly to their places as if nothing had occurred. The salesgirl who had started the trouble, now all smiles and helpfulness, promptly began to assist another lady, whose gentle manner, Mr. Owen decided, belied an intrepid spirit, to match a length of ribbon.

Turning once more to his companion, Mr. Owen was momentarily upset to find himself being happily beamed upon from that direction. What manner of man was he, Mr. Owen found himself wondering? Externally, the man appeared to be a person of refinement, not to say distinction. He was no taller than Mr. Owen himself, and of the same general physique, although he carried himself far more debonairly than Mr. Owen had ever dreamed of attempting at his most heady moments.

The gentleman's complexion, Mr. Owen noted, was darkly olive and smooth. Two brown eyes of a subtly insinuating cast, but now eloquent with well being, sparkled and snapped beneath fine, graceful eyebrows. About the man there seemed to hover a faint suggestion of danger, recklessness, and unscrupulous enterprise. Behind the brown eyes glittered, or seemed to glitter, an inner preoccupation with affairs not generally considered nice. The man's hair was smooth, like the rest of him, smooth and black. There was just a touch of scent—not bad—and at the temples a sprinkling of gray. Two rows of white, even teeth formed a background for a pair of firm lips which to Mr. Owen seemed capable of uttering the most hair-raising blasphemies with all the unconscious charm of a child murmuring to itself in its sleep. He was faultlessly attired in a morning coat and striped trousers. There were spats. This last item strengthened Mr. Owen's conviction that he was standing in the presence of a person whom one should meet with reservation and follow with the utmost caution. The gentleman now addressed Mr. Owen in an engaging tone of voice.

"You are, my friend, I see," he said, "somewhat puzzled by the little affair you have just witnessed?"

Catching the rising inflection in the other's voice Mr. Owen assumed his words to be couched in the form of a polite but superfluous inquiry.

"Quite naturally," he replied a little sharply. "I am not accustomed to seeing respectable-looking ladies set upon by a howling mob, and violently flung out of doors. Who wouldn't be surprised?"

"I wouldn't, for one," the gentleman answered equably. "And I could name thousands of others. We're quite used to that sort of thing here."

"Do you mean to say," demanded Mr. Owen, "that you permit your sales people to toss perfectly respectable customers out *ad lib?*"

"More at random," the gentleman decided, eyeing Mr. Owen with an amused smile, "although your *ad lib* is pretty close to the mark. Furthermore, respectability doesn't count with us here. We find it exceedingly trying." With a shocked feeling Mr. Owen found himself unconsciously agreeing with the speaker. Respectability could be trying. "And anyway," the gentleman was running on, "that old devil wasn't really respectable, not honestly so. She derives her income from some of the most unentertaining resorts—you get what I mean (Mr. Owen was afraid he did)—in town, or rather I should say from some of the least entertaining, for none of them is really unentertaining. Like whiskies, some are merely better than others. I never visit hers myself, but I'll take you to some dandy ones I've recently discovered."

"Aren't we getting a little off the point?" Mr. Owen hastily put in. "We were talking about the lady."

"What?" said the gentleman. "Oh, yes, I forgot. Well, remind me about the other things. We'll take those up later together with several other delightfully vicious resorts you'll find amusing. Now, about that old sea cow—that walrus woman. We simply loathe her. On and off, she's been annoying us for years."

"I doubt if she does any more," commented Mr. Owen, smiling in spite of himself.

"I hope, I hope most sincerely, she does not," the

man continued quite seriously. "You see, my dear sir, it is an old trade custom of ours—a tradition, in fact—that whenever customers become unendurably overbearing with any member of our sales force we throw 'em out on their ear regardless of the sex of the ear. It makes no difference with us whether it's a man's ear, a woman's, or a child's. I'm told my clerks call it the 'bum's rush,' but of course I make it a point to frown on the use of such expressions. I find them unnecessarily crude."

"But scarcely any cruder than the actual deed itself," Mr. Owen observed.

"My dear fellow," the other hastened to explain, "that's where you err. That's exactly where you err, if you will forgive my saying so. The action itself was justified. Neither my partners nor I can stand having our store cluttered up with a lot of rattle-brained, vacillating, self-important time wasters and ill-mannered bullies such as, unfortunately, so many persons are who habitually frequent department stores. You must be familiar with the sort I mean," the man went on. "She bustles into the store with seventy-nine cents in her purse and a parcel of goods to exchange and thinks she's God Almighty's social arbiter in the presence of a group of slaves. We chuck 'em out here before they can upset our salesgirls. We don't like upset salesgirls unless upset in the right way and in the right place."

"What's the right way to upset one of these salesgirls?" asked Mr. Owen.

"How charmingly put!" the other exclaimed. "I see you're a bit of a one yourself. Frankly, though, you don't need to upset most of our salesgirls. They seem quite willing to upset themselves with the most alarming alacrity. If anything, they're a little too eager, let us say, for the lack of a better word, to upset."

"I should think," interjected Mr. Owen in an attempt to change the subject, "you'd lose a lot of customers by such drastic methods."

"Oh, we do!" the gentleman exclaimed enthusiastically. "You have no idea. Perhaps that's one of the reasons we're tearing along into bankruptcy. I don't quite know. On the other hand, we believe in giving our customers an even break. We always inform them that they are at liberty to hit any member of our sales force with any object handy whenever the sales person shows the slightest inclination to gratuitous incivility, stupidity, or lack of interest. Whenever we find that a clerk has been knocked cold by several customers in the course of a few days we naturally decide that the clerk is not qualified to deal with the public and so, accordingly, we chuck the clerk out, too. We find it much more natural and efficacious to allow our clerks and customers to settle their little difficulties and differences among themselves. Besides, I find it rather amusing. I do so loathe monotony, don't you, Mr.—er——"

"Mr. Owen," the other replied hesitantly. "At least, I think it is—Hector Owen it was or used to be."

"Well, it really doesn't make a great deal of difference," said the other. "Nevertheless, it's convenient to know. Now, unlike you, I'm almost certain that my name is Horace Larkin—Horace and Hector, quite a coincidence, what? Oh, very good. Am I veering?"

Mr. Owen was looking at his companion with growing alarm and suspicion. The man was giving signs of mental instability which, added to his obvious moral looseness, did not make an admirable combination. Before he could find a suitable reply to Mr. Larkin's childish inanity his attention was diverted by the sight of a large, sinister, wild-eyed individual rushing down one of the aisles in the direction of the nearest doorway.

"Yes, yes," Mr. Larkin was murmuring contentedly, "I do so hate monotony. Now, what can this be about? That desperate-looking chap seems to be in a great hurry to get somewhere else."

The desperate-looking chap was, and as he dashed past the spot where they were standing a glittering object, falling from his pocket, rolled up to their feet. Quickly Mr. Owen's companion stooped and picked it up.

"Dear me," he said in a distressed voice, "someone's been stealing diamonds again. Now, isn't that too bad. No wonder we're going bankrupt. Diamonds are very valuable, you know. The things cost no end of money.

Why can't they steal something else for a change—groceries, for instance?"

A large blond gentleman wearing heavy black eyebrows and a fashionably tailored suit of tweeds, and a small, meek-looking individual who in spite of his faultlessly cut morning attire impressed Mr. Owen as being a trifle drunk, appeared in the open plaza and, spying Mr. Horace Larkin, marched up to him with gestures of agitation. Following them was a clerk who appeared totally disinterested.

"I know," began Mr. Larkin without giving the others an opportunity to speak. "And here I was just saying how I loathed monotony. Don't tell me about it. I also loathe being upset and I am going to be upset whether I loathe it or not. You know—that luncheon. Presently we all must go to it. All of us. Even you must go to that luncheon, Dinner." Here Mr. Larkin pointed to the smaller of the two men and added parenthetically for the benefit of Mr. Owen, "His name is Dinner. It really is. Makes things confusing when luncheon comes before or after it, but I can't help that now. Don't tell me," he went on to the others. "We've been robbed again, haven't we? Thieves shouldn't take diamonds. It's not at all sporting. They're too damn easy to carry."

"But don't you think we should induce someone to pursue this beggar?" the large blond gentleman mumbled. "Offer a sort of a bonus thing?"

"Yes," piped up Mr. Dinner, producing a gold flask of beautiful design and helping himself to its contents. "Yes," he continued over the crest of a slight huskiness. "Shouldn't we send somebody after this beggar to shout out in a great voice, 'Stop thief! Stop thief!' and act excited and all?"

Mr. Larkin gazed at the little gentleman with pity and affection, then his expression became serious.

"Why do both of you keep on calling this chap a beggar," he asked irritably, "when most obviously he's a thief of the worst character? Let's get this straight—did he ask for the diamonds, or did he take them without asking?"

"He took 'em without a word," said the clerk in a bored voice.

"There," resumed Mr. Larkin after a thoughtful pause, "the man must have stolen the diamonds. He's not a beggar."

"He certainly did," owlishly proclaimed the one known as Dinner, once more producing the flask. "And I think someone should scream about it."

"I very much feel like screaming about it myself," observed Mr. Larkin. "I really do. Anyway, we haven't anybody who is especially good at doing that sort of thing—screaming, you know. This chap was running very fast, very fast indeed—tiresomely so. None of us can run very fast, and we all loathe running."

Although the sensation of freedom and well being still persisted with Mr. Owen, he felt, nevertheless, as he listened to all this, that he was going not a little but definitely and completely mad. And the strange part of it was he did not seem to care, rather enjoyed it, in fact. However, he did think it time to interpose a slight suggestion.

"How about the police?" he asked. "Shouldn't someone scream after them?"

Mr. Horace Larkin hopelessly shook his head.

"We also loathe the police," he replied. "In all probability that chap was the police. By this time he has tucked those diamonds in the safe at headquarters. Did he steal many of them?"

"Almost a handful," answered the clerk. "Big ones."

"That's a lot of diamonds," Mr. Larkin murmured regretfully. "I feel very low about losing so many. They were good big diamonds. Is anyone minding the rest of the jewelry?"

"Not a living soul," breathed Mr. Dinner, his eyes browning large. "The counter is all alone. You see, we brought George, here, along to tell you all about it."

Mr. Owen was frankly stunned. These three men must be figments of his own disordered mind. Such simplicity was impossible.

"Dinner, put that flask back or we'll have to carry you to luncheon," Mr. Larkin commanded, then fell silent to ponder upon this fresh problem. "Well," he resumed at last, "that's not at all right. That's almost sheer carelessness. If someone doesn't watch all those precious stones we won't have any left, and that wouldn't look at all well for a big store like this." He turned to the clerk. "George," he said briskly, "you'd better hurry back to those jewels, what there is left of them, and make out a claim for the insurance company. Add as much as you think is safe to the value of the stuff stolen. Don't scrimp. I can't stand scrimping. We may be able to make a not inconsiderable piece of change out of this regrettable incident after all. Waste not, want not. You get what I mean."

Mr. Owen was appalled by the callous dishonesty of Mr. Horace Larkin. Up to this point he had looked upon him as something extra special in the line of lunatics. Now he regarded him in the light of a menace to society in general and to insurance companies in particular. Once more he felt himself called upon to project his greater wisdom and ethics into this mad discussion.

"But such an action," he protested, "would not be at all right."

The suavely polished Mr. Larkin nodded a reluctant agreement.

"It's not right, I know," he said. "I think it's simply terrible myself, but you know how it is. Everybody does it, almost, literally everybody—really nice people. You'd be surprised." In spite of his legal experience, Mr. Owen confessed he was. "And then again," Mr. Larkin added confidentially, "none of us likes insurance companies very much. It's such a bother to pay their premiums, and they get so annoyingly stuffy about it when you don't. You can see for yourself, if we don't cheat the insurance company, we won't make any money on all those lovely diamonds, and that wouldn't be so good for us, would it?"

"But wouldn't it be better," pursued Mr. Owen, "to arrange things so that your lovely diamonds wouldn't be stolen?"

"That's an idea worth thinking about," the gentleman in tweeds put in, his deep voice carrying a serious, labored note. "How about shooting a couple of customers suddenly just as a bit of a warning?"

Once more Mr. Owen was unpleasantly impressed with his company. Were all these gentlemen dangerous maniacs?

"If we did that," Mr. Dinner objected, "we might find it difficult to induce any of our customers to go near the diamond counter at all. I wouldn't go myself. People don't like to be shot for no reason."

"People don't like to be shot for any reason," Horace Larkin corrected, as if depressed by the unreasonableness of the human race.

"Why shoot 'em, then?" continued Mr. Dinner triumphantly. "Especially since they don't like it."

"But," contributed the blond gentleman, "it wouldn't do any good to shoot them if they did like it."

"It seems," observed Mr. Larkin, "that somebody has to be shot at some time, but don't ask me why. I don't know, and I don't like revolvers. In fact, I simply—"

"Loathe them," Mr. Owen supplied, in spite of himself.

"Yes," continued Mr. Larkin, "I loathe a lot of revolvers knocking about the store. Dinner, here, might take it into his head to shoot up the place during one of his drunken orgies. He's like that." Mr. Owen gazed at the meek Dinner with increased alarm and respect. "How's this for an idea?" Larkin went on, and at this point he fastidiously shot his white cuffs, waved delicately to a passing salesgirl, then turned briskly to his companions. "Suppose," he said, "we run a full-page advertisement in all of the better newspapers stating in bold face type that our diamonds and other precious stones are false as hell and hardly worth the effort to carry away. Someone can think up the right words. This gentleman here, perhaps," he indicated Mr. Owen. "He looks as if he knew a lot of words."

"Wouldn't that be a better advertisement to run about someone else's store?" Mr. Dinner suggested, blinking thoughtfully. "About some competitor, for instance."

"Sure thing," chimed in the gentleman in tweeds enthusiastically. "If we ran a whole series of them we might ruin their business."

"No go," replied the suave gentleman. "We can only do that by spreading rumors. If we print advertisements about our competitors we might get into trouble. You see, it's all very well to print lies about our own store, but if we print them about our competitors, they might sue us for libel."

"Be just like 'em, too, the dirty crooks," said the tweedy giant. "Well, here we all stand waiting."

At the mention of waiting, Mr. Owen experienced an uneasy feeling that the past was creeping silently up to surround him and carry him off. When had he last been waiting and where? To escape the memory, dim as it was, he turned to his three companions almost eagerly. He would cling to them and go mad in their own peculiar way. Anything would be preferable to that dull, anxious depression lying somewhere behind him in the shadows. He did not feel low any more and for so many months he had felt low—low, spiritless, and disillusioned. Here was no sadness, and certainly it seemed almost impossible to keep these men depressed for more than the lengths of an inane sentence. And surely for their own sakes as well as for the public's, some sober mind should stay with them. For a moment Mr. Owen was seized with the fear that they might forget all about him in their charming way, and walk off, leaving him alone. They needed a sympathetic companion no less than he needed their companionship—someone like himself to see that they did injury neither to themselves nor to anyone else. That idea about shooting customers—now, that was all wrong. It was not a right idea. Although he realized they were not quite sane, Mr. Owen found something insidiously appealing about their special brand of insanity. They seemed to be so perfectly happy in their madness, so contented and busy about it, so full of daft ideas and unhelpful suggestions. Perhaps, after all, they were sane and he had been mad all his life. What did it matter? However, as the deliberations progressed he found it difficult to entertain this idea. These men were mental cases, or else they possessed an altogether new type of mind. Of that there could be no doubt. Mr. Owen became aware that the blond gentleman was asking questions.

"But look here," the man was saying, "isn't this a bit of a hitch? If we print an advertisement saying that we have a lot of bum jewelry, won't that keep customers away as well as burglars?"

"Not necessarily," Mr. Larkin replied. "I thought that out, too. We can station attendants at the doorways to tell customers not to pay any attention to the advertisement because we were only fooling."

This answer apparently satisfied the objections of the tweeds. Mr. Dinner, however, was stubborn about it.

"But suppose one of the attendants tells a burglar?" he inquired. "We can't very well ask our customers as they come in if they are burglars or not."

"Not very well," Mr. Larkin replied slowly. "That wouldn't put them in the proper mood to buy. Maybe no burglars will come in on those days."

"On what days?" asked the gentleman with the eyebrows.

"On the days when we have to tell our customers who are not burglars," patiently replied Mr. Larkin.

"From the way things keep disappearing in this store," the blond man moodily commented, "I suspect all our customers of being burglars."

"Of course," observed Mr. Larkin, "we steal some of the things ourselves and then pawn them when we're short of cash."

"And we make presents, too," added the blond man. "Fur coats and such like to women."

"I know," Mr. Larkin agreed, "but in one way that saves us a lot of money. I think we're very fortunate to have a nice department store. There's hardly a woman in town who will say no for long with a whole department store to choose from."

"In all the world," supplied the meek Mr. Dinner.

"Then I guess we'll have to let this burglar escape?" said the large man.

"We don't have to let him escape," replied Horace Larkin. "He will take care of his own escape. In fact, I suspect he already has." He broke off and concentrated his gaze on one of the broad aisles. "But what new diversion have we here?" he asked. "You know, running a store like this keeps us dreadfully on the dash. I'll be glad when lunch times comes, and then again, I won't."

Following the direction of Mr. Larkin's gaze, Mr. Owen watched the new diversion approach with increasing interest. Four beautifully formed girls clad in the sheerest underwear were speeding down the aisle. Behind them sped four decidedly determined gentlemen almost, but not quite, draped in towels. As unprepared as he was for this sort of thing, Mr. Owen was even less prepared for what followed. One of the girls, when about three feet off, flung herself upon him and as far as he was able to establish began to climb up to his shoulders. He had a confused picture of bare arms and legs busily doing things with his body, and even at that moment he could not help wondering if the young woman thought he had a pair of stirrups strapped round his waist. Ducking his head momentarily beneath an energetically upraised knee he caught a glimpse of his companions and discovered with some satisfaction that they were similarly occupied. Mr. Owen's profession had made him more or less familiar with the various physical indications of assault. He found these distressingly present with the difference that the tables were now turned. Even while he was struggling, his legal mind was engaged with problems of what chance a man had for a successful verdict when suing a lady for rape. In a criminal action the man, he decided, would have no standing at all. A man could be so assaulted almost repeatedly without altering greatly either his social or physical status whereas with a woman it might make a lot of difference. On the other hand, no woman would want a husband who was going to be raped all the time. There might be something in that. He did not know. He was much too busy. To steady himself, he involuntarily thrust up an arm and laid a hand on the young lady who was by this time somewhere in the neighborhood of his neck. He could hear the deep breathing of his companions who were laboring with their respective burdens. No sooner, however, had he seized his fair rider than his hand was smartly slapped.

"Don't grab me so careless-like," she told him.

Mr. Owen was upset.

"How shall I grab you?" he faltered.

"Do you have to be told how to grab me?" she demanded. "Where would you grab a lady?"

"I never grabbed a lady," replied Mr. Owen. "That is, not one in your condition."

"Well, brother, you've missed a lot," said the girl pityingly.

"If you'd stop shoving down on my belt," Mr. Owen complained, "I might barely be able to keep my trousers up."

"I can't," gasped the girl. "If by shoving myself up I happen to shove your trousers down, it's just too bad."

"It's more than too bad," Mr. Owen told her. "It's far more serious than you think. The trousers are not all. In some strange manner you seem to have got your toes locked in my shorts."

"Don't make me laugh," the girl admonished. "I don't want to fall off now that I've got myself comfortably up."

"Ruthlessly up, I'd say," muttered Mr. Owen.

To save his trousers he placed his hands on his hips and stood swaying in front of a number of spectators, many of whom received the impression they were witnessing an act put on by a slightly out of practice acrobat and his partner for their special edification. Strange things were always taking place in this store. Those four men in towels—what were they doing there and why were they being restrained by so many attendants?

"It's all right, girls," Mr. Owen heard Horace Larkin saying reassuringly. "You may come down when you like. The gentlemen are being held. What is it all about, anyway?"

Fortunately for Mr. Owen's trousers his burden was the first to hit the floor.

"Those four would-be cave men wouldn't believe we were working," she exclaimed furiously. "They insisted on playing with us, and they began to take it too seriously. We got frightened and ran. Besides, it's office hours."

"A most commendable attitude to take," replied Mr. Owen, "especially during office hours. Perhaps, only in office hours. Where did this action take place, may I ask?"

"In the swimming pool," said another young lady, springing lightly up from the small body of the prostrate Dinner. "We came in to give our review and found them swimming about without a stitch. They wouldn't believe we were models. Started in right there and then. Would you believe it, Mr. Larkin?"

"Yes," answered Mr. Larkin. "From my point of view, it seems almost inevitable, under the circumstances. You know how easily one thing suggests another. May I ask why you were staging your delightful review in the swimming pool?"

"Major Britt-Britt told us to do it," chimed in a third young lady in scanty attire. "Last night he told us. He said that our department would be closed for redecorating and that until further notice we should hold our fashion reviews in the swimming pool, didn't you, Maj?"

"Call him Major, call him Major," said Mr. Larkin in a low voice. "There're a lot of customers knocking about." He turned smilingly to the Major, who was looking a little uncomfortable under his furious mop of blond hair and heavy black eyebrows. "And I fancy, Major," Mr. Larkin continued, "that from the pressure of business resulting from the universal popularity of this magnificent yet essentially reasonably priced modern mart of merchandise you overlooked the slight detail of notifying the proper authorities that the swimming pool should not be used by our naked customers during the period of the review?"

"It slipped my mind," muttered the Major.

"You big stiff," surprisingly observed Mr. Dinner, rising from the floor and instinctively reaching for his hip pocket, an action which Mr. Larkin was prompt in intercepting, "there's not enough room on that mind of yours for anything to slip off of. That girl nearly tore me to pieces with her great clutching hands. Can't tell me she was as worried about her confounded honor as all that."

"Don't be disagreeable," Mr. Larkin told the little man. "And don't talk so lightly about a lady's honor in public. It may be a confounded nuisance and a terrific social handicap, but some women still cling to it. What are we going to do about these four gentlemen, now? They strike me as being more offended against than offending. Under similar circumstances, I would have made the same mistake myself."

"You'd have acted worse," proclaimed one of the girls. "Don't I know."

Mr. Larkin coughed loudly.

"Not here," he said rapidly under his breath. "Not here. These people won't understand how we run this store. They're quite, quite narrow, my dear."

"But we told them to wait," one of the girls protested. "We kept telling them we were busy and asked them if they wouldn't wait."

"And they didn't want to wait?" Mr. Larkin asked, interested in spite of himself.

"No," said the girl. "They claimed they couldn't wait."

"They must be in a bad way," Mr. Larkin remarked as if to himself. "We seem to be doing everything in this store this morning except selling goods to customers. Another day like this, and we'll be in the hands of the receivers." Producing a notebook he hastily scribbled an address on a leaf, tore the leaf out, and handed it to one of the toweled gentlemen. "Sorry about all this," he continued easily, "but if you pop off right now I'm sure you won't have to wait. Better get dressed first, though—at least temporarily."

Eagerly making plans among themselves, the four gentlemen hurried off. When a safe distance had been put between them and the models Mr. Larkin sent the girls about their business; then, locking arms with Mr. Owen, he walked off down an aisle in the direction of his private office. Mr. Dinner and Major Britt-Britt followed in like fashion. Thus they made an impressive and dignified exit from the eyes of their admiring patrons, who seemed still somewhat puzzled over what it had all been about. As soon as the door to Mr. Horace Larkin's amazing office closed behind the four backs he turned courteously to Mr. Owen and took one of that gentleman's hands in his.

"My dear sir, I'm sorry," said Mr. Larkin. "I've been neglecting you terribly. What would you like to sell this morning?"

"What!" gasped Mr. Owen. "Do I have to sell something?"

"Certainly," replied Mr. Larkin gently. "We all have to sell something. You're a full-fledged partner, you know."

## CHAPTER IV

## *The New Partner*

"No," said Mr. Owen vaguely when he had recovered a little. "I didn't know."

"Neither did we," both Mr. Dinner and Major Britt-Britt said in unison. "Is this man our new partner?"

"Yes," replied Mr. Larkin in the manner of one taking a new automobile out for a spin. "Do you like him?"

Mr. Owen would not have been greatly surprised to hear himself referred to as Model A.

"How did it happen?" he asked.

"Well," began Mr. Horace Larkin, "last night it occurred to me that we could do with a new partner—some congenial chap to share with us our many responsibilities. Do you like my office?"

"What?" gasped Mr. Owen, startled by the abruptness of the question. "Oh, yes. It's lovely."

"I rather fancy it myself," confided Mr. Larkin, gazing appreciatively about him at the huge pillow-heaped divans, the colorful oriental hangings, and the gleaming rug-scattered floor. He even delicately sniffed the scented air. "Isn't that nude stunning?" he continued. "The one with the man."

"They both look nude to me," observed Mr. Owen, glancing at the painting indicated, then hastily averting his eyes in holy horror.

"Yes," said Mr. Larkin simply. "That's what's stunning about it. They're both nude together—mother naked. I do a lot of business here, a lot of interviewing. You understand, with my staff, of course."

"I'm afraid I do," replied Mr. Owen. "If you'll pardon my saying so, there's an unmistakable suggestion in this office of an old-time barroom."

"Is there, now?" said Mr. Larkin, greatly pleased. "Well, isn't that a coincidence? Because this room is literally alive with liquor. Let's all have a drink."

"Would you mind going on about how I became a partner?" Mr. Owen asked. "I can't help feeling curious."

"Yes," rumbled the monumental Major. "How did you pick him out?"

"Pardon me," said Mr. Larkin. "Pardon me. My thoughts veer so, I'm surprised I don't have a stroke. So I just made up my mind that the first likely-looking gentleman to enter the store in the morning should be our partner and have the privilege of sharing with us our many—"

"We know," interrupted Mr. Dinner rather cynically. "Heavy responsibilities. That, no doubt, will enable you to devote more of your priceless time to your staff work."

"How did you guess?" beamed Mr. Larkin. "Exactly what I had in mind."

"But wasn't I snatched through a doorway?" pursued Mr. Owen. "Or was I snatched through a doorway?" He was groping desperately in what remained of his memory. "Was it raining when I came in?" he continued. "I'm quite sure I remember the rain—steadily falling rain and a woman with heavy-lidded eyes."

"There was rain out there," Mr. Larkin replied, vaguely waving his hand as if in the general direction of some unknown shore. "But I'm sure I saw no woman with heavy-lidded eyes."

"Lucky for her you didn't," observed the Major, "or you'd have snatched her through, too."

"Is that nice, gentlemen, I ask you?" Mr. Larkin asked in gentle reproach. "I am sorry, however, about this heavy-lidded woman. I am fond of heavy-lidded women. They are born without morals and acquire them very slowly—if ever. Tell me, was she worth while?"

"Seemed like a good sort," said Mr. Owen. "A lonely sort. She was standing out in the rain. I don't think she'd have minded if you had snatched her through. She seemed to be looking for a place to go—a cheerful place."

"We all need cheerful places to go at times," observed Mr. Dinner in an odd voice. "Someone to snatch us out of the rain."

This unexpected contribution from Mr. Dinner gave Mr. Owen to feel that he might just possibly be somewhat dead and standing in the presence of the latest thing in angels. He could not, however, quite accept Mr. Larkin as God. That would be painting the lily.

"What door did I happen to come through?" he asked a little uneasily.

"I don't quite remember which door it was," replied Mr. Horace Larkin, and this time Mr. Owen was convinced that his vagueness was deliberately assumed. "Some door—one we very rarely use. Saw you standing in it looking rather at loose ends so I took the liberty of dragging you through. The door is not an exit."

For a few moments no one spoke. Mr. Owen was wondering with mingled emotions about the door that was not an exit. Did he really want an exit? Was there a single thing to which he cared to return—a single person or place? All washed out with the rain. There was a woman. He could not altogether forget Lulu. No one who had been forced to live with her could altogether forget Lulu. But what he remembered was bitter and distressful. To visit Lulu was an event; to live with her a disaster. She was a woman like that—popular only on occasions one had no desire to recall.

"I'm glad," he said at last, "you did pull me out of the rain. Your intervention was providential."

"Then everything is quite all right, isn't it?" cried Mr. Larkin. "But you haven't told us what you would like to sell. First, however, let me officially introduce you to your partners—our partners." He turned to the two gentlemen and eyed them with a faintly ironical glitter, then turned hastily back to Mr. Owen. "A thousand and one pardons, your name has entirely escaped me. My thoughts veer so it's a wonder I don't have convulsions."

Mr. Owen thereupon designated himself with that self-conscious feeling of deficiency characteristic of men when forced to pronounce their names in public.

"Owen," murmured Mr. Dinner. "That's an appropriate name to add to this firm. It's all we ever do."

"How clever he is," said Mr. Larkin, as if speaking about a dog. "By the way, you won't mind if we tack it on last? It will save us from changing the sign. It will read simply, 'Larkin, Britt, Dinner and Owen.' We'll have to shift the 'and' and squeeze up 'Britt.' He needs a little squeezing. Ha! Ha! It's quite jolly having a new partner. I feel better already."

"You're looking well," observed Major Britt-Britt caustically. "A regular human banquet."

"Do I now? That's splendid," replied Mr. Larkin. "Mr. Hector Owen, this is Major Barney Britt-Britt. He gambled his way out of the army. And this is Mr. Luther Dinner, an odd name and an odder type. He is a young and, I suspect, an intellectually feebler son. Myself, the senior partner in everything save sin and age, was once in the show business. We won this store at a poker game."

"Then you weren't trained in the business," said Mr. Owen.

"I should think not," replied Mr. Larkin, as if stung by the very idea. "We're really supposed to do nothing, that is, little or nothing. And we don't do much, really. Running a store like this is a very simple matter. Buy and sell, buy and sell. You'll enjoy it."

At this moment a studious-looking individual hastily entered the room and began to speak without ceremony.

"The accountants for our stockholders," he announced, "have uncovered those hidden assets you told me to hold out on them. They're raising hell about it."

"So would I," replied Mr. Larkin in an unperturbed voice, "if I were silly enough to be a stockholder. Don't blame them. Can't you hide those assets somewhere else?"

"You talk as if you could tuck assets up your sleeve like rabbits," complained the man.

"Do I now?" exclaimed Mr. Larkin. "I must be veering again. Anyway, I never knew you could tuck rabbits up your sleeve. Always thought it was hats. Can't these accountants be bribed?"

"They can," answered the man, "but it's too late now. The cat's out."

Mr. Larkin looked surprised.

"The cat's out," he repeated. "What cat? Didn't know we had one. I'm immensely partial to cats."

"I mean everyone knows," the man exclaimed. "There isn't any cat."

"Oh, then there isn't any cat," Mr. Larkin went on in a disappointed voice. "I'm sorry, but you keep talking about cats and rabbits and things until it's really no wonder I veer. Surprised I'm not revolving." He turned abruptly to Mr. Dinner. "Take a note," he said. "Remind me about cats."

Mr. Dinner promptly produced a notebook and stood waiting with pencil poised.

"What shall I remind you about cats?" he asked.

"To have some," said Mr. Larkin Napoleonically.

Mr. Dinner wrote laboriously in his notebook.

"How's this?" he asked reading aloud. "Remind H. Larkin to have some cats."

The senior partner considered this effort for a moment.

"It's very nice," he said at last, "but it might lead to a misunderstanding in case you were found dead some morning, which I for one hope you are. Change 'have cats' to read 'get cats.' I couldn't very well have cats even if I wasn't so busy. Where were we now?"

"It was about those hidden assets," ventured the man.

"But they're not hidden assets," replied Mr. Larkin, "God pity us all. It becomes harder and harder to get away with a thing. Tell me, don't we owe a number of bills?"

The man merely laughed, but that was as good as an answer.

"I don't see how you can laugh about it," Mr. Larkin complained, "because now we'll have to pay them. Take those unhidden assets and pay a lot of bills. Don't give our stockholders a penny. Ask them if they think this store is a bank, and tell them that once more Horace Larkin has saved them from bankruptcy—no, say, a pauper's grave." Dismissing the man, he turned once more to Mr. Owen, who was looking slightly dazed. "But you haven't told us what you want to sell," continued the senior partner.

"No, I haven't," said Mr. Owen dizzily.

"But you will?" coaxed Mr. Larkin.

Mr. Owen thought rapidly. Toys were rather cheerful things. They might be amusing.

"I might do well with toys," he suggested. "Toys of the mechanical sort."

Mr. Larkin's eager expression fell a little.

"I'm afraid you won't fancy our mechanical toys greatly," he remarked. "Do you want to play with them yourself, or sell them, or does it matter?"

"I don't know," replied Mr. Owen. "Does it?"

"If you want to play with them, it does," said Mr. Larkin. "You see we sell mechanical toys on the theory that they are made to be broken. So we buy only broken ones."

"But what good is a broken mechanical toy?" Mr. Owen protested.

"No earthly good," Mr. Larkin readily agreed. "No earthly good at all, but children seem to enjoy them. However, we can get you some unbroken mechanical toys." He cupped his lips in his hands and suddenly called out, "Horrid! Horrid! Where is that boy? And you, too, Green Mould."

Mr. Owen was certain that the senior partner's mind had slipped completely off its frail hinges until he saw two figures dart into the room from opposite directions and dash up to Mr. Larkin. One was an exceedingly horrid-looking boy and the other was an aged man, strongly suggestive of his name.

"They're mine," said Mr. Larkin with a note of pride, pointing to the pair. "All mine. Nobody else wants them."

Mr. Owen, surveying the unadmirable-looking pair, saw no reason why anyone else should. However, he kept his opinion to himself.

"I can't see that," he replied. "They'd make splendid museum pieces."

"They'd do much better in a graveyard," observed the Major feelingly.

"Or in jail," added Mr. Dinner.

"Give them time," said Mr. Larkin, "and they'll probably be in both. Horrid," he continued, addressing the younger of the two, "I want you to induce Green Mould to go down to the Galleries de la Lune and bring back lots of mechanical toys. Charge them to my account. I buy all my things there, anyway. They have better stuff than we have, and the prices are much more reasonable."

Mr. Owen looked at the speaker in amazement. The man was as great a danger to himself and his store when honest as when unsuccessfully hiding assets.

"And Blue Mould—or is it Green? I forget which—don't let the grass grow under your feet," Mr. Larkin continued severely to the old man.

"Wot!" piped up the ancient one in a shrill voice. "Right through the pavements?"

"No," scolded Mr. Larkin, "through the floor of the taxi cab. You're going to ride. Won't that be nice?"

Green Mould considered.

"Oo pays?" he demanded. "Ther last time I took er cab fer you it cost me all me cash. God knows when I'll ever get it back."

Mr. Larkin coughed delicately behind his hand.

"Is this the time to speak of trifles?" he demanded, reverting once more to his Napoleonic mood.

"When is?" asked the old man.

"Not now," Mr. Larkin replied.

"Nor ever," muttered Green Mould, shuffling from the room after his companion, Horrid. "Me own money is trifles. His is worse than counterfeit. It don't exist. Oo ever sees it? Yer can play with false money, but yer can't even smell his."

"This is one of those days," said Horace Larkin sadly, "when everyone in the world wants to take our money away from us. I don't like such days. By the way, my dear Mr. Owen, did you ever work for a living?"

"I'm a lawyer of sorts," Mr. Owen admitted modestly.

"Splendid!" cried Mr. Larkin, immediately regaining his blithe spirits. "Fancy that, a lawyer. You should be able to hide practically all our assets."

"He might even find a few," Mr. Dinner suggested hopefully.

"In the meantime," continued Mr. Larkin, "how would you like to sell some books? That's always fun. You'd be surprised at the great quantity of odd people who read books. Some even buy them. I wonder why? Major, will you take our new partner to the Book Department? Let him knock about there until luncheon."

At this moment there sounded a furious bang on the door. Mr. Dinner moved to open it, but was arrested by the voice of Mr. Larkin.

"If you open that door," he said, "a wolf might walk in—a wolf with a bill in his mouth."

A wolf did walk in, and it was not dressed in sheep's clothing. She was hardly in any clothing at all—a tall, good-looking woman artfully draped in a bolt or so of some clinging material. For a moment she stood arrogantly regarding the partners, who returned her gaze uneasily.

"Am I to fall in a stupor of exhaustion?" she demanded in a deep voice, advancing into the room.

"I hope not," said Mr. Larkin nervously. "Are you?

I hate stupors of exhaustion. Why not lie down? There's lots of room."

"Nobody else is lying down," retorted the woman.

"Do you want us all to lie down?" Mr. Larkin asked her rather helplessly. "Of course, we all could if it will do anything about that stupor of exhaustion."

"Why should I wish all of you to lie down?" the woman coldly demanded. "All of you?"

"We don't know," replied Mr. Larkin. "Have you any reason?"

"What reason would I have to lie down with all of you?" went on the woman.

"Oh, my God!" exploded the Major, then made a violent sound deep in his throat.

Mr. Larkin started nervously.

"Don't be like that, Major," he pleaded. "You veer me." Turning once more to the statuesque woman, he asked, "Have you any reason to want to lie down with all of us?"

"I see no reason why I should lie down with any of you," she replied in measured tones.

"Oh," said Mr. Larkin, a little set back. "You don't? I thought you did."

"Do you realize what you're asking me?" the woman continued inexorably.

"No," answered Mr. Larkin hastily. "Or, rather, yes. But for goodness' sake, don't tell us. I feel quite driven to the wall as it is."

"I'd like to drive you through the wall," the woman replied without any show of feeling.

"Would you now?" asked Mr. Owen, glancing round at the walls as if gauging their resistance. "Through the wall. Fancy that."

"I put it up to this gentleman," the woman cried, advancing languorously on Mr. Owen.

"Don't put it up to me," he protested hastily. "I'm new at this business. And besides I have a feeling I'm married."

"What's that got to do with it?" the woman asked scornfully.

"With what?" gasped Mr. Owen as the woman draped two arms round his neck and leaned so heavily against him he was forced to brace himself as if slanting against a gale.

"You know," murmured the woman with a feminine sort of leer.

"My God!" cried Mr. Larkin. "She's coming unwound. In fact, she's nearly finished. Gentlemen, you must leave at once. This is a most important interview. I could never sit through that luncheon unless I got this off my mind."

"It seems the senior partner gets all the breaks," Mr. Dinner observed as he and the Major escorted Mr. Owen to the door. "She's the head of our Designing Department. An excellent piece of goods."

Mr. Owen was not sure whether the man was referring to the body or to the material she had been wearing when she had first entered the office. His parting glimpse was epic. Mr. Larkin was holding one end of the material while the lady, now completely herself, was clinging to the other. Mr. Larkin seemed to be veering again, but this time in the right direction.

## CHAPTER V

## *Pornography Preferred*

MR. OWEN FOUND HIMSELF CAGED BEHIND FOUR counters. He was literally surrounded by books. As far as his gaze could reach, there were books and still more books. The mere thought of reading even a fraction of them numbed his literary faculties. All the books in the world seemed to have been gathered into that department. He found himself unwilling to open the cover of even one of them. He thought of giant forests denuded for the sake of these books; of millions of publishers and editors crushed beneath the weight of their spring and fall lists, of numberless bookstore owners resorting to theft and murder or else going mad in their efforts to keep from sinking in seas of bankruptcy beneath the steadily rising tide of current fiction. He thought of haggard-eyed book reviewers turning their bitter faces to those strange and awful gods to which book reviewers are forced to turn in the affliction of their tortured brains. He heard these abandoned men calling in loud voices for a momentary recession, at least, of the soul-rotting flood of books. He even thought of authors, and his heart was filled with indignation against that indefatigable, ever hopeful tribe of word vendors. If it wasn't for the diligence of authors so many hearts would remain intact and so many hopes unblighted. Mr. Owen decided it would be better not to think of authors. No good would ever come of it. Also, with a feeling of shame, he thought of the reading public, and his mind began to veer very much in the manner of his senior partners. Luckily his thoughts were taken off the reading public by the conversation of two gentlemen who were fingering various volumes in a decidedly furtive manner. One of these gentlemen was tall, hungry-looking, and artistically untidy. The other was exactly like the first only not as tall. Feeling themselves under scrutiny, the pair looked up guiltily.

"How is *The Broken Bed* going?" the tall one asked in a diffident voice.

"What?" replied Mr. Owen. "I don't sleep in a broken bed."

"No. No," said the other in tones of pain, "I was referring to Monk's latest. I don't care where you sleep."

"Nor do I care where you sleep," replied Mr. Owen tartly, "or if you ever sleep. Please stick to business. You were referring to Monk's latest what?"

"I was referring to the works of Monk," answered the tall person in the manner of a god offended.

"Oh," said Mr. Owen, momentarily stunned. "You were? Well, we don't refer to them here. You must be in the wrong department."

"Do you mean to stand there and tell me to my face," cried the man, "that you don't sell *The Broken Bed* here—not one single *Broken Bed*?"

"I'm rather new at this business myself," Mr. Owen explained, thinking it better to be patient with the man. "But I know they sell broken mechanical toys. They might even sell broken beds. Why don't you try the Furniture Department? If they haven't one there they might be willing to order a broken bed for you. They might even break one of their good beds. Almost anything can happen in this store."

"My dear sir," said the tall man, evidently deciding to be patient himself, "it seems you don't understand. I am referring to Monk's works."

"I know," put in Mr. Owen, "but I do wish you'd stop."

"One moment," the man continued with a wave of his hand. "This may jog your laggard wits. They recently made him into an omnibus."

"Who?" gasped Mr. Owen, starting back.

"Monk," replied the other triumphantly. "There! They made Monk into an omnibus."

"How could they do that?" Mr. Owen wanted to know.

"Why, they make all the best ones into omnibuses nowadays," he was told. "It's being done."

"But I don't see," answered Mr. Owen. "How could they possibly make this chap Monk into an omnibus?"

"He became so popular," replied the other simply.

"Still I don't see it," pursued Mr. Owen. "Just because a man is popular, why should they make him into an omnibus? Doesn't it hurt terribly?"

"Why should it hurt?" exclaimed the other fiercely. "They just take him and squeeze him together tight and compactly, and there you are."

"I know," said Mr. Owen, unable to keep the horror from his voice. "But look at him. The poor fellow must be in an awful condition. I don't even like to think of it."

"No, he isn't," replied the other, frowning dangerously. "Not if he's properly done. There you have him for all time conveniently at hand—the best of his works. The rest of him that doesn't matter you can toss aside."

Mr. Owen shivered and stared at the speaker with dilated eyes.

"Will you please go away," he said quietly. "I don't care to hear any more."

"Nonsense," spoke up the smaller of the two madmen for the first time. "They made *him* into an omnibus. He's Monk."

"Oh," said Mr. Owen, speaking gently as if to a child. "He's Monk and he's an omnibus, too. What might you be, a tram car?"

"No," the little chap replied in all seriousness, "but I hope to be an omnibus some day. You know, if they don't make you into an omnibus you're simply no good."

"I shouldn't think you'd be much good if they did," observed Mr. Owen. "Why don't you run along now and play in the Toy Department?"

"What do you think we are," cried the tall lunatic, "children?"

"Not at all," Mr. Owen said soothingly. "You're an omnibus all right. I can see that at a glance. But don't you think you'd be happier in our Motor Vehicle Department? You might run into a Mack truck there. Wouldn't that be fun?"

Upon the reception of this suggestion the tall man uttered a loud complaint and dashed off wildly through the store, pushing and being pushed. The little chap followed him. A good looking salesgirl sidled up to Mr. Owen and invited incredible confidences with her wickedly shadowed eyes.

"You're the new partner," she began, "aren't you? What was troubling those two half-wits?"

"One kept telling me he was an omnibus," faltered Mr. Owen. "And when I admitted he was—called him one, in fact—he started in screaming and ran away."

The girl smiled sympathetically and patted Mr. Owen's arm.

"Don't mind them," she replied. "They're just a couple of authors. You know, they come around here and innocently ask how their books are going, and then get mad as hell because we haven't even heard of them.

They should tell us they're authors, in the first place. Then we could think up some comforting lie."

"But this chap insisted he was an omnibus," Mr. Owen continued. "Said they did things to his—his—I forget now, but however it was, they did things to the best of him and then he was an omnibus."

"This is an omnibus," the girl explained, picking up a stout volume. "It's one of those quaint ideas that occasionally get the best of publishers. Whenever an author isn't good enough to have his old books bought individually and still isn't rotten enough to be taken off the list entirely they publish an omnibus volume of his stuff, and surprisingly few people ever buy it."

"Oh," said Mr. Owen. "Then I was a little wrong. He started in with asking for a broken bed."

"That's Monk's latest drip," the girl told him. "It doesn't matter, though. He didn't want to buy it. He was seeking information."

At this moment a middle-aged lady sailed up to the counter and knocked off several books which she failed to replace. The salesgirl eyed her.

"What would be nice for a young lady sick in bed?" she demanded in a scolding voice.

"How about a good dose of salts, lady?" the girl replied promptly out of the side of her mouth, and winked at the shocked Mr. Owen.

"Or a nice young man?" chimed in another salesgirl.

"I'll have you to know this young lady comes from one of the best families," the woman retorted indignantly.

"Why did they kick her out?" Mr. Owen's companion wanted to know.

"They didn't kick her out," cried the woman.

"Then how did she get to know you?" the other girl inquired.

"Are you deliberately trying to insult me?" the woman demanded in a voice of rage.

"I was," said the girl with the shadow-stained eyes, "but I've given it up."

"I asked," said the woman, struggling to control her words and mixing them completely. "What would be nice to give to a sick book in bed?"

"A worm, lady," replied Owen's friend. "A book-worm—a nice, succulent bookworm."

"But can't you understand?" cried the woman. "I don't want worms."

"Neither do lots of other people," the girl replied philosophically, "but they can't help themselves. I didn't know you had worms."

"But I haven't any worms," said the woman.

"Then why don't you want some?" she was asked.

"Who wants worms?" snapped the woman.

"Perhaps this woman is trying to sell you some of her worms," Mr. Owen suggested.

"That's an idea, too," agreed the girl. "Say, lady, are you trying to sell me some worms?"

"Certainly not!" expostulated the woman. "I don't want to sell some worms."

"See?" said the salesgirl with a hopeless shrug of her shoulder. "She says she won't let us have any of her worms."

"But I didn't have any worms to begin with," cried the woman.

"Oh," replied the girl, with ready understanding, "you picked them up as a hobby."

"No," declared Mr. Owen. "She mean, she wasn't born with worms."

"It's a pity she was born at all," observed the salesgirl. "She and her old worms. Who brought up these worms, anyway?"

"You did," the woman told her. "I asked for a book, and you brought up worms."

"And where did the young lady in bed go?" the girl asked. "Is she still sick?"

"You told me to give her a dose of salts," the woman retorted furiously.

"Did I?" replied the salesgirl. "Well, give her a couple of doses and worm yourself off. This is a book counter and not a worm clinic. I'm tired of you and your worms and your dying young women and all that. Besides, I want to talk to this gentleman. You're in the way. Come back tomorrow when you've made up your mind."

"The management will hear about this," the woman threatened.

"The management has heard," the girl replied. "This gentleman is one of the owners. Isn't he lovely?"

Impotent with anger the woman rushed away.

Owen looked blankly at the salesgirl.

"Is there anything wrong?" he asked her.

"Oh, no," she replied, her eyes gleaming with unholy amusement. "There's nothing at all wrong. Can't you read?" Here she pointed to an overhead sign. "That damn fool came to the Pornographic Department. Take a look at this book."

She selected a book at random, turned the pages until she found an illustration, then passed the book to Mr. Owen. He glanced at the picture, gave one frantic look about him, then turned his back on the girl. The poor man's brain was paralyzed by the picture the girl had put under his nose, a picture she should not have looked at herself and which most certainly she should not have shown to him. With the book still held forgotten in his hands, Mr. Owen strove to think of other things. It was obvious to him that he was never going to turn round and face that girl again. What disturbing eyes she had! He wondered whether it would not be better for him to crouch down back of the counter and to wait there until one of the partners came to take him away. Dimly he realized that someone had been asking him a question, the same one, several times. He looked up and discovered he was being glared at by a thin, bitter-faced lady who gave the impression of being mostly pince-nez.

"Do you have the *Sex Life of the Flea?*" the woman asked sharply.

Mr. Owen now noticed that the woman held a slip of paper and a pencil in her hands. "My God," he wondered, "Is this horrid old crow trying to interview me on my sex life? What a place this is."

"No, lady," he answered disgustedly. "I don't have the sex life of a louse."

"But I must have the *Sex Life of the Flea,*" the woman insisted.

"I hope you enjoy it," he retorted, "but I shall play

no part in it. None whatsoever. Personally, I don't care if you have the sex life of a mink."

"I've finished with minks," snapped the woman. "I'm doing fleas now."

"Have you mistaken me for a bull flea or whatever the he's are called, by chance?" he shot back. "Or have you gone batty like everyone else? If you want a flea's sex life why not take up with some unmarried flea and have done with it?"

"You've gone batty yourself," retorted the woman.

"Madam," he replied, "I certainly have. Now, run away and look for this flea. I'm busy."

The woman sniffed, tossed back her head, and subjected Mr. Owen to a parting glare.

"You," she said witheringly, "would not even understand the sex life of the Bumpers—*Chloroscombrus chrysurus.*"

"I doubt it," admitted Mr. Owen. "It doesn't sound very restrained."

"And as for the courtship of the Squid," she tossed in for good measure as she prepared to march away, "I know you are ignorant of that."

"I'm not alone in my darkness, madam," he told her a little nettled, "and, furthermore, I'm not a Peeping Tom."

"Will you kindly hold that book a little higher?" a fresh voice asked at his other side. "I want to study the detail of the illustration."

Mr. Owen wheeled and found himself confronting the gravely critical face of a lovely young girl. With his last shred of chivalry he endeavored to remove the book from view, but the girl hung on gamely.

"What's the matter?" she asked innocently. "Don't you want me to see it?"

"Of course not," he scolded. "I don't want anybody to see it. Can't look at it myself."

The girl took the book from his now nerveless fingers and studied the picture intently. Fully expecting her to shriek and hurry away as soon as she understood what it was all about, Mr. Owen watched with fascinated eyes.

"Those Arabian lads certainly had some quaint

ideas," she observed in a casually conversational voice. "So complicated—almost too elaborate, I would say, but perhaps they had a lot of time on their hands and nothing better to do. And after all is said and done, what is there better to do?"

"Don't ask me, lady," said Mr. Owen hastily. "I wash my hands of the whole affair."

"You seem to find something wrong with this picture," the girl went on. "Is it out of drawing?"

"It's out of reason," he answered coldly. "Please stop memorizing it."

"I don't have to memorize it," the girl replied proudly. "I'm thoroughly conversant with the technique of Arabian erotology."

"Oh," replied Mr. Owen feebly, then prompted by the belief that anything would be better than this clutchingly graphic illustration which they were shamelessly sharing between them, he asked, "would something in Squids interest you, or Bumpers, perhaps?"

The young lady judicially considered this proposal.

"No," she said at last. "I don't think I'd get much of a kick from the erotic life of the Squid."

"Sorry," said Mr. Owen, and he really was. "Then how about something especially filthy in the line of Bumpers? That might tide you over."

"Hardly," replied the girl. "Haven't you a dirtier book than this one?"

"My dear young lady," said Mr. Owen with deep conviction, "they don't print any dirtier books than that one. Even to be standing together in its presence makes me feel that for all practical purposes you and myself are nine tenths married."

"Does it affect you that way?" the girl inquired with professional interest.

"I don't know what way you mean," he replied cautiously. "But I do know I'll never be quite the same."

"You're too impressionable," the girl assured him. "Now, I ran across a book the other day that would have opened your eyes. It was ever so much dirtier than this—to begin with it described——"

"Don't!" cried Mr. Owen, clapping both hands to his

ears. "Are you proposing to stand there in cold blood and describe to me a book even dirtier than this one?"

"Perhaps when I've finished," smiled the girl, "your blood won't be so cold."

"Oh," muttered Mr. Owen, panic stricken by the implication in the girl's words. "Oh, dear. Oh, dear. I want to get out of this department. How can I do it? Where shall I turn?"

His hands fluttered helplessly over the books, and all the time he was painfully aware of the fact that the salesgirl with those eyes was observing his distress with quietly malicious amusement.

"Tell that creature all about it," he said to the young lady distractedly and pointed to the salesgirl. "She'll probably cap your story with the Nuptials of the Whale or Everyman's Manual of Rape, for all I know. Don't hang around here any more. I'm in no mood for any monkey business."

"Then I'll call on you when you are," the smiling young lady replied. "I like that sort of business, and it's so refreshing to find a man who is still fresh and unspoiled—you know, not blasé."

"Don't you dare come back," Mr. Owen called after the girl as she gracefully swayed away. "My sex life is null and void."

Apparently the girl did not hear, but various other customers did, and stopped to stare interestedly at this man who was thus publicly proclaiming his truly lamentable condition.

"I hope you don't mean that," the salesgirl murmured, undulating up to him with her trim, flexible torso.

Mr. Owen, after recovering a little from the effect of the torso, noticed for the first time that a small section of hell had crept into her hair and left its flames glowing among the waves. A dangerously alluring girl, he decided. She was certainly not the proper person to team up with when selling pornographic literature. Especially when illustrated. Or maybe she was. He did not know.

"I wish you'd stop sidling up to me like an impassioned and overdone piece of spaghetti," he complained. "And what has my sex life to do with you, I'd like to know?"

"That's rather a leading question, isn't it?" she answered, a challenging glitter in her eye.

"I don't know," said Mr. Owen. "If it is, don't answer."

"I feel that I must," she told him gently.

"Oh, God!" breathed Mr. Owen.

"So far," said the girl, "our sex lives have never crossed, but they might at any minute."

"What!" cried Mr. Owen. "You mean right here and now? Oh, no they won't, my girl. Nobody is going to cross my sex life in the middle of a department store. You keep your sex life and I'll keep mine."

"But you seem to have no sex life."

"Then don't worry about it. Let the sleeping dog lie."

"What sleeping dog?"

"Don't ask me," Mr. Owen told her bitterly. "Any sleeping dog."

"Oh," said the girl. "I thought you meant your sleeping dog."

"Well, I didn't," he retorted irritably. "I never had a dog either sleeping or awake."

For a moment she studied him appraisingly.

"Did you ever have a girl?" she asked.

## CHAPTER VI

### *Satin*

"I'M SOMEWHAT HAZY ON THAT POINT," MR. OWEN replied. "Seems as if I had. Why?"

"Nothing at all," she answered. "I was merely wondering if your sex impulses had ever been thwarted."

"What's that to you?" he asked.

"Again, nothing at all," she assured him. "Only it makes one a little cracked when that happens."

"You don't look so seamy," Mr. Owen was ungallant enough to observe as he considered the girl's gracious moulding.

"Why should I?" she demanded.

"Don't ask me," he answered defensively. "I don't know whether you should or shouldn't. It's none of my business."

"It certainly is some of your business," she told him, returning his gaze with an appraising eye. "You don't think I'm going to let you or any other man thwart my sex impulses, do you?"

"I don't give a hang about your horrid old sex impulses," he retorted. "Have I tried to stop you?"

"From what?" she wanted to know.

Mr. Owen looked blankly at her.

"From whatever you want to do when you carry on like that," he answered lamely.

"Well," she snapped, "you haven't been any too encouraging. You haven't puffed or panted or rolled your eyes or tried to find out things like other men do."

"Do you want me to rush about after you like an exhausted masseur?" he demanded.

"No," she replied, "but you haven't even insulted me so far."

"Would that be possible?" he asked.

"No," she replied dispassionately, "but it's nice, just the same. A girl gets to expect it. Your partners make indecent proposals whenever they get the chance. Nothing discourages them."

"Do you try?" Mr. Owen asked quickly, surprised by the keenness of his interest.

"Why do you want to know?" she demanded, drawing near the man.

"I don't," he disclaimed hastily. "I don't care if you encourage the War Veterans of the World."

"Who are they?" she asked with sudden interest, then her eyes snapped dangerously. "Oh," she continued, "so you don't care, do you? Well, I'll fix you. I'll damn well lay you out with the dirtiest book I can find."

"Then what will you do?" Mr. Owen inquired.

"Lay myself out beside you," she fumed.

"With an equally dirty book, no doubt," he caustically added.

"Yes," she said, snatching up a heavy volume of *A Thousand and One Nights*. "This ought to settle your hash."

It probably would have, had not Mr. Owen ducked at the last minute. *A Thousand and One Nights* consequently descended upon the head of a near-sighted but otherwise unremarkable gentleman, whose nose, previously nearly buried in a book, was now completely interred. When presently the nose found strength enough to rise from its lewd resting place, the gentleman behind it glared at the innocent Owen through tears of rage and pain.

"That," said the man, as if explaining the incident to himself, "was an unnecessarily dirty trick."

"It was an unnecessarily dirty book," Mr. Owen replied soothingly. "It barely missed my head."

"Well, here's one you won't miss," grated the gentleman, and before Mr. Owen could duck he received full upon the top of his skull the entire contents of Fanny Hill, illustrations and all. As he staggered back from the blow he felt a heavy tome being slipped into his hand. Several other salesgirls were arming themselves with erotic literature for the defense of their assaulted leader.

"Pat him with this," a voice said in Mr. Owen's ear. "It's a bronze-bound Boccaccio. If that doesn't settle his hash I'll have a swell Rabelais ready."

"You're bound to settle somebody's hash," Mr. Owen muttered with a grunt as he drove Boccaccio down upon the other gentleman's head. "Better his hash than mine. I hope that did it!"

Apparently it had. The twice-flattened nose descended to rise no more of its own volition. Boccaccio had made a lasting impression. The body was speedily removed, and business went on as usual. Mr. Owen thanked the salesgirls for their ready support, then turned back to the one who had made him her special province.

"Just where were we?" he asked, then remembering that they had not been at such an agreeable place, added. "Let's begin a little farther back."

"How much farther back?" she asked. "Before all this rotten pornography?"

"Oh," said Mr. Owen hopefully, "then you're not so fond of pornography yourself?"

For a moment the girl looked at him defiantly.

"Suppose I'm not?" she demanded. "I can take it or leave it, just as I like. You don't have to wallow in pornography to be pornographic yourself. I'm a very erotic woman, I am. So erotic I can hardly stand being in the same section with you. I don't know what might happen."

"Don't let it," pleaded Mr. Owen. "I haven't quite found my sea legs yet."

"You haven't even looked at my land ones," the girl shot back.

"Let's not go into that any more," he begged her. "Do you mean that you find it difficult to be caged in here with me, or would you experience the same feeling with just any other man?"

"With any other man," she replied, "so long as he wasn't dead or too badly damaged."

Mr. Owen's face fell. His disappointment was obvious.

"Oh," he said somewhat flatly, "that's nice if you like it."

"Not that you don't affect me differently," she went on, smiling up at him. "I find my sex life rapidly approaching yours. It may be today. It may be tomorrow. It may be the next day at the very latest. Whenever it is, they're going to meet like a couple of ten-ton trucks."

"Does it necessarily have to be as violent as all that?" he asked uneasily. "Sounds sort of rough to me."

"It will be rough enough, no fear," she replied. "There's something about you that arouses my most primitive instincts. I don't know what it is, but it makes me simply filthy. Feel as if I want to shock you out of your wits."

"You have already," said Mr. Owen, "and I don't even know your name."

"It's Honor Knightly," she told him, "but people call me Satin because of my skin. I'll show you that later—all of it, if you like."

"No," said Mr. Owen, a little terrified. "Only some. It is like satin, though, all smooth and everything."

"You don't know the half of it," she boasted. "I'll open your eyes to something extra special in the line of skin!"

"You're too good to me," murmured Mr. Owen unenthusiastically, as he thought of the tremendous amount of skin he was slated to see on or before the day after tomorrow at the latest.

"Oh, I get fun out of it, too," said the girl almost gloatingly. "I get a lot of fun."

"I'm sure you must," remarked Mr. Owen. "But, tell me, Satin, do all young ladies about here talk like you?"

"Oh, no," the girl declared. "Most of them are not at all afraid of calling a spade a spade—perfectly unrestrained, they are."

"Not like you," he suggested.

"Not a bit," she admitted. "I like things clean but nice. You know—ladylike."

"Have you a decent dictionary?" a studious-looking gentleman inquired, leaning over the counter towards the girl.

"No," said the girl briefly. "All our dictionaries are indecent. Full of obscene words."

"I know all those," said the man.

"You do like hell," snapped Satin. "How about this one?"

She leaned over and whispered a word in the man's ear.

"What does it mean?" he asked in an awed voice.

Once more she whispered in the man's ear.

"My word," he said, his eyes growing round. "Does it mean all that?"

"And more," the girl replied. Turning to Mr. Owen, who was curious in spite of himself, she added, "Now, if I wasn't a lady I'd have said all that right out loud."

"Thank God you didn't," murmured the gentleman.

"On second thought, I think I'll buy one of those dictionaries."

"It's called the Little Gem Desk Dictionary Of Obscene Words," she told him, passing him the book. "It's standard. You'll find it quite a comfort, especially when you're mad."

"I've a friend on the faculty who loves indecent words," the studious gentleman informed her, tucking the book in his pocket. "Of course, when nicely used."

"Most members of faculties love indecent words," Satin declared. "It comes from dealing with the young."

"What are you doing for luncheon?" the gentleman asked her, to Mr. Owen's annoyance.

"Too bad," said Miss Honor Knightly with sincere regret. "I'm dated up today. You see, among my other means of making extra pin money," and here Mr. Owen found himself wondering about those ways, "I act as executive secretary for the Kiarians. They're holding their monthly luncheon today, and I have to take notes of the proceedings. It's an awful trial. I'm glad I know a lot of dirty words. One needs them at a Kiarian meeting, I assure you."

"I should imagine," replied the gentleman, "it would be even worse then dealing with the young. Some other day, perhaps."

"You'd be surprised," Satin informed Mr. Owen, when the gentleman and his dirty dictionary had taken themselves off, "how many invitations I get since I've taken charge of the Pornographic Department."

"No, I wouldn't," Mr. Owen assured her.

"Yes, yes," Honor went on, happily reminiscent. "I'd never suffer from insomnia if I took advantage of all my opportunities."

"Do you ever suffer from insomnia?" he asked, white nights from the past dimly stirring his memory.

"Terribly," said Satin, "when I'm all upset and erotic. But I won't any more now that you are here. There'll be no need of insomnia to keep me awake. I like things clean but nice."

"Oh, you like things clean but nice," Mr. Owen observed moodily. "I'll admit you make them clear enough. I'd never mistake one of your spades for a teething spoon, by any chance. But don't delude yourself. I'm not going to be here for long. I'm going away."

"Then I'm going to ask the partners if they won't give you to me," the girl declared.

"Oh, they'll say yes," Mr. Owen told her, "but it won't mean a thing. They're like that—impulsive. Then they forget."

"But I don't," said the girl. "And your number's up. Don't *you* forget."

"It must be a high one," Mr. Owen answered in a really mean spirit.

She looked at him.

"When my sex has dominated yours," she told him, looking rather mean herself, "I'm going to make you suffer for your rotten little wisecracks. See if I don't."

A page boy appeared to inform Mr. Owen that the partners were awaiting his pleasure. As he prepared to follow the boy he observed with some satisfaction the expression of irritation on Miss Honor Knightly's undeniably pretty face.

"You haven't told me that word," he tossed at her casually. "You know, the one you whispered in the man's ear."

"No?" she replied. "Well, lean over and I will."

Mr. Owen leaned over and waited. Why did he want to know? he wondered. His orderly mind assured him it was because she had told the other man. Was it possible he was morbidly jealous? He felt her breath fanning lightly on his cheek. Her lips brushed the lobe of his ear. Then her teeth seized it and, so far as he was concerned, bit it off. In his anguish Mr. Owen involuntarily released several of the dirtiest words he knew.

"It was none of those," she told him. "And now you will never know."

"How can you talk so clearly," he asked her huskily, "with the lobe of my ear in your mouth, or did you swallow it?"

"How common you are," she remarked coldly. "I don't like vulgar men. The boy is waiting."

Tenderly feeling his ear, Mr. Owen followed the boy

to the senior partner's private office. Here he was enthusiastically received and escorted up to one of the largest cocktail shakers he had ever seen. The Major, owing to his strength and size, was wrestling with this frost-coated vessel.

"It's nice to drink a lot of cocktails before luncheon," Mr. Larkin was telling everyone. "Of course, if you drink a whole lot of them you get quite drunk, but then, getting drunk is sort of nice, too."

Mr. Owen received this surprising shred of information with a proper display of interest as he accepted a glass from the hands of the hovering Dinner. After he had swallowed its contents he was inclined to agree with Mr. Larkin.

"It's nice to get drunk before dinner, too," quoth the Major, his deep voice rumbling pleasantly through the room.

"One can't get drunk before Dinner," the senior partner put in. "Dinner is always drunk."

"No," the small man objected. "He's always getting drunk, but he never quite is—not dead, I mean."

"Come! Come!" cried Mr. Larkin hospitably. "Drink up, everybody. To the new partner and the old ones. We simply have to get a skinful to stand that Kiarian luncheon."

"Oh," said Mr. Owen, visions of Satin in his mind and prints of her teeth in his ear. "Is that where we're going?"

"It is," replied the Major gloomily. "I'd much rather take you to a sporting house or a gambling dive."

"So would I," agreed Mr. Larkin. "I told him to remind me about brothels. Now, don't forget everybody, bring up brothels."

Mr. Dinner produced his notebook and made a painstaking entry.

"I have it down in black and white," he announced, looking up from his book. "Here it is," and he read: "Everyone is to remind H. Larkin about brothels."

"That's almost too black and white," observed Mr. Larkin. "In case you were found dead, I wouldn't want people to get the idea I had to be constantly reminded about brothels. No normal man should be as absent-minded as all that, should he? I know I'm not."

"No," said Mr. Dinner, his eyes blinking thoughtfully. "What you need is someone not to remind you of them. Suppose I put down a note like this: Everybody is to try to keep H. Larkin's mind off brothels. How would that do?"

"It won't do," Mr. Larkin replied after a thoughtful pause. "People might get the impression I thought altogether too much about such places, and I wouldn't like that, would you, Mr. Owen? You wouldn't like it noised abroad that you just couldn't think of anything else even if you seldom did."

"Certainly not," Mr. Owen agreed, and tossed off another cocktail. There was nothing out of the ordinary about this conversation. They were all jolly good fellows, sound, sensible men, and they drank delicious cocktails.

"You see?" cried Mr. Larkin. "He agrees with me. Put that notebook away, Dinner. There are some things I should be allowed to handle for myself. Besides, after we've finished that shaker, I think we'll all be primed to call on Hadley at the bank and demand a line of personal credit for our new partner. He has to have some money, you know, or else he'll be spending all of ours."

The two other partners looked at Mr. Owen with frankly alarmed eyes. Evidently it was a decidedly disagreeable possibility.

"No," murmured the Major, "that wouldn't be so good."

"Good," gasped Mr. Dinner. "It would be just awful. Let's rush to the bank."

# CHAPTER VII

## *Establishing a Line of Credit*

BY THE TIME THE LAST QUARTET OF COCKTAILS HAD been drained from what Mr. Owen had at first feared was going to be an inexhaustible shaker but which now he regretted was not, the partners felt themselves suitably set up to call on Mr. Hadly, the president of the bank with which the store did business in its casual way.

"We'll establish a line of credit for you, Mr. Owen," growled the Major like a jovial thunderstorm, "or I'll tear the hinges off the safe with my own two hands."

"And I'll help you," vowed Mr. Dinner. "What good is a bank unless you can establish a line of credit with it, I'd like to know?" As no one seemed prepared to tell him, he added, disgustedly, "They're so drunk I can't even hear them."

"I do feel so good," exclaimed Mr. Larkin. "I believe the four of us could establish a line of anything if we set our minds on it. What say you, Mr. Owen?"

"I say stick to credit," said Mr. Owen wisely. "Once we have our credit we can set about establishing other things—a reign of terror, for example. Some sadistic strain in my composition has always craved for a reign of terror. Also, I've always wanted to carry a cane."

"Let's all carry sticks," cried Mr. Larkin. "Heavy ones. They might intimidate that skinflint, Hadly."

He rang a bell on a flower-heaped desk, a girl entered, received the order together with various flattering but uncalled-for observations from all the partners, and in a surprisingly short time returned with four heavy sticks, so large and heavy, in fact, that Mr. Dinner experienced some difficulty in handling his and himself at the same time.

"Speaking of sadism," remarked Mr. Larkin easily,

clipping on a pair of light yellow gloves, "did you ever beat a defenseless child?"

In spite of the cocktails, Mr. Owen shuddered as he vigorously shook his head.

"Neither did I," went on Mr. Larkin, "but I've heard it's lots of fun."

"You might try it on my nephew," volunteered the Major. "He's an exceedingly snotty child. Last time I played cards with his father the young scamp pulled four aces from my sleeve."

"Any child should be beaten who does a thing like that," observed Mr. Dinner. "Maybe his father put him up to it."

"Quite possibly," replied the Major. "There always was a mean streak in my brother. Anyway, he'd been losing heavily all evening, what with one thing and another."

"If you'll give me a little room," put in Mr. Larkin, "I'll make an honest effort to veer myself through that door. We really must be going."

The senior partner thereupon veered through a private door giving to the street. Behind him veered his three companions, diligently swinging their sticks. Mr. Owen could not remember ever having veered onto so pleasant a thoroughfare. He drew a sharp breath and tried to remember all the things he ever heard about Paris. This street, he felt sure, was far better than anything Paris had to offer. Surely there had never been such inviting-looking women seated at such convivial-looking tables. And as he walked past them he became inwardly elated on discovering that the women gazed at him with eyes of undisguised approval.

It was jolly to be looked at that way for a change. He could not help wondering if the cocktails had not only improved his mental outlook but also his physical appearance. If they had, he decided to become a confirmed drunkard. Too few women had paid any special attention to him in the past. Only the out-of-luck souls had seemed to drift his way. Now he was coming into his birthright. He was being admired by the opposite sex. And he, in turn, was admiring. He was returning these women's glances with brightly acquisitive eyes.

He was lusting after them all. The world at last was his barnyard. Why didn't everyone get undressed and start in to chase one another? He could not decide which one he would chase first. Probably he would try to run in all directions at once.

It was a friendly sort of day, with a fair blue sky overhead. Beneath it the boulevard gave the impression of running away into friendly places. Other streets branched from it. He caught glimpses of spacious parks and plazas and lovely, interesting buildings. It seemed to be the sort of city he would have built himself, had he been given a free hand. Even the theaters wore an especially attractive aspect. One announcement read: "The only piece of cloth in this show is the curtain." Another play was called *Just As We Are,* and Mr. Owen, looking at the photographs of the girls, decided they would be just like that in this wholly desirable metropolis. He was very favorably impressed with everything. Delighted.

Their progress was necessarily slow, owing to the wide acquaintance of the three partners with various ladies and gentlemen they encountered in the course of their walk. Even Mr. Dinner, as small as he was and as drunk as he was, appeared to be greatly in demand. At one table Mr. Owen was introduced to a lady who in his exalted state impressed him as being the most beautiful woman in the world. When he extended his hand to take hers she deftly slipped her café bill into his.

"Pay that and I'm yours," she said in a thrilling sort of voice.

Mr. Larkin took the bill from the amazed Mr. Owen, scrutinized it closely, then clapped his hand to his forehead.

"Do you mean for life?" he asked the woman.

She shrugged her handsome shoulders eloquently.

"Nobody wants me for life," she replied.

"They might want you," the senior partner declared gallantly, "but, my dear, only a few men could afford to feed you. Is that just this morning's bill, or have you been living here for years?"

"You know how it is," she smiled. "Just dropped in

and felt thirsty. Got a bit hungry. Ordered a few things. That's all."

"The way you say it sounds cheap as dirt," Mr. Larkin said, returning her smile with interest. "If you hadn't let us see this bill we'd never have suspected you were sitting there filled to the scuppers with five quarts of champagne—of the best champagne, let me add, not to mention various other small but costly items."

"I know," protested the woman, "but I have to act this afternoon."

"What in, a free for all?" he inquired. "Or are you fortifying yourself for the entire chorus?"

"Oh, of course," retorted the woman, "if you don't care to pay it——"

"But we do," broke in Mr. Owen.

"You mean you do," the Major amended.

Mr. Larkin quickly passed the bill to Mr. Owen.

"I don't know how much money you have," he observed, "but you'd be simply mad to have as much as that."

Mr. Owen did not have as much as that. And it was such a nice day too. A man should have no end of money on such a day as this and in the presence of such a woman. He looked about him helplessly. Mr. Larkin took the bill and called for the captain.

"Charles," he said smoothly, "this is our new partner, Mr. Owen, Mr. Horace Owen—no, I mean Mr. Hector Owen. I grow confused in the presence of so much beautifully concealed champagne. Anyway, it doesn't matter. They both begin with H. Why did I call you, Charles?"

Charles, who was evidently both fond of Mr. Larkin and quite familiar with his ways, bowed and smiled quite happily.

"Has it to do, perhaps, with the presence of Madame Gloria?" he asked.

"Tremendously, it has," cried Mr. Larkin. "The very woman herself. Now Mr. Owen, our new partner, desires very much to sign her check. He will sign the store's name and his own initials, H.O. Even I can remember them. As this bill stands now, it is a worthless scrap of paper. Signed, it becomes even more so. If it doesn't bring money, we may be able to outfit your staff. Is everything understood?"

"Fully," the captain replied with another bow.

"And Mr. Owen gets the woman," went on Mr. Larkin. "Remember that, Charles. She's his until bent with age. This is a monolithic bill. It makes one crawl to think of it. Sign, Mr. Owen, sign."

Mr. Owen signed the bill, and Charles, still smiling, departed with a generous tip provided by Mr. Dinner, who seemed to be the senior partner's peripatetic desk and cash register.

"You owe the firm five dollars in cash," said Mr. Dinner, making a note, "but you might as well give it to me."

"When he gets that line of credit," Mr. Larkin told the small man. "Which reminds me, that line is yet to be got. We must spurt. We must actually tear along."

"Thank you," said Madame Gloria sweetly to Mr. Owen. "I am yours for life."

It was exceedingly indelicate, thought Mr. Owen, the way everyone kept referring to his ownership of this woman, including the woman herself.

"We'll take that up later," he explained to Madame Gloria.

While pondering upon how fast they must tear along, Mr. Larkin had fallen into a mood of deep abstraction. At Mr. Owen's words he looked up thoughtfully.

"Did you say up or off?" he inquired. "The size of that bill makes off almost obligatory." He paused and beamed upon the fair lady. "You may call your friends back now," he said. "I've detected them hiding about in places for quite some time. You've established your line of credit. We must now establish ours. The next time you give a barbecue I hope it will occur to you to stick one of our competitors, or at least wait until we've collected the insurance for some diamonds we lost this morning. Don't know which damaged us most, you or the thief."

As they hurried from the presence of this adorable

woman, Mr. Owen was dismayed to see four gentlemen and three ladies converging upon her table from various places of concealment. Then all of them sat down with cries of gladness and anticipatory expressions.

"That's the way we do things here," Mr. Larkin explained. "We boggle at nothing and nothing boggles us. A nice word, boggle. I'm fond of the two g's."

Mr. Larkin said so many things that made any sort of answer seem hopelessly inadequate. Hector Owen was not prepared to commit himself about boggle. He had never considered the word. However, almost any word was a good word on a day like this.

A short time later, in the office of the bank president, Mr. Owen found himself being presented to a large but florid gentleman whose impressively worried expression concealed a weak but generous character. Although habitually called a skinflint by the partners, the appellation had no justification as applied to Mr. Hadly. Anyone who did not immediately respond to the amiable proposition of their inflamed imaginations was automatically classified as a skinflint or worse.

"Well, gentlemen," he began fussily when they had seated themselves in his luxuriously appointed office, "I suppose you have called to see me about those bad checks we took the liberty of informing you about in this morning's mail."

"The liberty!" exclaimed the Major aggressively. "I call it decidedly bad taste. An imposition! Checks can't stay good forever, I say—"

"One moment, Major," cut in the suave voice of the senior partner. "Save that for later. Your words might befog the issue—even sink it entirely." Here he turned to the president and literally showered him with smiles. "You'll forgive the poor dear Major," he continued. "He's such a God damn fool. You were saying in your nice, friendly way something about checks. Ah, yes, I remember. It was something about bad checks, wasn't it? Well, let's not talk about them. We would never get anywhere that way. They're like spilled milk, no good sobbing over them. Let the dead bury the dead. And another thing, we omitted the detail of opening the mail this morning. You see, we take turns, and this morning we forgot whose turn it was. So we didn't open the mail at all. There it still is. Quite unopened. Naturally, we can't go on. You can see that for yourself, my dear, good Hadly."

"Although for the life of me I can't," his dear, good Hadly replied in a weary voice, "I'll try to if you'll endeavor to bend your brilliant faculties on this."

"Did you hear that gentlemen?" Mr. Larkin demanded proudly. "For once a bank president has spoken the truth." He addressed himself to Hadly. "If you'll overlook those checks I'll do more than bend my faculties. I'll wrap them about anything you may have to say."

"Good!" exclaimed the president. "Wrap 'em around this. Your stockholders have placed in my hands for collection all of the guaranteed coupons for dividends due them since you first took over the store. Naturally, I must do something about it."

"I should say you must," remarked Mr. Larkin, deeply moved. "You must throw those coupons right back in their double faces. Those coupons are not worth the paper they were printed on. Never were. If the truth were known, the words printed on them are not worth as much as the paper. I didn't make up the words, anyway. As I remember, Dinner did, and he was drunk at the time. Everyone should know that a drunken man's words shouldn't ever be taken seriously. If we believed what you said when you were only half drunk you'd be owing us the bank."

"As it is," replied Mr. Hadly, unable to keep a note of bitterness from creeping into his voice, "I've practically given it to you."

"Well, we've given you things, too," put in Mr. Dinner hotly. "Shirts and socks and even the drawers to your legs. And you still owe us for a mink coat you gave to that foreign—"

"One moment," Mr. Hadly interrupted, glancing uneasily at the door. "Let's save our recriminations for the barrooms. I give you boys credit—"

"How did you know?" the Major asked in surprise. "That's just what we came for. We wanted to establish a line of credit for our new partner. And here you go giving it to us before we've even asked."

"I wish the Major were dead," said Mr. Larkin, gazing dreamily into space as if seeing laid out upon it the large, dead body of his partner. "Everything would be so much simpler then. And if Dinner would only sicken and die, I might even yet to be able to snatch a few moments of happiness from life. However——" He broke off with a shrug and turned to Mr. Hadly. "I didn't want it to sound so bald when the matter was first presented to you. It wouldn't have sounded nearly so bad the way I was going to put it—the way I am going to put it, in fact. You see—"

"I'm not going to do it, whatever it is," the president broke in desperately. "And that's flat."

"I should say it is," Mr. Larkin agreed. "So flat it's silly. Now, listen, if you please. No more temper. I don't like it. You know how I am about temper. Easy on, easy off, or whatever you say."

Mr. Larkin stopped and looked at the president as if expecting an answer. Not knowing what else to do, Mr. Hadly nodded, although he obviously hadn't the remotest idea what he was nodding about. However, he had always found things went better if he nodded occasionally when Mr. Larkin was in full cry. The nod seemed to satisfy the senior partner, for he continued in his best manner.

"You see," he said, "Mr. Owen here, as our new partner, quite naturally has at heart the best interests of the bank with which we do business. Just how we do business and what business it is we do, need not enter into this discussion. We must all remember that. For it is very important that we should not embarrass the issue with facts. As soon as we talk facts we get to calling each other nasty names which are even harder to stand than the facts themselves. Is that understood?"

From the various expressions on the faces he inspected it was almost impossible to ascertain whether it was understood or not. Nevertheless, it was not denied.

"Very well, then," he resumed. "To continue. Mr. Owen, being who and what he is, does not want to give the wrong impression of the bank to our innumerable important friends. He does not want people to think he is dealing with a stingy bank, a penny-pinching, close-fisted, blood-sucking institution such as any bank would be that refused him a line of credit. I hope I'm not boring you with these obvious little details?"

"Not at all," said the president politely. "You've merely sickened me."

"Good!" exclaimed Mr. Larkin. "That's one way of breaking down resistance. But don't start me veering. I'd hate to begin rotating like crops." He paused and cleared his throat. "Nor," he resumed, "does our Mr. Owen want it to get about among his friends and influential business connections that the president of his bank is a man of low character, with the appetite of a swine and the instincts of a torturer. He doesn't want people to say as he passes them on the street, 'There goes old Owen, poor fellow. It's a damned disgrace how that chap's bankers keep him short of cash. I wouldn't deal with bankers like that if I had to go out of business. Hadly, from what I can learn, is a big hunk of cheese.' It would hurt him to hear things like that. It would hurt us all. But most of all it would hurt the bank. Most of all it would hurt Hadly, here, the president of the bank. And we don't want to do that."

"May I ask," inquired Mr. Hadly in a weak voice, "what you do want to do?"

"Merely to establish a line of personal credit for Mr. Owen," replied Mr. Larkin, "that would enhance the prestige of the bank we honor with our account. I will not permit it to be said that we do things on a small scale."

"You have, of course, collateral to secure this credit?" Hadly inquired more for the pleasure he would derive from infuriating the partners than from any hope of security.

"Are you mad?" three voices screamed in varying degrees of rage.

"You've already got in those beastly vaults of yours," boomed the Major, "practically everything we own in the world save our women and personal attire."

"Let's beat him up with our sticks," suggested Mr. Dinner, almost in tears. "He's gone too far this time.

He'll be asking us for our list of telephone numbers next."

"No," said the senior partner. "I've got something that will hurt him more than that. When my new yacht goes into commission next week we won't invite him to come along. That will break his heart. That will simply burn him up."

"How much does he want?" asked Mr. Hadly wearily.

"How much can you spend?" Mr. Larkin promptly demanded of Mr. Owen. "I mean without stinting— without giving the wrong impression?"

"I don't know," faltered Mr. Owen. "I don't need a great deal. Never had much to spend."

"He doesn't know what he's saying," Mr. Larkin said hastily to the president. "Your sordidness has deranged him. I think he should have for his personal use about fifteen hundred a month."

"Fifteen hundred!" gasped the president. "What does he intend to do—drink, gamble, and run around with women?"

"What would you want him to run around with?" the Major demanded. "Cows?"

"I don't know," muttered the president. "I don't want him to run around at all."

"No," observed Dinner scornfully. "You want him to stay home and grow old economically."

"No, I don't," retorted Hadly. "I don't mind a man having a bit of fun now and then, but with fifteen hundred dollars a man can't have anything else but fun. Wouldn't one thousand be enough to keep up the prestige of this bank? We wouldn't expect too much, you understand."

"Let's toss a coin to see whether it's a thousand or fifteen hundred," Mr. Larkin suggested.

"All right," replied the president. "A gambling chance is better than no chance at all."

For a few moments the five gentlemen waited uneasily to see who would produce the coin. They waited without result. No one produced the coin.

"Go on," said the Major at last to Mr. Hadly. "You

furnish the coin, or isn't there such a thing knocking about this dump?"

"I do wish you'd prevail upon your partners," Mr. Hadly complained to Mr. Larkin, "to moderate their manner of address somewhat. After all, I'm not quite a dog, even though I am the president of a bank. They really do owe me something."

"They owe you everything," Mr. Larkin replied hastily. "As I remarked before, it would be better were they dead and buried in their graves."

"You didn't say a word about graves," said Mr. Dinner.

"No?" asked the senior partner. "Well, I don't greatly care whether they bury you or not, so long as you're dead. However, I can't expect to get everything at once. Give me that coin, Hadly, and we'll toss for this line of credit."

"It's half a dollar," said the banker, looking closely at the coin before handing it over. "I shall expect it back."

"God," muttered the Major. "You're so damned cold-blooded you could freeze ice cubes in the hollow of your tongue."

"Gentlemen," cried Mr. Larkin, tossing the coin in the air, "I cry tails."

"You would," declared the Major. "How does she lie?"

"Who?" asked Mr. Larkin, forgetting to look at the coin he had deftly caught in his hand.

"The coin! The coin!" cried the Major.

"Pardon me," said the senior partner, gazing down into his hand. "I was thinking of something else. Dear, dear me, now isn't this odd. It fell tails up. Mr. Owen, you're lucky."

"So are we," declared Mr. Dinner. "We can all borrow from him."

"But first he must have a check book," said Mr. Larkin. "Hadly, that's a dear boy, send for some check books. We all want some check books. And ask the head teller to step in. He should meet our new partner."

When the teller appeared, armed with a stack of

check books, he was introduced to Mr. Owen. He was a sardonic-looking person with a pair of glittering eyes and a tongue that was awed by no man, regardless of how much he was worth.

"Not at all sure whether I'm glad to meet you or not," he told Mr. Owen. "Your partners' checks are bouncing all over the bank, and now I'll have to play leap-frog with yours, I suppose. Don't you birds ever get tired of spending money? I know I am, of trying to find it for you."

"Our new partner has lots of money to spend," said Mr. Dinner proudly. "He's just established a splendid line of credit, and he owes me five dollars already."

"Write him a check," put in Larkin, "or you'll never hear the end of it."

"And while you're settling up," Mr. Hadley suggested, "you might as well let me have that half dollar back."

"I'd like to sit next to you in hell," said Mr. Larkin admiringly to the president, "but I fear you would pick my pockets even while we shivered."

"Our hands would probably become entangled," replied Hadly, smiling at last, now that the unpleasant business was over. "Glad to have met you, Mr. Owen. Bear in mind that just because you have fifteen hundred a month you don't have to spend it all."

"Certainly not," said the Major. "We don't expect him to. We have all sorts of ideas about the disposition of his funds."

"I want a check for five berries," Mr. Dinner dully declared.

"Give him his check and let's pound along," put in Mr. Larkin. "That damned Kiarian luncheon has to be outfaced. Come along, gentlemen. We must thud. Drop round to see our new partner, Hadly, old crow. You'll find him immensed in a book in the Pornographic Department."

And with this merry leave-taking Mr. Larkin hustled his partners from the presence of the president of the most powerful bank in the city. At the door Major Britt-Britt paused and looked back at Mr. Hadly.

"When people come to see us," he announced, "especially old and valued friends, we'd consider ourselves lepers if we didn't give them a drink."

The door closed on the president's unprintable retort.

"Oh, dear me, yes," Mr. Larkin murmured happily as they strolled down the street. "That's how we do things here. It gives me a deal of pleasure to do old Hadly in the eye. Just the same, I don't believe all bank presidents are conceived in cold storage. Hadly really is a charming fellow."

"How long does this credit last?" asked Mr. Owen.

"Indefinitely, my dear fellow. Indefinitely," the senior partner assured him. "Forget all about it. We can do anything with that bank except dynamite the vaults. They wouldn't like that."

"Let's catch a spray of drinks before we join the Godly," Mr. Dinner suggested.

"Not a bad idea," said the Major.

"A good idea," agreed Larkin. "Then we'll feel better equipped to establish a reign of terror among the Kiarians."

## CHAPTER VIII

## *The Burning Beard*

"THERE'S NO DOUBT ABOUT IT, I DO FEEL GIDDY," SAID Mr. Larkin, giggling behind his hand as the partners pushed their way through the crush of smartly dressed gentlemen in the get-together-room of the Kiarian banqueting quarters. "At any moment now I may begin to veer like a tidy little typhoon. Don't see a face I like. They're all smug and acquisitive. Look! What *is* Dinner doing?"

Mr. Dinner was merely doing what appeared to be the normal thing to a drunken mind. Unable to attract the attention of his friend the Major, the little fellow, stooping over, was vigorously jabbing his cane at his huge partner between the legs of a stout gentleman. This endeavor to establish contact by means of a short cut proved effective but disconcerting. The stout gentleman, looking down to see what was disturbing him, uttered a cry of frightened amazement. What incredible metamorphosis was he going through, he wondered. In his endeavor to get away from whatever the thing was, he turned sharply and thus entangled the cane between the legs of another earnest Kiarian. The Major thereupon seizing the free end of the stick gave it a violent upward tug. The shrieks of the two impaled gentlemen rang through the room. Mr. Dinner, now deeply absorbed in his occupation, which had become in his addled brain a battle of wits and deftness, yanked up his end of the cane with equal determination. The noise the gentlemen made merely whetted his enthusiasm. Even at that late date the situation might have been saved had the two Kiarians not attributed their unhappy plight to the other's deliberate intent.

"Is that a nice thing to do?" one of them demanded furiously, endeavoring to ease himself on his objectionable as well as painful perch.

"Nice," grated the other. "You've nearly ruined me, and still you keep on doing it. Do you want to get poked in the eye?"

"I don't much care where I get poked now," the other man said in a hopeless voice. "Please stop doing it."

"I'd rather have been stabbed than to have had this happen," his vis-à-vis retorted. "If you don't take that stick away I'll do something to you."

"You are doing something to me already," cried the stout man. "You're doing plenty. Don't twiggle it like that."

"But he isn't doing it at all," a Kiarian spectator helpfully informed the speaker.

"Oh, dear," Mr. Larkin observed reflectively to Hector Owen. "Dinner can think of the damnedest things to do with a stick. Those gentlemen must be in great distress."

"I hate to think of it," said Mr. Owen. "Look how the Major's pulling. He'll cut those men in two."

From the sounds the men were making this was not difficult to believe. Drink had lent strength to Dinner's arms and added to that already possessed by the Major's. The gentlemen, turning on the stick, were imploring their tormentors to abandon this contest in which they themselves had never expressed the slightest desire to participate.

"Oh, very well," said the Major to his small partner. "You can have your old stick."

With this he abruptly released his hold, and the two gentlemen fell weakly to the floor, from which they were presently assisted by a number of sympathetic Kiarians.

"Certainly I'm going to have my stick," little Dinner declared stoutly. "And no big bully is going to take it away from me either."

"May I ask," inquired Mr. Larkin, "how you managed to get two Kiarians on the end of your stick?"

"They got themselves there," said Dinner. "I didn't get them there. Must have thought they were playing horse. I think some of these Kiarians drink too much. Come along. Let's get our badges."

Without even so much as glancing at the tortured men, Mr. Dinner led the way to a table at which an official was importantly giving out badges bearing the Christian name or the nickname and the occupation of the member presenting himself. The senior partner received one that informed the world he was "Larkie" and that he passed his days as a merchant. This trophy he immediately pinned on the back of an innocent bystander. Mr. Dinner's was affixed with strategic craft by the Major to the seat of another gentleman's trousers. Whenever he bent over, this gentleman announced to the gathering at large that he made a practice of referring to that section of his body simply as Lu. The Major, with much unnecessary adjusting, pinned his badge on the breast of a pretty cloakroom girl who did not seem to mind. Taking it all in all, Mr.

Owen decided his partners were men with excessively puerile minds and futile ways. Why they had insisted on their badges and waited in line to get them only to make them objects of ridicule and derision was more than even his somewhat confused mind could understand.

On the way to the luncheon room they were accosted by numerous members who, in spite of the absence of badges, addressed the partners in cloyingly familiar terms, anyway.

"Well, B. B.," cried one gentleman, clapping the Major on a shrinking shoulder. "It does my eyes good to see you, old boy. How's the Little Lady?"

"You must be not only dumb but also blind," the Major told him. "If you ever saw my wife you'd damn well know she wasn't little, and if you'd ever heard her line of talk you'd never call her a lady. Go fawn on somebody else. I don't like that way of talking."

As surprised as he was at this display of brutal frankness on the part of the Major, Mr. Owen was even more so by the language of Mr. Dinner. A gentleman named Buddy was addressing the small man in hearty accents.

"Hello, Lu," this person cried. "Tickled to death to see you."

"You're a liar," said Dinner coldly. "You know you hate my guts."

And with this he turned his back on the much discomfited Buddy. Another well meaning Kiarian had cornered the glowering Major.

"It isn't the heat," the man was saying, "It's the hu——"

But the man never finished his sentence. The Major knocked him down with a single blow, wiped his hand with an expensive silk handkerchief delicately scented with eau de Cologne, and deliberately walked away.

"We can't let them get too friendly with us," Mr. Larkin informed the astounded Owen. "If we did, they'd ruin our lives."

"I don't see why they want to know you at all," said Mr. Owen, "if you treat them that way."

"You don't know Kiarians," the senior partner replied. "They'd forgive a murder for the sake of prosperity and sell their wives for a boom in business."

"What do you think of our city, Mr. Owen?" a person calling himself Benny wanted to know a few minutes later, during the course of an introduction.

"Tell him it smells," whispered Mr. Dinner, at Mr. Owen's shoulder. "I want to watch his face."

"It smells," said Mr. Owen obediently, and he, too, watched Benny's face. It merely became more foolish, if possible, than it had been before he asked the question.

"You should never have brought him along," Benny told Mr. Larkin when he had recovered from the shock. "He'll never mix with the boys."

"Go away," said Mr. Larkin in a dead voice, "or I'll pull your inquisitive nose."

"But I didn't mean it smells, really," Mr. Owen explained when the man had tottered off.

"I know," replied Mr. Larkin, "but it does when he's around. If you say the first thing that comes into your head at one of these luncheons you're pretty sure to be right."

"Why do you ever come?" asked Mr. Owen.

"To annoy people," said Mr. Larkin, "and to be annoyed in turn. It's good for everybody. Yet sometimes, when I come away from one of these luncheons, I get the feeling it must all have been a dream—that these people didn't really exist but were culled up from a fit of depression. Why, they even sing at one. All together they sing—boosting songs, patriotic songs, mother songs. You'll hear them soon yourself."

Mr. Owen did, and although there was too much of it and the songs were either too optimistic or sentimental, he had to admit to himself the singing was pretty good. Nevertheless, he wished it would stop.

Mr. Larkin enlivened his table by surreptitiously pouring some essence he had purchased for his cigarette lighter into his neighbor's glass of water. The other partners were as innocent of this affair as was the owner of the water himself. And the owner was a personage of note, a man high up in the deliberations of the Kiarians. His inspirational speeches were listened to frequently and indefinitely. He was a man with a long square beard, lots of white to his eyes, and a deep, beautiful voice. He was large and he was lofty. He was the president of one of the most progressive advertising agencies in town and had grown used to having himself referred to by his initials which through some trick of fate chanced to be W. C. Just previous to the serving of the soup this magnificent gentleman felt himself called upon to discover how well his voice sounded in public today. Accordingly he rose, and with a fat hand holding an unlighted cigar, silenced the singing mouths.

"Kiarians!" he cried. "I am no longer your chairman, your leader."

"Good!" croaked a disguised voice from somewhere in the neighborhood of the sleepy-looking Mr. Dinner.

The bearded gentleman paused, frowned heavily, then filled his lungs with air.

"Kiarians!" he burst forth again, and Mr. Dinner, who had been perfecting the art in secret, promptly began to quack like a duck.

"Kiarians!" cried the man. "Is there a duck in this room?"

"You haven't begun on your soup yet," said the Major in a loud admonitory voice. "What do you want with a duck?"

"I don't want a duck," thundered W. C.

"But you did ask for a duck," said the Major, stubbornly sticking to his guns.

"I asked if there was a duck," the man retorted.

"Well, is there?" Mr. Larkin inquired pleasantly.

"How should I know?" snapped the great man. "There were duck-like sounds in the room. If it wasn't a duck I'll eat it."

"May I eat it if it is?" the Major asked brightly.

"What!" exploded the man. "I have no duck for you to eat. I want to get rid of this duck."

"Will somebody please throw that duck out," Mr. Larkin called in a voice of authority, then murmured to Mr. Owen, "Isn't this amusing? It's better than I hoped."

"What duck?" asked several earnest voices.

A volley of unpleasant sounds shattered the brooding silence of the room. Mr. Dinner, startled himself by his remarkable performance, appeared from behind his napkin and looked about him with an innocent face.

"Kiarians!" called W. C., now at the end of his patience. "You speak as if I personally knew this duck, as if deliberately I had brought this duck among you, as if this duck were my boon companion." He paused, then flung at them, "How should I know what duck?"

"Lord love a duck!" cried Dinner for no apparent reason.

W. C. shivered. His temper was out of hand.

"I hate a duck," he shouted. "I'd like to wring its neck." A fresh burst of protesting quacking from Dinner greeted this impassioned avowal.

"There it goes again!" cried W. C. "Am I to be mocked by this pest of the barnyard?"

"Maybe he's in your beard," suggested Major Britt-Britt in a penetrating voice, "and is squawking to get out. I know I would if I were a duck."

"I wish to God you were," thundered the incensed Kiarian, "and in the barnyard, where you belong."

"You'd be the first worm I'd gobble," said the Major with surprising self-control, and added thoughtfully, "Even if it killed me."

"Kiarians!" once more cried the bearded gentleman, who had never before been talked down by any man and who proudly refused to be defeated at the bill of a fowl. "Now that the duck has stilled its brazen voice I will again raise mine."

Mr. Dinner was quacking tearfully behind his napkin, but the great man pretended not to hear the sounds. Mr. Larkin was watching him closely, waiting for that inevitable moment when the hand would raise the glass of water to the bearded lips. That moment was not far off. The senior partner held a match pressed to the side of a match box.

"Kiarians!" thrilled the orator's voice, his hand reaching for the glass. "I no longer govern your deliberations." The glass was raised slightly from the table. "I no longer give you the light—"

Mr. Larkin struck, and as if performing some well polished feat of legerdemain W. C. lifted a flaming glass which promptly ignited his beard. The applause in the room was tremendous. Kiarians rose and cheered. They had never before suspected good old W. C. of such ability in sleight-of-hand. Admirers in the room cried out, but none cried louder than W. C. himself.

"Don't applaud, you damn fools!" he shouted through the fumes and smoke. "Somebody put me out!"

"Do you mean throw you out?" the Major inquired lazily. "Like the duck, for instance?"

Mr. Dinner, in his drunken excitement, was quacking unrestrainedly. Mr. Owen, still undecided whether he was witnessing a trick or a burning Kiarian, remained quietly in his seat. The senior partner had risen and was holding a bowl of soup carefully poised beneath the burning beard.

"Now," he said in a voice of great composure, "if you'll be so good as to lower your head a trifle, then plunge the beard in this bowl of delicious soup, I think we'll have you extinguished in a jiffy. It would be better, if you closed your eyes. The fumes will be terrific, I fear."

But before closing his eyes W. C. caught a vivid picture of the city's greatest advertising leader solemnly dipping his glorious beard into the depths of a bowl of soup. What an imperishable memory he would leave in the eyes of the assembled Kiarians! This was the end of his career as a public character. He could never hope now to complete the autobiography which one of his copy writers was doing for him on office time and without extra pay. The eyes he turned on the senior partner were filled with rage and hate.

"What do I care," he growled, "if the soup is delicious?"

Making a virtue of necessity, he bared his teeth in the semblance of a smile for the consumption of the watching Kiarians, then plunged his beard in the soup. Even as he did so, thoughts of moving-picture comedies of the slap-stick variety flashed through his mind.

There was a sizzling sound and a burst of smoke and through it all gleamed the white teeth of the advertising genius whose lips were contorted in a maniacal grin. Strong men caught their breath, while weak ones turned away. Mr. Dinner quacked like a duck and sleepily rubbed his eyes. One especially enthusiastic Kiarian cheered in a loud voice, a well meaning display which only seemed to increase the mental anguish of the smouldering man.

"The beard is now extinguished," Mr. Larkin announced. "Pardon me if I cry a little. W. C.'s personally conducted bonfire has made my eyes water."

"It's fairly sickened me," commented the Major in a rough, coarse voice. "Barring none, that beard is the worst I've ever smelled. I'll bet it hasn't been dusted off since Queen Victoria died."

This observation on his personal habits of cleanliness was too much for W. C. He raised his massive head and glared at the Major. The beard emerged from the delicious soup tastefully garnished with vegetables and spaghetti. Mr. Owen, for the sake of his own sensibilities, was moved to offer the gentleman a napkin.

"You wouldn't look quite so awful," he said in a sympathetic voice, "if you used this on what's left of those whiskers."

Automatically W. C. accepted the napkin and thoughtfully applied it to his damaged beard.

"May I do it for you?" Mr. Larkin asked, advancing on the man. "I'd dearly love to dry your poor dear beard."

The advertising genius started back with a cry of horror. The sparks of madness were gleaming in his eyes.

"I'll dry my own beard," he cried through wisps of smoke still straining through the hard dying tangle of hair. "Keep your hands off it. Don't come a step nearer."

"You wouldn't have to ask me twice," Major Britt-Britt informed the world. "It certainly is a mess."

"About the most revolting beard I ever saw," claimed little Mr. Dinner. "I wish he'd hide it somewhere."

"And I wish the lot of you would stop saying things about my beard," the great man retorted. "It's bad enough to have it burned, without having it discussed."

"That's right," agreed Mr. Larkin. "No beard looks its best immediately after a fire. We expect too much of W. C. He's done enough as it is."

At this point Mr. Mark Crawly, universally known as Big Boy, presiding officer of the local Kiarians, deemed it expedient to introduce some semblance of order into all this acrimonious chaos. Mr. Crawly was a nice chap. One could not help liking him a little. He possessed what all Kiarians loved most—a fine front. Inside, Mr. Mark Crawly was just plain dumb, which was no handicap among his fellow members. He could say stupid things in a firm, manly voice and get away with them. Years ago his firm had recognized the value of his smile as a business getter and had elevated him to the position of general sales manager. It occasionally took new members of his staff almost a month to discover that he had only a vague idea of what it was all about. He smiled business in and competition down. Above his desk was a Keep Smiling sign. In the *Nut and Bolt Trade Journal* his words were often quoted. "'Meet depression with a grin and smile a boom into being,' says Mark Crawly at the Tenth Nut and Bolt Convention." Had it not been for his hard-working subordinates he would have smiled his firm into bankruptcy, but that, of course, was not generally known. Big Boy Crawly now addressed the still slightly smoldering W. C. in particular and the room in general.

"Gentlemen," he began, "we all like and respect our W. C."

Mr. Dinner giggled a little at this, but Mr. Crawly frowned.

"We are sorry about his beard," he resumed, "yet even now I'm not sure whether he did it on purpose or not."

An animal-like howl burst from the advertising man's singed lips.

"Do you think I'd deliberately set fire to my beard," he asked in an impassioned voice, "to amuse you damn fools?"

"I assumed you were trying to amuse us," Big Boy Crawly replied good-naturedly. "It was funny, you know. How did it catch?"

"It was very dry," announced Dinner in a solemn voice. "That beard was a public menace."

"It was nothing of the sort," shouted W. C. "I've worn that beard for years."

"When was it last dry cleaned?" Major Barney inquired.

"It never was dry cleaned," retorted the other.

"I feared as much," said the Major. "The damn thing burned of its own accord like a heath fire. Spontaneous combustion sort of—that's how I figure it out."

"The Major means," Mr. Larkin explained to the room, "that the regrettable fire which broke out in the beard was due to the accumulation of years of débris. Am I right, Major?"

"As always," the big chap replied. "Wonder if he had it insured?"

"Was the beard insured, W .C.?" the senior partner inquired, turning politely to that infuriated gentleman. "Not against theft, of course, but for fire?"

"Bah!" ejaculated W. C. "Bah!"

"He's bleating like a sheep," cried Mr. Dinner, who was professionally interested in animal noises. "There's no end to the things the man can do."

"One moment," called Mr. Crawly. "I asked W. C. a simple question, and you gentlemen have made the thing seem terribly involved. W. C., can you tell us how your beard caught fire?"

"How should I know?" shot back the mighty man in the agony of his soul.

"Aren't you even interested?" Major Barney asked innocently. "I know if I had a beard and it happened to go off like yours did, I'd never rest until I'd discovered the cause. The damn thing might do it again."

"It would be awful to have it happen in bed with a woman," Mr. Dinner observed reflectively. "What would she think?"

W. C. sprang to his feet. Beard or no beard, he would put a stop to this. These people were not going to continue talking about himself and his beard as if neither of them were present.

"Kiarians!" he cried, showing the whites of his eyes. "Let's abandon this talk about beards and turn to other things."

"We haven't settled that matter of the duck yet," Mr. Dinner suggested. "We might take that up."

"Someone was making duck noises," W. C. replied. "I've thought that out, too. There is no duck."

The volley of quacking and squawking that greeted this denial far surpassed all previous demonstrations. W. C. paused and shook himself like a punch-drunk fighter.

"I may as well sit down," he observed at last in a hopeless voice, "if that duck is going to interrupt every word I say."

"It seems to be coming from the direction of your table," a Kiarian called out.

"You look under the table, Dinner," the Major commanded, "and I'll look under whatever remains of his beard. That duck must be one place or the other."

"If you touch my beard I'll cut your throat!" cried W. C., grabbing up a knife.

"A pretty way for a man to talk," complained Mr. Dinner. "We were only trying to help."

"I wasn't going to touch his old beard," explained Major Barney in an injured voice. "I was just going to peep under it."

"Kiarians!" almost screamed the distracted man, "Are you going to allow these ruffians to turn this dignified meeting into a discussion of my beard? Are you going to permit them to torture me about it—to throw my beard in my face?"

"Better than burning it in ours," put in Major Barney.

"Very well, then," called out the senior partner in a conciliatory voice. "Let's table the beard now that he's finished souping it."

"How do you do that?" asked the unintelligent Dinner. "Do you mean flatten it out and iron it?"

"Bah!" exclaimed the great leader. "And bah again."

"Why again?" asked Major Barney. "We heard the first bah, and it didn't mean anything either. I like the duck better."

Mr. Dinner lifted his napkin and behind it quacked his thanks. W. C., with a despairing cry, flung up his hands and sank heavily to his chair. Then he brought his hands down and rested his head in them. He would never appear in public again, he vowed to himself. But he did. He appeared many times until at last he died in public and had a public Kiarian funeral and then was promptly and publicly forgotten as such men should be.

He could never have been tolerated in private.

## CHAPTER IX

## *The Kiarians Continue*

ALMOST COINCIDENT WITH THE COLLAPSE OF THE excellent W. C., as that gentleman was commonly called, was the arrival of Honor, or Satin, Knightly. As she walked the length of the hall the eloquent sheen of her frock quoted faithfully the lines of her body. And by the time she had seated herself at a small desk near the speaker's table there was not one of those Kiarian boys who had not committed sin in his heart save, perhaps, W. C., who was muttering things in his beard.

Having been penned up with this girl at close quarters, Mr. Owen now had the opportunity to study her from a distance. He found Satin exceptional in every detail. To be too close to the girl destroyed one's critical faculties. At such times there was room in the masculine mind for the entertainment of only one thought. And Satin herself did not make things any easier. She was far too vividly aware of herself and her quarry for relations in the abstract. She had her lips and her eyes

and various other things. They were at their tireless
best now. Why let them go to waste? Why let time
gather in an unused credit? Satin saw no reason. She
was also convinced that her creator never had any reason in mind.

As Mr. Owen studied the girl, he felt as if he were
wandering through the fragrance of an old lost orchard
in search of the shadow of his youth still lurking
among the trees. He could appreciate keenly what the
years of soured domesticity had done to him by the
very freshness and harking back of his present vision.
Old scenes, old songs, and lost impressions came well-
ing up from some long neglected depth of his being.
At the moment the desire to be loved was more urgent
than to give it. He had done enough of that and found
it unrequited. This had left him somewhat uncertain of
himself in the rôle of a lover. He needed to be convinced, and he had a strong, happy conviction that
Satin Knightly could be most convincing when once
she set her mind on it. He had begun to feel that
falling in love was a sort of automatic process that
functioned only when one was young. He had doubted
up to now the recapturing of those poignant, all envel-
oping emotions, those sensations that seemed to be
tangled up with every reaction to one's surroundings,
one's private thoughts and aspirations.

Now he was not so sure. Satin was working strange
magic in him. And if it chanced to be black magic, he
did not greatly care. He felt all the better for it—all
the younger. He wished, however, that she was not in
the Pornographic Department. In such surroundings it
was difficult to sustain for long the preliminary stages
of romance on a decently exalted plane. In the Pornographic Department they began low and ended even
lower. He doubted if there were any preliminary stages
in Satin's conception of courtship. She seemed to believe that a lavish display of skin constituted the normal wooing. Should it prove too difficult to guide the
young lady's conduct into the channels of conventional
decency, he would be forced to conform to hers, which,
when all was said and done, amounted to the same
thing. As for his partners, they were simply animals.

He liked them, but could find no good in them. They were animals, simple and impure, and would always remain animals. He pitied them a little in the generosity of his newly born emotions.

In the meantime the animals were enjoying themselves according to their fashion. The senior partner had collected the ashes of W. C.'s beard into a neat pile which he now scraped into an envelope and politely offered to their rightful owner.

"Wouldn't you like to keep these?" he asked in his suavest tones. "They're the ashes of your beard—about a foot's worth in all."

"Take 'em," Mr. Dinner urged. "You're about one tenth cremated already, you know."

"Sure thing," contributed the Major. "He should send them to the family vault as a sort of first shipment. The rest of him can come along later, either whole or part by part."

"I want to be an urn when I die," declared Mr. Dinner. "Can I be an urn?"

"No," replied Mr. Larkin. "You'd go much better as a flask or a cocktail shaker."

"Let the Major be a cocktail shaker," the little fellow pleaded. "I want to be an urn, a nice urn in a niche."

"You won't make enough ashes to use up a thimble," Major Barney remarked.

"All right," declared Dinner. "I don't care. Just tuck me in a thimble and stick that in an urn, because that's what I want to be, an urn—" then he added thoughtfully—"in a niche."

"I do wish you'd stop repeating that word over and over again," came the gloomy voice of the advertising man. "I don't know why they ever placed me at this table. The lot of you are no better than idiots."

"You can't be any better than an idiot, can you?" asked the Major. "Unless, of course, you're a maniac, and they're just plain crazy."

"I wonder what he'd like to be?" continued Mr. Dinner, pursuing his mournful topic. "Ask him if he'd like to be an urn along with me. I don't care what company I keep once I'm safe in an urn."

"I don't think W. C. wants to be an urn," put in the senior partner consideringly. "I have a feeling he'd rather go as a gas tank or even a bathtub. Either would be more suitable for a public character."

"Then why not let him go as an ash can or just simply as a kitchen sink?" persisted Mr. Dinner.

"By God!" cried W. C. "I'll not stand for that. No, sir, I won't. You're irreverent, sacrilegious vulgarians. I'll not sit another minute at this table. Let me out of here."

The great man rose unsteadily, stepped on the plate of soup Mr. Larkin had thoughtfully placed on the floor, then staggered away to the speakers' table, where a place was quickly made for him.

"I guess he didn't want the soup anyway," said Mr. Larkin, looking thoughtfully at the mess on the floor. "It was all full of beard."

Mr. Owen shuddered fastidiously. The partners obviously were not at their best at meal times.

"Wonder how soup would go with beard?" wondered the inquiring Mr. Dinner. "I shouldn't think I'd like it."

"Not with that beard in it," agreed the Major.

"I don't think I'd care for soup with any beard in it," vouchsafed the senior partner.

"You haven't seen all the beards in the world," Dinner shot back in a challenging tone of voice.

"I don't care to taste any," Mr. Larkin replied with dignity. "I am not a beard taster."

"Is there such a thing as a beard taster?" asked the Major, who was easily interested.

"I don't see why there shouldn't be," Mr. Larkin replied with more confidence than he felt. "There are coffee tasters and tea tasters and wine tasters. It seems only reasonable there should be beard tasters."

"It may seem reasonable and all to you," Mr. Dinner persisted, "but what I want to know is, what do they want to taste these beards for?"

"They might not want to taste the beards," replied Mr. Larkin. "They might have to taste the beards."

"Why?" asked Mr. Owen, drawn in, in spite of himself. "Why should any man be forced to taste beards?"

"Simply as a means of livelihood," said the senior partner triumphantly. "Necessity—economic necessity."

"You mean as professional beard tasters?" the astonished Major demanded.

"I can't think of anyone being mean enough to beard-taste for pleasure," replied Mr. Larkin. "That would be the same as taking the beard out of honest men's mouths."

"I'm an honest man," Mr. Dinner declared, "and I'd consider it a favor if anyone yanked a beard out of my mouth."

"No self-respecting man would let you taste his beard," replied the senior partner cuttingly.

"Oh, I don't know," retorted Dinner. "I guess I could taste a beard as well as the next."

"But what I don't understand is," deliberated the Major, "what's to be gained by tasting a lot of beards?"

"There you have me," agreed Mr. Larkin. "That's the one weak point in the argument."

"Not at all," cried Mr. Dinner, suddenly switching to the side of the beard tasters. "A man might want to have his beard tasted for any number of reasons."

"Name me one," demanded the Major.

"Well," replied Dinner, floundering a little, "it is easily possible that a man might like to have his beard tasted to see if it's getting brittle or to see if it's getting tough or to remind him of what he had for the previous meal or to discover lost collar buttons and neckties and other misplaced articles—"

"Men with beards don't have to wear neckties," the Major interrupted.

"Men with short beards do," argued Dinner.

"They can claim they're wearing bow ties," shot back the Major.

"Ah, Dinner," interposed the senior partner. "He has you there. A very good point."

"Of course, if they want to lie about it they can," said Mr. Dinner moodily.

"May I ask," put in Mr. Owen, "what in the world is all this coming to?"

"We don't know," replied the Major, "but don't interrupt."

"I feel I'd be neglecting my duties if I didn't," said Mr. Owen. "You'll go clean off your heads if this keeps up much longer."

"Nonsense," snapped Dinner impatiently. "We often go on for hours like this at the office."

"When there's too much to do," Mr. Larkin explained.

Mr. Dinner's flask, which had been going the rounds during this conversation, was now empty. Accordingly, Mr. Larkin produced his and passed it to Mr. Owen.

"Drink some of that," he said, "and everything will seem much clearer."

Mr. Owen drank and discovered to his delight that Mr. Larkin had spoken the truth.

"I defy Dinner to tell me," resumed the Major, "of one single instance where beard tasting has served a useful end."

Mr. Dinner took a pull at the flask and pondered over this challenge.

"I can conceive of a case," he declared at last, "where an especially adept beard taster simply by tasting a beard could tell whether it was going to rain or not."

"Brilliant!" exclaimed the senior partner. "Dinner, that was brilliant—oh, very good. Very good indeed."

The Major looked momentarily discomfited. He turned hatefully upon his small antagonist.

"Where would you find such a sensitive beard?" he growled. "One so delicately attuned to nature."

"On a prophet," retorted Dinner without batting an eye. "You know, one of those birds that never shaved."

"You mean a rabbi," snorted the Major. "Who'd want to taste a rabbi's beard?"

"Maybe some especially devout member of his congregation," replied Mr. Dinner. "Who knows?"

"You don't, for one," said the Major. "And I don't care."

"Then," Mr. Larkin suggested smoothly, "it's about time to change the subject. Perhaps we may be able to annoy a few of these damn Kiarians."

Big Boy Crawly, the chairman, was once more on his feet. He was preparing to launch himself forth on a wave of oratory having to do with the character and accomplishments of the speaker of the day, a powerful figure in the automobile world, an entire trade journal in himself, not to mention a couple of house organs.

"Kiarians!" cried Big Boy Crawly. "Need I introduce to you the speaker for today?"

"Not so far as we're concerned," the senior partner consented agreeably, rising to his feet and confronting the room. "And besides, I have a few words to say myself."

"Mr. Larkin," replied Mr. Crawly, the smile flickering on his face, "you are out of order, I fear. The questions and discussions come after the speech."

"Please sit down," said Mr. Larkin in a pained voice, "You know how I am about interruptions. They make me veer most noticeably—fairly spin on my axis. Already I feel like a revolution. I might even do a little foaming on the side. You look as if you were going to do considerable foaming yourself, Big Boy. Do sit down." He paused then continued rapidly, as if fearing another interruption. "Kiarians!" he suddenly bellowed in a fair imitation of the great voice of W. C. "No one regrets more than I do that a familiar landmark has today been destroyed before our very eyes."

"Please sit down," cried Mr. Crawly.

"Be still, you," shouted Mr. Larkin, "or I'll cut your smiling heart out. This is sacred, Kiarians!" he unleashed again. "No one regrets more than I do, and in this I include my slightly drunken partners—"

The enthusiastic quacking of a duck greeted this pronouncement.

"No one regrets more than we do," continued the senior partner, "that the magnificent beard of W. C.—the only beard we had among us—should have taken it upon itself to catch fire and burn up, virtually in our laps. I would suggest that in future our great advertising play boy, instead of depending entirely on soup, be provided with a neat pocket fire extinguisher of his own, suitably engraved with the Kiarian emblem and some nice little sentiment such as, the Beard that Burns at Banquets Lights the World."

"Oh, for goodness' sake," cried Big Boy Crawly, "Mr. Larkin, won't you please sit down?"

"No, I won't," snapped the senior partner. "I won't sit down. I'll veer round this room like a jolly old whirling dervish. By rights you should be doing what I'm doing for you—saying a few kind words about that poor, dear beard of our excellent W. C. You all seem to have got used to addressing him that way. As for me, I frankly confess I still feel a little embarrassed whenever I have occasion to say it. You know what I mean. However, I'm nearly finished now, anyway. I merely wanted to say it was a good beard, but better soup. The soup was delicious. It was better than the beard because it put the beard out. Anyone can see that."

Dignified Kiarians in various parts of the room were now on their feet. Why had not the Lord God of Business and Boosting struck this man dead as he blasphemed? "Sit down! Sit down!" they hurled at the senior partner as he calmly stood his ground and with a coy, friendly hand waved back to them.

"You Kiarian boys are acting simply childish," he chided them gently. "Do keep still. I want to talk about this beard. For some reason, to talk about this beard fills a fundamental craving in me. I'm frantic about it. Never did I see anything work so perfectly. It was splendid. You know, I'm told that when that beard was quite itself W. C. used to use it to measure the length of advertisements. He'll use it thus no more I fear, unless on very small advertisements. And right here and now I suggest we give a standing vote of thanks to W. C. and his beard for the splendid entertainment they have provided. You will forgive me if I don't join you in this, because I am dying on my feet. I thank you."

The senior partner sat down amid a profound silence, which was rudely broken by the din raised by the members of his party. Mr. Owen and the duck led all the rest.

"You certainly are a pretty talker," Major Barney

assured Mr. Larkin heavily. "All those words—all spoken aloud. Think of it."

"This isn't a bad luncheon," Mr. Dinner observed, apropos of nothing. "I find I'm actually enjoying myself. I hope you all realize that I've been doing the duck."

"No!" cried the senior partner delightedly. "Have you been, now? Splendid! Major, you kiss him. You're sodden with drink. No fooling, though, I'm glad you can do a duck. I wish you could do a braying ass for the benefit of our next speaker."

Mr. Crawly was on his feet, but his smile seemed to have slipped, giving him something of the appearance of a saint with a tilted halo.

"Kiarians!" he bawled. "Now that I've been informed that Mr. Larkin was trying to be funny—I mean, to amuse us—I am sure we will all forgive the high spirits of one of the most influential merchants in our city."

"Sure they will," interpolated the cynical Mr. Dinner. "They still owe us for their drawers."

"Knowing that you agree with me in this," the speaker continued, "I will now give you one whose vision, whose courage, whose industry have placed his name among the leaders of our great progressive nation. With such a stout defender of our time-honored traditions in our midst, the snarling wolf of communism can go and—and—" the speaker paused in search of something sufficiently painful and demeaning for the communistic wolf to do.

"Sit on a tack," suggested the Major.

"Exactly," agreed the speaker lamely, "that's what it can do. Kiarians, I give you that great man of wheels—that automotive giant, Thomas W. Spratter of Sprattsburg, Sprattsylvania!"

The lull was filled with a deafening din as Mr. Spratter arose. It was plain to see that these men were basking in his success and power, that they were hoping to grab off a little of their own simply by being in the same room with him. Later they would refer to him casually as, "My old friend Tom Spratter."

"Why doesn't someone laugh?" Mr. Owen asked

most surprisingly. "Now, I think that's funny. That man has a funny name, and he comes from a lot of funny places."

"At last Owen has joined us," observed the senior partner complacently. "He too is a little drunk. Soon he'll become disorderly."

Mr. Spratter, too, was a large, square man, and everything about him was square, save, perhaps, his dealings. He had a square head and a square chin and a square carriage to his shoulders. He stood squarely on his feet and looked his inferiors squarely if arrogantly in the eye. Few persons on seeing him for the first time would have suspected that here was the greatest trafficker in muscle, brains, and souls the world had ever produced, a man who would have sent Attila home in tears to rock the cradle, an almost omnipotent enemy of the spiritual and intellectual life and aspirations of a nation. Even had the observer known all this, it would not have greatly mattered. The man had made good. What more need a man do? And then, of course, he was very rich. That was nice, too.

"Gentlemen," began Mr. Spratter, in a voice like a rough, square brick, "I will not mince matters."

"There," exclaimed Mr. Larkin nervously. "I knew he wouldn't mince. That's bad. That's very, very trying. He should mince a little, if only for my sake. I don't know how people get through the day without mincing a lot."

"Are there voices in this room?" demanded Mr. Spratter.

"If the speaker is hearing voices already," Mr. Larkin called back with the utmost urbanity, "I fear he will be seeing things soon. Mental cases usually do, you know—angels and what not. Let's stick to burning beards. That's preferable to madness."

If anything, the rugged industrialist settled on his track more firmly. There was a nasty smile on his lips.

"I'll handle this," he said. "If the communist or the socialist or even the single taxist who has just spoken will step up here, I shall take pleasure in knocking him down."

No sooner was this invitation released than the four

partners, led by Mr. Larkin, elaborately pulled the tablecloth over their heads and sat crouching beneath it. Frightened cries mingled ironically with the vociferous lament of a duck.

"Gentlemen," continued Mr. Spratter, utterly unperturbed, "my subject is Progress and Prosperity as opposed to Economics and Science."

The burst of approval that greeted this was loud and universal save for the four drunken partners and the duck.

"Gentlemen," resumed Mr. Spratter, "I think at my time of life I have the right to say, I have toiled mightily and wrought in full measure." Mr. Spratter's publicity man had a forgivable yen for the Bible. "Yet in all the years of my struggling and success," the square voice went on, "never once have I lowered the knee to the narrow, unpatriotic dictates of science and economics. Gentlemen, do you know who the greatest scientist is, who the greatest economist is, who the greatest philosopher is?"

In the rhetorical pause that followed, Mr. Owen's timid voice made itself heard.

"Professor Snozzle Durante," he offered.

"What!" thundered the automobile man scornfully. "That murderer! That monster! That socialist! Never! The greatest of them all is Old Man Common Sense. Hear me, everybody! Old Man Common Sense—horse sense, if you like."

"I think of the two," vouchsafed the senior partner, poking his head out from under the tablecloth, "I like horse sense the better. It's more playful, but I bet you'd have said best, and you'd have been wrong, as usual."

"Yes, sir," went on the great man, ignoring this interruption. "Old Man Common Sense can chop a lot of kindling and make the chips fly."

"There's something infinitely precious to me about dear old homely language," said Mr. Dinner affectedly. "Let's spit and swap horses. We'll make believe the horses."

"I wouldn't take all the Stuart Chases in the world,

all the John Deweys, all the Thomas Hunt Morgans," cried Mr. Spratter, "for one grain of common sense."

"Where wouldn't you take them?" the Major wanted to know. "And how do you know those lads would go with you?"

"Shut up!" cried Spratter. "Gentlemen! These men would deny that our great spirit of rugged individualism, our hail fellow, knock-down game of competition, our inherent confidence in the survival of the fittest have produced a race of industrial giants and two-fisted business getters."

"This makes me sick," said a voice that sounded surprisingly like Hector Owen's. "Give me another sip before I kill that butcher in human guise."

"Gentlemen, I say," the great voice boomed on, "rather than knuckle under to the findings of modern science, the advice of malicious economists, and the destructive drive of red-tainted philosophers, rather than do that, let's turn back the hands of the clock! Let's turn 'em back, I say!"

"Oh, good!" cried Mr. Dinner. "That's something to do. Let's all turn back the hands of the clock and keep on turning and turning until they come off."

"No!" protested Mr. Larkin. "Don't let's turn back those hands until after he's finished talking. He's simply trying to trap us into giving him more time."

"If I had those interrupters out at my plant," shouted the speaker, "I'd starve them into submission and—"

"Sell their families into slavery," Mr. Owen helped out.

"Can John Dewey build an automobile?" the speaker wanted to know. "Can Stuart Chase quell a mob of infuriated workers? Can—"

"Can you do card tricks?" demanded Mr. Dinner.

"That's a logical critical method," put in Mr. Larkin. "Let me ask one. Could Abe Lincoln change a tire? No. Very well, then. The man was a washout."

"Silence!" roared the speaker, "or I'll have you jailed for disorderly conduct."

Once more the four partners sat huddled at their table, Dinner quacking pitifully in a subdued voice.

"Men," continued Mr. Spratter, "the Spratters have been fighters from way back."

"Right!" once more Mr. Owen interpolated. "From way back behind the lines."

"During the last war," the great man snarled at his tormentors, "the Spratter poison dart killed more men, women, and children than any other offensive weapon used."

"On which side?" someone wanted to know.

"On both!" retorted Spratter, forgetting himself for the moment.

"Wish I had one now," said Major Barney.

But Mr. Spratter had no intention of letting the discussion be taken out of his hands.

"Kiarians," he broke in, "I am the guest of your loved and respected W. C."

"You should be," said the Major disgustedly.

"And an insult to me," boomed Spratter, "is an insult to him."

"Which is a convenient and time-saving arrangement," commented Mr. Owen who felt himself getting better and better.

"I will not let anyone insult our W. C.!" cried Spratter doggedly. "Therefore I'll ignore these ruffians. And now, men, now, Kiarians, now I come to the burden of my message. Prosperity is with us here and now! She has always been with us! The dear little lady has never left our side. She is waiting for us all both individually and collectively. Her arms are wide open. On her lips there is a smile. Invitation glows in her eyes."

"Wow!" exclaimed the licentious Major. "This is getting good. Wonder what part of her he's going to take up next?"

"Yes, sir," the speaker went on gloatingly. "There she lies, the——"

"He's got her down now," muttered Mr. Dinner in a voice loud enough to be clearly heard, and it must be said for the credit of the Kiarians that a few of them giggled nervously, as they contemplated the recumbent figure of the lady in question.

"Yes, sir," repeated Mr. Spratter with passionate convictions. "There she lies, ready and waiting. All you need to do is to step up and tinker with her engine——"

"What!" cried out the senior partner. "My God, what a thing to suggest!"

"I said tinker with her engine!" Mr. Spratter shouted back.

"I know you did," replied Mr. Larkin, getting control of himself. "That's just the trouble. Don't you realize what a terrible thing you've said?"

"I find the word tinker especially objectionable," put in Mr. Owen with legal distinctness. "I suggest the speaker be requested to moderate his language."

"Sounds fairly brutal to me," observed the Major. "Not a thing to do to a lady."

"Nonsense!" cried Mr. Spratter. "There she lies, I tell you. All you need to do is to——"

"I can't stand looking at her," wailed Mr. Dinner, putting his hands over his eyes. "The poor, poor thing. What is he going to do to her now?"

"I will speak," thundered the automobile man. "All you need to do is to tinker with her engine—a slight adjustment here and there—and then step on her gas. Put your foot down hard."

The last words were said in a voice of grating triumph. Once more the senior partner was on his feet.

"Step on her gas," he repeated in a voice trembling with incredulity. "Am I hearing his words aright? Does he really suggest that?"

"Why not?" demanded the manufacturer. "Why not step on her gas?"

"Why not?" cried Mr. Larkin witheringly. "Are you so utterly lost to chivalry and common decency as to ask me that?"

"How would you like to have someone step on your gas?" asked Mr. Dinner. "Put their foot down hard, as you said?"

"I don't need to have anyone step on my gas," Mr. Spratter retorted proudly. "I'm always pepped up."

"May I ask," demanded Mr. Larkin coldly, "if myself and my partners are to be debased by such bawdy proceedings? We have stood for having her engine tinkered, but, by God, as a loyal Kiarian, I will not allow anyone to step on her gas—to put his foot down hard."

"Who is this woman, anyway," asked a kindly old gentleman, "to whom all these things are going to be done? I'm afraid I'm a little deaf."

"I've forgotten, myself," called Mr. Larkin, "but it doesn't matter who she is. It's a damned dirty trick."

"The woman is Prosperity!" called Thomas W. Spratter, grimly sticking to his unhappy personifications. "That's who she is."

"I know," persisted the old gentleman, not knowing at all. "But what is she going to be doing about it all this time? Won't she act up and call for help?"

"You don't understand," cried Mr. Spratter. "She isn't a real lady at all."

"She wouldn't be," observed the old fellow, "if she let you do all those things to her."

"Nevertheless, I protest," put in Mr. Larkin. "On behalf of myself and my partners, I protest. Just because a woman isn't a lady, I see no reason why she should be stepped on and tink——I just can't say it," he broke off. "If the rest of you want to do it," he added, "I can't stop you, but we will have no part in such ungentlemanly conduct."

"All I said was to tinker with her engine and to step on her gas," said Mr. Spratter, feeling rather hopeless about it all. "You'd think I was suggesting a crime."

"Oh, yes," retorted Mr. Owen with fine irony. "To you it may be an every-day occurrence. To you, Mr. Thomas W. Spratter of Sprattsburg, Sprattsylvania, it may come under the head of pleasure. All this stepping on and tinkering with ladies may be your quaint idea of fun, but, answer me this—what would your wife say? What would any decent woman say? You may get away with it in Sprattsburg, but I dare you to try it out here."

"Gentlemen," called Mr. Spratter, appealing to the room. "My time is greatly limited. This fruitless argument has taken nearly all of it. Soon I must hurry with our excellent W. C."

"I can't stand any more of this," Mr. Dinner complained to Mr. Owen. "I'm going to put an end to it all."

And with this he bent over and struck a match to the nearest portière.

"Sheer genius," murmured the Major, setting fire to the tablecloth. "I'll forgive you, Dinner, for that beard-tasting fiasco."

Mr. Owen, not to be outdone, ignited his napkin and tossed it under the nearest table, where it started to burn merrily among the frantic feet of the Kiarians. Mr. Larkin promptly lost interest in speaking in the face of this fresh diversion. Taking an envelope from his pocket, he lighted it with great care and deliberately held it to another hanging. Then he arose and calmly addressed the assembled Kiarians, who were already uneasily sniffing smoke.

"I'm afraid we'll all have to go," he said. "It seems that some sparks from the late beard of our excellent W. C. have been smoldering in the hangings and things for some time. Emulating his spectacular example, the room has broken out into fire in several places. It's no longer a question of whether Mr. Spratter needs to go or not. He'll damn well have to go. *Sic semper tyrannis!* I am greatly pleased."

It is doubtful if the Kiarians either heard or cared about how much Mr. Larkin was pleased. By this time the room was filled with smoke and flames. It was not so well filled with Kiarians. Mr. Spratter evidently had needed to go because his square figure led all the rest. In their anxiety to depart, the business getters had overlooked the fact that a woman was in their midst. Hector Owen, however, had not been so forgetful.

"I'm going to save Satin!" he shouted, staggering among the tables.

"We'll all save Satin," boomed the voice of the Major.

"My God, yes," cried Mr. Larkin. "She has the most thorough knowledge of indecency of any woman in our Pornographic Department."

Together the four partners laid violent hands on the young lady and, using her as a battering ram, drove their way through the milling Kiarians.

"Don't worry," Mr. Owen told her. "We'll get you out unharmed."

"And also undressed," she responded. "There's little under my skirt, but what there is I'd hate to show in public."

However, she had spoken too late. In their anxiety to do the right thing the four partners were tugging altogether too hard for the resistane of light summer attire. As a result, their burden's garments parted in various quarters, so that when the partners passed through the lobby of the hotel they gave the appearance of four gentlemen diligently engaged in carrying away a naked but unprotesting woman. Once on the street they set her on her feet and started to brush her off here and there, as men will.

"Heavens!" exclaimed the senior partner. "What happened to her clothes? She didn't come like this, I hope."

"You have part of my skirt in your hand," Satin casually observed. "The others have other things."

"Put them on, my dear child, at once," continued Mr. Larkin. "It's a sight to make one veer. Besides, this is no place for frivolity. The hotel is on fire. We can't drop back in there. A taxicab would do nicely at this moment."

The Major stopped a cab, and the partners piled in behind the thinly disguised Satin.

"We'll all be late at the store," lamented the senior partner. "It always happens this way. Something inevitably breaks out and this time it was a fire. I like a good fire. We'll be able to watch it from the roof."

As the taxi turned a corner it nearly ran into a fire engine. There were much cursing and shouting and clatter.

"I'd love to be a fireman," Mr. Dinner observed wistfully.

"So would I," agreed the senior partner. "The engines seem to veer nearly as much as I do."

There was a smothered scream from Satin.

"Why, Mr. Owen," she said. "I'm more surprised than insulted."

# CHAPTER X

## *From the Roof Top*

"HORRID!" CALLED MR. LARKIN THE MOMENT THE partners and Satin had reached his private office. "Horrid! Take Blue Mould up to the roof, but don't let him fall off. He'd splash all over one or more of our customers. If they were going out it wouldn't matter much. If they were coming in it would make a lot of difference. Is everything clear, or have I failed at some point?"

"Don't know about that," said Horrid. "What do you want us to do on the roof, old Blue Mould and me?"

"Look for a fire, of course," Mr. Larkin explained with a show of impatience. "Naturally. What does one go to roofs for? Where's your native sagacity?"

"Me native what?" asked the horrid office boy.

"It doesn't matter," explained Mr. Larkin hastily. "You haven't any. Will someone please throw something over that nude girl? Bare flesh burns me up. If it's a good fire, let me know. If not, I don't care to hear a word about it. If she sold books the way she is in the Pornographic Department we might be able to make two ends meet. What a luncheon! Well, gentlemen, to your places. We must make up for lost time. Dinner, wherever your place is, have someone bring you a chair. You'll look better off your feet. Breathe into space, if at all." The senior partner paused for breath in the midst of this executive outburst and surveyed Honor Knightly. "Splendid legs!" he said as if to himself. "Oh, legs, legs, legs, what would we do without them?"

"Drag ourselves along," replied the Major laconically.

"Or walk on our hands," added the senior partner.

105

"But I really wasn't asking for information. I was merely exclaiming, rather ecstatically, I thought. Do something about her legs. She owes us her life, and we owe her a dress. Someone figure that out. It doesn't seem right. Have we made up any lost time yet?"

"All," asserted Mr. Dinner. "Or nearly. May I have a slight pick-me-up? The stuff is dying on me."

"You should die with it," exclaimed Mr. Larkin. "Give him a great drink, Major. It may paralyze him. Give us all a drink—even those legs."

"Those legs would like a drink," said their fair owner. "What with smoke and Kiarians and nudity, my mind is all agog."

"I'm very much agog, too," asserted the senior partner. "It's a good word. Two g's in it like boggle, only in different places. Put something on."

The Major passed the drinks around, and everybody sat down to enjoy them, Satin draped in a Spanish shawl snatched from one of the divans.

"Of course," observed Mr. Larkin, frowning worriedly into his glass, "I hope you all realize that this is rather a poor way of making up for lost time. If anything, it's a better way to lose a lot more of it. I would be a great deal better off without any partners at all. Then I would have more money to spend and very much less lost time. Do I hear any resignations?"

"Horace," the Major assured him affectionately, "you'd be lost yourself without us."

"Would I, do you think?" Horace inquired rather anxiously. "Well, don't leave me, then—not for a moment—although, damn me, I sometimes wonder if we are running this store quite right. It's such a very big store, I should think there ought to be a great deal more bustling about and rushing places, more orders issued, and all that. It would be nice, too, if one of us knew something about figures. Our books are far more mysterious to us all than a set of detective novels. I fear our accountants cheat us terribly. You see how it is. I have to think of these things occasionally, but not, thank God, very often."

"Mr. Larkin," Satin asked him, "may I have Mr. Owen?"

"What an extraordinary request, my child," Mr. Larkin answered. "What do you want him for?"

Satin, holding the shawl tightly about her, hipped herself across the room and, bending over the senior partner, whispered into his ear a few moments. Mr. Owen did not greatly care for this sort of thing. He looked about him uncomfortably.

"Oh!" exclaimed the senior partner at last. "For that! I might have known." He paused and glanced consideringly at Mr. Owen. "Of course," he continued, "the dew is no longer on the rose—the first blush is gone, but a slightly faded man is preferable to a fickle one. How is your health, Mr. Owen?"

"You talk of me as if I were a horse," Hector Owen protested.

"Oh, no," replied Mr. Larkin. "If you were a horse we'd talk about you in an entirely different way. We might even go so far as to examine you. People do, you know. The horses never mind. They have no shame. I admire and envy horses. They have four legs. Miss Knightly doesn't want a horse. She'd rather have you. I don't know why."

"I have my suspicions," said Mr. Dinner. "Want me to air them?"

"No," cried the senior partner hastily. "Fumigate them instead. It happens you're right. She does—and for that."

"Not a bad break," observed the Major, looking the girl over from head to toe. "Not a bad break at all. Think you feel up to it, Owen?"

"For God's sake!" exclaimed Hector Owen. "Why consult me? Wouldn't it be better to drag my clothes off and auction me on the block?"

"It might be at that," Mr. Larkin declared. "Wonder how much you'd knock down for? The women in this town are simply mad about new faces and all. You know what I mean?"

"I fear I do," said Mr. Owen. "Let's change the subject."

"And you must not forget," went on the senior partner, "you own Madame Gloria for life. That's a lot of woman to own."

Upon the reception of this information Satin swung about and furiously confronted Mr. Owen.

"Has he had relations with that trull?" she demanded.

"Only such as are possible at a sidewalk café," Mr. Larkin explained rather nervously. "They were in the presence of the public all the time. There weren't any beds about or anything like that."

"Was there an undercurrent of beds?" the girl wanted to know.

"Merely a slight strain," said Mr. Larkin. "You know how Madame Gloria is—one never gets very far away from a bed with her. I'm surprised at times she doesn't go about in one."

"I know how she is," Satin pronounced coldly. "And I know how she will be if she tries to drag a bed between me and him."

"If it were exactly in the middle," Mr. Larkin remarked thoughtfully, "you might both race for it. He'd be in the bed."

"Do you think I'd stay in the bed?" Mr. Owen demanded.

"I don't see why not," said Mr. Larkin, "if it were a comfortable bed. You'd be sure to have one of them."

"You might even get both," put in the Major. "It might be a dead heat."

"I could beat that old trollop to bed," cried Satin, "with a suit of armor on. But there's not going to be any race. That man, such as he is, is all mine, and may God pity both him and that Gloria wench if I ever catch them together."

"Haven't I any voice in the matter?" Mr. Owen asked. "No *locus standi?*"

"I don't know what your *locus standi* is," she retorted, "but it doesn't sound very decent to me. I've practically reared you in pornography, and I certainly don't intend to let another woman reap the benefit of my teaching."

"Has he picked up much dirt?" Mr. Larkin asked with interest.

"Not as much as he's going to," the girl replied.

"The trouble with him is, he hasn't the right kind of mind."

At this moment Horrid stuck his head in at the door.

"There's a lot of smoke," he said.

"Then there should be some fire," commented the senior partner. "Or maybe it's the other way round. Let's go up and see."

"I want a new dress," declared Satin.

"You need a new dress," agreed Mr. Larkin. "Have we any decent dresses in this store? If not, send out to some other shop and charge the stuff to us. I'll send Mr. Owen down to the Pornographic Department as soon as we've had a good look at this fire."

"If he doesn't come down," said Satin, "I'll come up and drag him down."

For a few moments after the partners had left, the girl wandered restlessly about the room, picking up this object and that, examining it curiously before casting it aside in favor of another. She went to the table and poured herself a fresh drink.

Meanwhile, the partners were comfortably seated on the roof of the store, looking at a lot of smoke. There was little else to look at. From time to time the ancient Green Mould, who Mr. Larkin suspected but was not sure should be called Blue Mould, filled their wine-glasses from a bottle selected from several others set in a large tub of ice. The partners did themselves well.

"It's a nice idea to sit on the roof of one's store," observed the senior partner gently, "and contemplate fires while quaffing champagne. There should be more fires."

"Or at least some fire," put in Mr. Dinner in a small, complaining voice.

"If the three of you sent down to the Musical Department," remarked Mr. Owen, "for some fiddles, your happiness might be complete."

"We should have done better than that," complained the Major. "We started four separate and distinct fires in that hotel. Not one of them is making out worth a damn."

"I doubt if an honest fire would burn in such a thick Kiarian atmosphere," Mr. Larkin asserted. "Does

Owen want some fiddles? He can have some if he does. I find phonographs much easier. Don't have to use so many fingers and hardly any ear."

Knowing he would miss nothing if he never listened to any of these conversations, Mr. Owen was gazing out over the city. Everywhere he saw broad, tree-shaded thoroughfares linked together by parks and plazas. Through the green of the trees he caught splashes of black, crimson, tan, and orange—vivid bursts of color from the awnings and parasols flanking the graceful streets. Over the hotel they had so informally quitted, a plume of smoke hung in the light, clear air. Smoke still trailed from the windows of the banqueting hall in which high-pressure salesmen had given place to high-pressure hoses. Through the main avenue of the city a body of bright jacketed troops, their accoutrements flashing in the sun, moved rhythmically to the music of a glittering band.

"They never fight, those soldiers," the Major explained regretfully. "Can't get them to fight. All our troops are like that—too fond of clothes. You see, we've changed our mind about fighting here. Decided to give it a miss. Only sworn and accredited pacifists are allowed to join the army. When other nations get mean about things, our standing army of pacifists can talk them deaf, dumb, and blind before they can even get mobilized. Of course, a lot of sweethearts, wives, and mothers don't like the idea. They can no longer heroically sacrifice their sons, lovers, and husbands for the sake of their country. So many women are such gluttons for death and bloodshed. Frankly, I don't see a thing in it, and I've killed lots of men in my time. It's a thoroughly ill-tempered occupation. In the place of sacrificing their men folk we allow women a little more latitude in betraying them. We don't even call it betraying any more—merely changing their luck. Naturally, we must have soldiers, bands, and uniforms. Such things fill a fundamental craving. I like a parade myself as well as the next."

It was a long speech for the Major, but inasmuch as he was a military man Mr. Owen listened with interest. His eyes were fixed on the hills which, breaking here and there, gave glimpses of the sea. Gazing down on this beautiful city Mr. Owen found it difficult to think of war. Surely here was a place made to order for peace and play.

"Those palaces over there on the hill," said Mr. Larkin, pointing to a magnificent row of buildings in the distance, "are the homes of our retired mayors and political leaders. All built by graft. Graft, you know, my dear Owen, is also a fundamental craving. Self-interest is its brother. We used to attack graft in the old days. Now we encourage it. The only stipulation the voters make is that our grafters must share enough of their spoils with the people, spend enough on public welfare, roads, construction, amusements and holidays to keep us all happy and contented. Thus we have all the fun of being dishonestly yet well governed. Dishonesty is so much more positive than its opposite, don't you think? I love to steal watches. Have you one?"

"No," replied Mr. Owen, "you just took it. I felt you."

"Then you can have it back," declared the senior partner. "There's no fun in it if you know."

Instead of returning Mr. Owen's inexpensive watch, however, he presented him with a handsome new one.

"It's a better watch than yours," Mr. Larkin explained. "Got it at luncheon from our excellent W. C. You can have it if you don't mind about the initials."

"What happens to your politicians when they fail to share their graft?" asked Mr. Owen, gratefully accepting another man's property.

"What happens?" repeated Mr. Larkin in surprise. "Naturally, we run them out of town. They bore us. We don't find them amusing. You can see that for yourself. Everybody likes to eat, drink, run about with women, and have a good time. As soon as the majority of people find themselves being cramped, we have a bloodless revolution and get bad friends with the government. It's lots of fun."

"And those buildings down there in the valley," broke in Mr. Dinner, his voice embodying the satisfaction he felt, "belong to the prohibitionists and other like vermin who endeavor to thwart nature. They're jails. Very uncomfortable places."

"Do you put all prohibitionists in jail?" asked Mr. Owen.

"Not all," replied Mr. Dinner. "Not the honest ones, but there are not very many of those. These chaps down there are mostly political hypocrites, professional reformers, people with weak stomachs or otherwise mentally or physically incapacitated for enjoyment. There are a lot of anti-vice boys and girls down there. No end of them. People who would rob us of our sex. That's not right. We got to have our sex. A few years back we weren't even allowed to travel with it. Now we can take it anywhere. We found it was making woman dumb, keeping them in one place all the time. Now they can see things. And they do."

"I can imagine," said Mr. Owen.

"I'm convinced you can," commented Mr. Dinner.

"How long are these prohibitionists and reformers in for?" asked Mr. Owen.

"Most of them can come out any time they want," was the surprising answer, "but they don't want to. They're ashamed. They get laughed at so much. You see, a person who votes one way, then goes home and acts another is not only a damn fool but also a damn fraud. Such people have no standing in this community. Anti-enjoyment people don't mind jail so much, anyway. There's something sadistic about jail routine that appeals to their perverted instincts."

"I see," said Mr. Owen. "In your madness there is a grain of sense. May I ask what that great walled enclosure over there is used for?"

"It's seldom if ever used," explained the Major, "but we keep it just the same. It's for the exclusive enjoyment of diplomats and statesmen either foreign or domestic. As a matter of fact, the grounds are open to all patriotic people and munition manufacturers. Whenever they get especially bloodthirsty we invite them to go in there and blow their Goddam heads off. Yet in spite of the fact that we have stocked the place with all sorts of flags and guns and gases—the very things they love so dearly—they seldom if ever can be induced to go in. We have to pitch them in whether they like it or not. Then we take pot shots at them from the walls. After that we bury them upside down and declare a public holiday."

"At the same time," observed Mr. Larkin, "it's good to do a little work, isn't it? We don't seem to be able to get around to doing any. For the last half hour I've been wondering if sitting on this roof can, by any stretch of imagination, be called attending even loosely to business. I've about come to the conclusion it can't. We've merely gone from one way of not making up for lost time to another. That isn't right. That's very, very bad. People might get the impression we were loafers. Let's go in and look at the store for a change."

"All right," agreed Mr. Dinner. "It's not such a bum shop."

"I like it," declared the Major. "We've ever so many things to sell that nobody wants to buy. There are always enough left overs for all of us."

Tossing their wineglasses to the roof, the four partners rose and departed to look at their store. Green Mould and Horrid gagged down the remains of the wine.

## CHAPTER XI

## *The Partners Are Helpful*

IN THE TOY DEPARTMENT THEY NATURALLY LINGERED a little—which one of them started the lingering it would be difficult to decide. Probably it was by general consent. It is almost impossible not to linger in a toy department. They lingered long enough in this one for a lady, who seemingly had just remembered something, to accost Mr. Larkin.

"Have you something for a mechanical boy?" she asked, all of a breath.

Mr. Larkin looked puzzled.

"A mechanical boy?" he asked politely as if to give the woman another chance as well as himself.

"Yes," almost panted the woman. "A mechanical boy he is."

"Is he, now," murmured Mr. Larkin. "Too bad—too bad. A mechanical boy. Fancy that. How mechanical is he, madam?"

"Oh, very," replied the woman proudly. "Entirely."

"God spare me," breathed Mr. Larkin. "An entirely mechanical boy. What does he run by, madam, steam?"

"What?" cried the woman. "He doesn't run at all."

"Oh," exclaimed Mr. Larkin, his face lighting up. "I see it. You want this mechanical boy repaired, is that it?"

"It is not," said the woman coldly. "I want a mechanical toy for the boy."

"Does it play with mechanical toys?" asked Mr. Larkin, greatly interested.

"Naturally," replied the woman.

"Must be a remarkable sort of a mechanical boy," observed Mr. Larkin with a sigh. "I'll have to admit that. Will someone else talk with the lady? We're not getting along so well."

"Certainly," volunteered the Major, stepping forward. "Is this a clockwork boy, madam, or an electric one?"

"Both," said the woman promptly. "He's good at both."

"Oh, he is," muttered the Major, slightly taken back. "I never saw one of those."

"You never saw this boy," said the woman. "Never saw the likes of him myself."

"You must be right," admitted the Major, then turning to his senior, added in a low voice, "Shall we go? I'm afraid she'll get angry soon. I don't seem to understand either."

"You great big dummy," said Mr. Dinner, in turn confronting the woman. "Madam," he continued with great assurance, "you just can't have a mechanical boy that works by both clockwork and electricity, and if you have, it should be solving the fourth dimension instead of playing with toys. In other words, we place little reliance in what you have told us. Please come to the point. Make it snappy."

"All I want to do is to buy a mechanical toy," said the woman in a hopeless voice. "Here I've been talking to three grown men, and I don't seem to be any further along than if I'd been talking to three stuffed owls that had never———"

"Don't let her go on," interrupted Mr. Larkin anxiously. "She'll never stop if she once starts going on. They never do. I know them. The stuffed owls are very bad. God only knows what she'll take up next. Get her mind off us. Ask her how she feels—anything."

"Would you like a broken mechanical toy, madam?" asked Mr. Dinner.

"What would I want with a broken mechanical toy?" demanded the woman.

"We don't know," said Mr. Dinner, stepping back among his larger partners. "If that boy is such a wonder he might like to find out what's wrong with this mechanical toy. No one round here seems to know."

"A good idea," put in Major Barney. "I've been told on reliable authority that it's more fun to get mechanical toys to work than to watch them do their stuff. Don't you think so, madam?"

"No I don't," retorted the woman. "I think you should have your minds examined—all of you."

"Does she now?" Mr. Larkin murmured thoughtfully. "All of us. That's a lot of minds to have examined. It would take so long to find Dinner's, if ever. And then it would be such a great disappointment when found."

"Don't want it examined," said Mr. Dinner. "If they found anything wrong with it, I'd go crazy wondering what it was."

"You don't have to wonder," replied the Major. "It's merely an alcoholic husk."

Mr. Larkin stopped a salesgirl.

"My dear child," he began gently.

"Don't call me that," she tossed back. "I believed

you once when you did, and now I have one of my own."

"Oh, dear," said Mr. Larkin. "How unfortunate. Now I remember your face."

"You should remember much more of me than that," the salesgirl flung back.

"Goodness gracious!" exclaimed the senior partner, looking anxiously about. "What a sale this turned out to be! Mechanical toys, at that. Imagine!" He turned back to the girl. "We'll have a nice long talk," he told her, "all about infant mortality. But not now. I must think. This woman wants a mechanical boy, but I fancy she'd be glad to take a stuffed owl in its place. Give her anything she wants or she'll never get home." He now addressed himself to the woman. "This perfectly charming girl will fit in just splendidly with your plans. Her mind is good and her memory altogether too good. Good-night, madam. I hope we'll all feel better tomorrow."

Once more he turned and walked rapidly away. By the time he had reached the end of the Toy Department he was almost running. His companions were close behind. A floorwalker looked after them and sniffed the air enviously.

"I hope we make that sale," said the senior partner, leading them down a flight of stairs to the next floor. "To my dying day I'll never be sure in my mind about that mechanical boy—whether he was or wasn't, you know—not even sure what the woman wanted."

"Simply a mechanical toy," replied Mr. Dinner, in a superior sounding voice. "I would have fixed her up in a minute."

The Major looked at him scornfully.

"She was preparing to tear you limb from limb," he said.

"And I for one wouldn't have lifted a finger," Mr. Larkin asserted impersonally. "Now, look here, Mr. Owen, this is the Fur Department. Women come here for furs, but most of the time men come with them. It's a very important department. Events leading up to the loss of more honor are initiated here than in any other department in the store. It's remarkable the things women will do for fur. As a matter of truth, I've never found out what they won't do for fur, and I've suggested about everything. Yes, yes, indeed. Women are savages for fur. If our present rate of women had lived in the prehistoric days there'd be no fur-bearing animals left at all. Give a woman a piece of fur——"

"They're very much like that where I come from," Mr. Owen broke in quickly, as a picture of a fur coat which he had never bought flashed disturbingly through his mind.

"It's the competitive instinct," contributed the Major with a surprising display of philosophy. "What one woman wears the other woman wants until she has it. Then she wants something else. And if the price of the best fur coats were reduced to five dollars you wouldn't be able to drag one on their backs. Yet the fur would be just as good."

"They don't wear them to keep warm," observed Mr. Dinner. "That's one sure thing. If you gave some of 'em a snout they'd look just like animals."

"Men are quite as bad," said the senior partner. "Especially young men who don't have to work for their money. At football games and other mob activities I've seen hundreds of young chaps overtaxing their maturing strength and spoiling their chances in life beneath the weight of strange-looking garments that would give a bear the creeps, assuming they ever crept, which I doubt."

"But women have to have something to give in for," suggested Mr. Dinner.

"Why don't they give in for an orange, as they used to when I was a boy?" demanded the Major.

"There we go," remarked the senior partner with a shrug to Mr. Owen. "Always getting personal. Now these furs all come from the best animals." Here he indicated the Fur Department with an inclusive wave of his eloquent hand. "All animals of the better class. I've often thought that if you could prevail upon elephants to grow hair everything would be much nicer. It fills me with regret to think that every piece of fur here displayed represents another step in the gradual extinction of animals whose only fault is that they have never learned how to shave."

"I wonder," mused Mr. Dinner, "what women would do if men suddenly began growing fur? Think they'd murder us all?"

"No," replied the senior partner quite seriously. "They'd hardly go so far as that, but I do think they'd try to drag us about on their backs with our arms tied around their necks."

"Why couldn't they tuck 'em in—our arms, I mean?" asked Mr. Dinner.

"That would never do," replied Mr. Larkin. "The furs would begin to pick the clothes off their wearers. A pretty sight that would be."

"How are we going to keep our hands warm, then?" persisted the small Dinner.

"Your hands would be covered with fur," the senior partner told him.

"Ugh!" muttered Mr. Dinner. "I wouldn't like that. Great furry hands like a beast's."

"It will probably never happen," interposed Mr. Larkin in a quiet voice. "There's no good building bridges before we've burned them, is there?"

Mr. Dinner and the Major looked uneasily at one another. This sort of question invariably set them puzzling—taxed them, as it were, beyond their capacity.

As they rounded a corner they came upon a scene of domestic discord. The partners stopped, enthralled, their worst instincts delighted. Two couples, the female members of which were exceedingly pretty women, were facing each other in battle array.

"May I ask why you are buying a fur coat for my wife?" one of the men demanded in a deadly cold voice.

"Apparently for the same reason you are buying one for mine," the other man smoothly replied.

"I'm buying a coat for your wife to keep the poor woman warm," replied the other with withering sarcasm.

"I don't have to buy a coat for your wife to keep her that way," retorted the other husband, growing a trifle common.

"Is that so?" was the brilliant rejoinder. "Well, your wife is hot stuff herself—once she gets away from you."

"Yeah?" shot back the other. "Well, your wife told me that to live with you was the same as living with an eating cadaver—a snoring dead man."

"That's funny," laughed the other nastily. "Your wife told me much the same thing. She said if it wasn't for the neighbors she'd have a hearse parked permanently at your door."

"At that," declared the other proudly, "she said it nicer than your wife did."

"Your wife can't say anything any nicer than my wife can!" was the perplexing reply to this.

"I do think," interposed one of the women involved, "that Jane would have shown better taste had she gone to another store. She knows very well that I always deal here."

"So sorry," said the one called Jane in a sweet voice. "I should have remembered meeting you here with still another woman's husband."

"I was selecting a coat for his wife," lied the first woman glibly.

"My mistake," replied Jane. "You wore one just like it all last season."

"We had planned to dress as twins," said the other lady.

"And doubtless were so successful her husband couldn't tell you apart," Jane remarked with a killing smile.

"Are you accusing me of improper conduct?" the other demanded icily.

"Why, no, my dear," said Jane. "Merely complimenting you on a long and successful career."

"Do you know what they're talking about?" one of the husbands asked the other.

"No," replied the man. "I'm getting tired as hell. They always go on like this."

"I'm dying on my feet," admitted the other. "Let's give them the air."

Fearing the loss of two simultaneous sales, Mr. Larkin felt himself called upon to exert a soothing influence. Leading the gentlemen aside he spoke to them in a low voice.

"If you gentlemen will step down to our Refreshment Department," he told them, "I'll send word that the drinks are on the house. In the meantime, I will take care of the ladies. They can charge the coats either to their own husbands or—if they find it more amusing—they can stick to the present arrangement. I'll see that neither of you gets done in the eye."

"What's the Refreshment Department like?" asked one of the men suspiciously.

"Dear me, don't you know?" exclaimed Mr. Larkin. "Why, there's nothing like it in any store in the city. It's a real innovation. It's run especially for gentlemen who are mad enough to go shopping with ladies. You'll love it."

"Why?" asked the other husband.

"I forgot to say," the senior partner apologized. "It's a sort of alcoholic harem with a continuous burlesque show. You won't find a decent woman in the place."

"Then don't tell our wives," said one of the men. "They'd break their necks getting there."

The two men hurried away, and Mr. Larkin turned to the ladies.

"Now that they've gone," he said, smiling dazzlingly upon each, "We can all get together."

"Where?" breathed one of the women so readily that Mr. Larkin put it down as an instinctive response to any agreeable suggestion.

"My office is busy now," he hedged, glancing at his watch, "but any morning in the swimming pool would make a good beginning."

"Are all men bad?" the one called Jane asked coyly.

"Not bad enough for you, I fear," Mr. Larkin answered gallantly. "Now, if you ladies will just step into those curtained enclosures, I'll take your lines for the fur coats. Dinner, you and the Major can have the one named Jane. Owen and myself will handle this beautiful blonde."

For a few minutes strange noises came from behind the enclosures. A series of giggles, small shrieks and startled ejaculations filled the air. Customers of both sexes paused and looked enviously at the curtains. Even the salesgirls, as accustomed as they were to the enthusiastic methods of the partners, did not remain unmoved.

"My God," came the voice of Jane. "The way these men go about it you'd think they were measuring one for a pair of tights instead of a fur coat."

Presently Mr. Owen came staggering from his booth and stood outside mopping his brow with a handkerchief.

"It's too much for me," he admitted to a salesgirl. "I know nothing about measuring."

"Neither do they," said the salesgirl.

"I'm not at all used to this sort of thing," Mr. Owen continued.

"No?" said the girl with interest, favoring him with an insinuating eye. "How'd you like to practise?"

"My God," muttered Mr. Owen, "what a store!"

The senior partner came bustling up to Mr. Owen and the salesgirl. He handed the girl a slip of paper on which some figures had been hastily scrawled.

"Give those women a couple of coats," he said. "Make the price right. It was worth it. These figures might help, but I doubt it. I was veering slightly when I jotted them down. Charge them. And," he added looking severely at the girl, "that is the way to make sales. Remember—on your toes."

"I think I see what you mean," replied the girl. "Thank you very much."

Gathering his partners about him, Mr. Larkin moved away with dignity and aplomb.

"Let's collect Satin," suggested Mr. Larkin, "and ask her to buy us a drink."

And thus ended Mr. Hector Owen's first working day in his new occupation. Most people are of two minds. Hector Owen was of many. Of one thing, however, he was sure. He did not want to find himself on the other side of that dimly but hauntingly remembered door—waiting there in the rain.

# CHAPTER XII

## *Satin Slings an Eel*

MANY LITTLE DIFFICULTIES NEVER GET THEMSELVES quite ironed out. Gangsters, judges, and other disturbing elements have long been aware of this. But women are even more so. As a matter of fact, women seem to glory in it. And of all things in the world, a great many of their little difficulties have to do with men, actually with men who are notoriously not worth the snap of one's fingers, especially a woman's fingers.

Nor do women need to be particularly interested in the same man to precipitate a deluge of these little difficulties—to arouse emotions of jealousy. Far from it. Both of them may heartily detest the poor beast, as they have no hesitancy in telling him the first moment they get him alone. The more women fight over a man, the more that doomed wretch eventually suffers. He pays for all their trouble. He suffers if they do and he suffers if they don't. For him there is no escape. If women don't fight over him, his market value declines. His wife grows restless—she becomes cold and unduly critical. On the other hand, many an odd fish with nothing in God's world to recommend him save his trousers has found himself in the center of the most alarming competition, merely because one woman has conceived the idea that another woman wants him.

For this reason it is barely possible that jealousy between women is not such a personal manifestation as is commonly supposed. With men it is entirely different, entirely personal—too personal, if anything. Men know exactly what they want, and although their motives are generally of the lowest, they usually know what they are getting at. With women, jealousy has more of the professional quality. It is the jealousy of the artist. It

122

springs not so much from a woman's love of a definitely selected male as from the disinclination to see one of her sex get away with anything, no matter how undesirable it may be. In other words, women have a proprietary interest in the entire class of males, whereas men, in their casual and shiftless manner, follow the female of the least resistance.

It so happened that Mr. Hector Owen, seated with Satin Knightly and his three partners at a table in a smart sidewalk café, found himself the unwilling center of one of these distressing conflicts. He was not greatly amused. Few men are, to hear themselves boldly discussed as if they were not present. Nor was he, as are so many of his sex, conceited enough to take any credit for the unbecoming conduct of the ladies.

Madame Gloria played a prominent part in this action. She made her entrance while Honor Knightly, pornographic expert, was buying the four partners a drink and, in turn, was being bought drinks by them. There had been lots of drinks already. There were prospects of lots more. Madame Gloria, accompanied by several ladies and gentlemen of her profession, wearily seated herself at the next table. This was unfortunate, for the moment Satin's madly bright eyes rested on Madame Gloria and noted that she was good, they began to snap and sparkle dangerously—venomously. The fact that Madame Gloria was a truly beautiful woman, although perhaps a shade faded, did not soften the quality of Satin's hostile gaze. She had, however, the grace to allow her enemy to seat herself before opening the attack.

"I understand," began Honor, her voice unrelieved by the slightest inflection, "that this person owns you for life. What about it?"

Satin indicated this person by leaning so heavily against him that Mr. Owen found it wiser to cling to his chair rather than to be pushed off it to the floor. In a small flurry of panic the senior partner, whose experience in the past with women gave him small hope of the immediate future, fluttered his hands nervously and rolled his eyes to heaven.

"Here," he predicted in a low voice, "is where we all begin to veer like a series of cock-eyed gyroscopes."

Madame Gloria observed Satin with one of her most perfectly refrigerated smiles.

"Are you personally interested in the answer, my dear?" she inquired.

"I am," said Satin distinctly. "And that lets you out. This man is mine. Understand that—all of you. He's mine. Of course, I don't want him much, but just the same, I'm going to have him. One encounters new faces so rarely."

"Very well, my child," Mr. Larkin proposed in a fearfully soothing voice. "Excellent, excellent, my dear girl. You take his face, and Madame Gloria can have what's left of him, although I very much fear that with her much won't be left of him long."

"Come! Come!" muttered Mr. Owen ineffectually, then added, by way of emphasis, "I say now—come, come!"

"No," replied Honor firmly, utterly disregarding the weak objection of the gentleman under discussion. "I'll have little use for his face unless I find it necessary to slap it occasionally. I want all."

"Couldn't some mutually satisfactory division of the man be arranged?" interposed Major Barney, pursuing the senior partner's difficult anatomical compromise.

Once more Mr. Owen was moved to objections as he gulped down a strong drink.

"Why not draw and quarter me?" he suggested. "Or put me on the spot? From the way things are going, I might as well be hanging in cold storage. Am I some butcher's chunk to be sliced and hacked at the convenience of two women?"

"You'd be better off if you were," Mr. Dinner uttered gloomily. "They're going to do you no good, those two trulls."

"I find this conversation jarring on my artistic sensibilities," put in Madame Gloria languidly. "Why drag it out here of all places?"

"Why drag it out at all?" demanded Mr. Owen in a shocked whisper.

"Now that we've started," replied Mr. Larkin sadly, "it has to be dragged out."

"What has?" mumbled Mr. Owen.

"It!" cried Madame Gloria dramatically. "Everything! We must know all, see all, and hear all."

"Not about me, you don't," exclaimed Mr. Owen, rising from the table. "I'm leaving now. Oh, yes, I am. I'm going right away."

"Sit down!" Satin snapped at him. "And don't mind that woman. I'll drag it out as much as I want. This——"

"Do you think I'm worrying about which one is going to do the dragging?" furiously interrupted the indignant man.

"Will you please be still?" the girl demanded. "This matter must be settled here and now. Drag it out, say I!"

"How do you mean?" asked Mr. Owen, now thoroughly aroused. "Who are you talking to anyway?"

"My good woman," explained Madame Gloria with softly malicious patience, "it has been settled already, this little affair. Can't you get it through your silly head that I am his for life and he is mine?"

"What fractional life interest can he possibly have in you?" Miss Knightly wanted to know. "You're an over-subscribed issue already. For years you've been floating yourself all over town."

"Really," protested Madame Gloria. "This is too insulting. When I give myself to a man I give myself entirely. Everybody knows that."

"Everybody should," Satin tossed back with a smile. "That is, every able-bodied member of the male population, not to mention a few cripples. When you give yourself, lady, you give yourself like a ton of bricks, you horrid old hooker!"

"Oh!" gasped Madame Gloria, not a little offended. "Is that so?"

"Yes, it's so," Satin informed her. "And here's something else: If he's yours for life, he's not going to live very long."

"I don't care how long he lives," Madame Gloria replied most convincingly. "I wouldn't mind killing him myself the way he sits there without a word to say in defense of the woman he owns."

"But, my dear lady," protested Mr. Owen, "you gave yourself to me of your own free will."

"That's a rotten thing to say," cried Madame Gloria, appealing tragically to the members of her party. "You were with me, all of you. Tell them it's a lie. He had no chance—no opportunity. Out here on the sidewalk—think of it! The man's quite mad."

"Why get so technical, Gloria?" asked a gentleman at her table who was obviously all for peace. "Frankly, I can't see what either of you two women want with him at all."

"I don't either," replied the lady of the stage, "but that doesn't matter. It's not as if I belonged to myself. I don't. I belong now to my public. I have that to think about, and my career, my reputation. Would it look well to see in the papers, 'Gloria Loses Her man'? Wouldn't that burn you up? Why, I've never lost a man to any woman."

"I wouldn't mind it so much," the gentleman replied, "not when you consider the man."

"I know," went on the actress. "He's admittedly a flop and all that, but I don't want my public to get the impression that the first overripe tomato that comes along can drop in the lap of one of my interests."

"I'll be damned well damned if I'll stand for all this!" Mr. Owen exploded, gulping down another drink. "That man has insulted me twice."

"Insulted you, hell!" exclaimed Satin. "That bedridden trollop of an actress called me a tomato—an overripe one, at that. If it wasn't her stock in trade I'd tear her clothes off!"

"Are you afraid, my dear," asked the bedridden trollop sweetly, "that my figure would put yours to shame?"

Satin rose furiously and began to unhook her dress while the three partners beat desperately at her hands.

"Come on!" she cried to Madame Gloria. "I'll make your body look like a mal-conditioned cow's!"

"Why, if I did such a thing in public," scoffed the lady, "men would hang diamonds round my neck."

At this tense moment a waiter, having proudly exhibited a moribund and loathsome eel to some strong stomached patron, passed by Satin on his way to the kitchen. Mastering her instinctive repulsion in the magnitude of her rage, she seized the snake-like object by its tail, twirled it expertly above her head, then gave it with a lashing motion to the actress, horror-riven in her chair.

"How do you like that round your neck?" Satin asked her, sitting down and fastidiously dipping her fingers in a fresh highball, then gulping it down considerably less fastidiously.

An eel is not so much a matter of character as it is of feeling. This is especially true of an eel wound round one's neck. One may have no character at all to speak of and yet object strongly to having an eel like that. Although Madame Gloria's character was far from good, she had every justification in assuming that the eel was not going to improve it any. Satin had asked her how she liked the eel round her neck. Madame Gloria was far too busy to give her an individual answer. However, she did make a fairly convincing public protest. Emitting a piercing scream, she clutched with both hands at her neck, only to encounter eel. Immediately she uttered another scream and decided she would rather be strangled to death than risk a similar experience. Thereafter she moved her hands impotently in the air and from time to time made noises. Mr. Larkin was of little help in this crisis. He was sitting with a napkin pressed delicately to his eyes.

"That was a decidedly offensive thing to do," came his awe-touched voice. "How can people think up such things? Just imagine—an eel round one's neck. What retribution!"

But by this time the eel was no longer round the fair neck of Madame Gloria. The eel was in quite a different quarter of the lady. It had slid down the neck of her dress in the general direction of her stomach, where it was much worse not only for itself but also for Madame Gloria. People who have had eels in both places claim that an eel on the stomach is, if anything, more undesirable than the same eel round the neck.

Such people would have experienced no difficulty in getting Madame Gloria to subscribe to their views. In the past she had electrified many in audience by the abandon of her dancing, especially in and about the present locality of the eel. She now cast aside whatever little restraint she had exerted over her movements and did some really shocking things with her torso. At various tables patrons unacquainted with the circumstances leading up to the gratuitous demonstration, cheered the gyrating woman on to even more devastating endeavors. For the first time in her life Madame Gloria was deaf to applause. It was not until the cause of her anguish fell with a moist flop at her feet that she desisted from her abdominal revolutions and rushed shrieking down the street in the direction of her automobile. After her trailed her party, leaving Satin and her horrid weapon in full possession of the field.

Madame Gloria had departed, and the first round had gone to Satin, yet deep in the heart of the actress burned an intense desire to rehabilitate herself in the eyes of her audience to which she owed so much. And she swore to herself that at a time no later than that night would she assert her rights to the body and person of one Hector Owen. She would watch for her opportunity.

"Now," said Honor Knightly, looking coldly upon Mr. Owen, "you're mine tooth and nail. Make no mistake about that. If it hadn't been for your cowardly vacillation all this would never have occurred. You've succeeded in making me extremely nervous and jumpy, you and your horrid old eel between you."

"It wasn't my eel in the first place," disclaimed Mr. Owen. "I wouldn't lift a finger for all the eels in the world."

"Oh, no!" shot back Miss Knightly in a nasty voice. "Well what would you do for this one?"

With a vicious lunge she recaptured the fallen eel. Once more the air whistled as the flashing body became the radius of a circle. Patrons at near-by tables buried their heads in their arms and waited for the inevitable crack. Fortunately for her intended victim, but not so for an unknown drunkard, the eel escaped her clutches and landed without warning in his soup. Drunk as he was, the man had enough sense left to know that he had not ordered eel with soup on it or soup with eel in it or eel in any other form. Therefore, putting the worst interpretation on this sudden appearance of reptilian life in the first thing he had attempted to eat for days, he broke into a cold sweat and collapsed to the sidewalk, where he lay calling on God until dragged off by the waiters. Henri, the head deity of the café, approached Mr. Larkin's table and deferentially registered a mild objection.

"Is it," he said, more in the nature of a suggestion than a request, "that the eel, you could let him rest tranquil for a small little? To our patrons he is more than enough already."

"Count me among the strongest objectors, Henri," Mr. Larkin replied with feeling. "I think it's simply disgusting myself."

"What's so wrong with a little eel?" asked Major Barney.

"I can't begin to tell you," Mr. Larkin replied. "As Henri says, he is simply more than enough. Please, Henri, hurry back with at least two quarts of champagne. And keep all eels away from this young lady. It's not her fault. It's a weakness—like a red flag to a banker, or is it a bull? I'm forever getting them mixed—bulls and bankers, you know. Not red flags. Anyway, what does it matter? And Henri, for God's sake, draw a sheet over the body of that eel, either dead or exhausted, on the table. He is doing no one any good where he is. He is an eel the most depressing, is he not, my old?"

My old, with a dazzling smile, showed the stuff that was in him by departing with the eel mercifully swathed in a tablecloth. Mr. Larkin breathed a sigh of relief and beamed upon his companions. "What a lot of things life is full of," he observed, "and what a lot of liquor we are."

"And we're going to get even fuller," gloated Satin, "and then I'm going for him in a big way."

Once more Mr. Owen braced himself against the pressure of her body. The situation was growing serious. By the time they had completed the ruin of the first bottle of wine he had formulated a plan of action.

"You'll have to excuse me a moment," he said, rising from the table.

"Why?" demanded Honor.

"Is that necessary?" he asked, elevating his eyebrows.

Mr. Owen had been absent less than five minutes when she sprang to her feet and seized a passing waiter.

"Where's the gentlemen's room?" she demanded.

"You're a lady," the waiter informed her. "It's another room, madam."

"At this moment I'm not a lady," she told him. "And what is good enough for a gentleman is good enough for me."

"I know, madam," said the waiter, who evidently had ideas of his own on the subject. "It's maybe all right for you, but what about the gentlemen? Are they to enjoy no privacy at all?"

"If a man's a gentleman," declared Honor, "he shouldn't want to enjoy privacy with a good-looking girl about. Anyway, I don't want to annoy your blessed gentlemen. I merely want to stand outside."

"Very good, madame," said the waiter, "but I don't see what that's going to get you. All the way back to the right."

Satin hurried away and took up her position by the door where she stood her ground in spite of the curious glances of various gentlemen passing in and out. After she had waited what she considered was a reasonable time she sent for Mr. Larkin. That gentleman appeared nervously with his partners.

"You're the most restless woman to take places," he complained. "Never a moment's peace and quiet. If it isn't an eel it's a gentlemen's room. What won't you be wanting next?"

"I want that partner of yours," she grated. "And I want him quick. I don't care what he's doing. You go in there and tell him if he doesn't snap out with a click I'll go in and drag him out."

Mr. Larkin departed on his mission, only to return within a few minutes a much puzzled man.

"He's not there," he said. "He's not in the gentlemen's room."

Satin made a dash for the door, but the partners held her back.

"Think!" cried Mr. Larkin. "Think of what you're doing."

"If I can stand the Pornographic Department," she retorted, "a gentlemen's room should be child's play to me."

"But the gentlemen take it quite seriously, I assure you," protested the senior partner. "And besides, Mr. Owen is not in there."

"Then where is he?" she demanded.

"Gone," said Mr. Dinner.

"To a hotel, perhaps," supplied the Major.

"A stand-up, eh?" muttered Satin. "I'll cook his goose. Let me out of here."

With a sigh of relief Mr. Larkin watched the girl hurry from the café. Then he turned to his partners.

"Let's finish that other bottle of wine," he suggested, "and then go and collect what she has left of our new partner. He's a very foolish man if he entertains the idea he can get the best of one woman, not to mention two."

"That's a funny thing, too," quoth Mr. Dinner. "A woman doesn't mind giving you her best but hates like hell to have you get the best of her."

"Splendid, Dinner!" cried Mr. Larkin, leading the way back to their table. "Write it down in your little book. Even the fact that it's true cannot rob such an utterance of its brilliancy."

A few minutes later another cork popped. The partners, minus Mr. Owen, were industriously at it again.

# CHAPTER XIII

## Mr. Owen's Buff

MR. OWEN DID NOT KNOW THE FIRST THING ABOUT this city into which he had so recklessly thrown himself. He was not even sure that he had made good his escape. Had he seen the closed automobile draw up in front of the hotel into which he dodged he would have been somewhat skeptical on the point. And had he seen Madame Gloria, her fair face set in lines of grim determination, emerge from the car and sequester herself in the lobby of the hotel, his skepticism would have increased to the conviction that from the trap he had crawled into bed with the trapper.

A short time after these two seemingly unrelated arrivals the hotel was treated to a third. Satin, with blood in her eyes and champagne almost everywhere else, rushed impetuously through the wide doors, caught sight of Mr. Owen's unassuming back, and ducked behind the nearest convenient chair. This happened to be occupied by a nervous gentleman whose sole desire in life was to be left alone. Satin was breathing hard. Feeling a draft on the top of his head the gentleman reluctantly put on his hat, a precaution which annoyed him a little owing to the existence of a headache directly beneath it. The draft ceased, but the sound of wind—a small, self-contained and irritatingly spasmodic wind—continued. Satin had been covering considerable ground. Beneath her fine upstanding chest her lungs were carrying on. The gentleman's annoyance increased. He arose and peered over his chair.

"Why are you breathing on me?" he demanded.

"Got to breathe somewhere," the girl explained.

"But not on me," said the gentleman firmly.

132

"If you put your newspaper over your head," she told him, "you won't feel it."

"I've already put on my hat," he replied with a suggestion of bitterness. "Isn't that enough?"

"Apparently not," said Satin. "Do you want me to explode back here?"

The gentleman considered this possibility dispassionately.

"I wouldn't mind," he told her at last. "Better to get it over once and for all."

"I've finished panting now," she assured him. "Do me a bit of a favor, and I'll send you a dirty book."

"How did you know I like dirty books?" asked the gentleman in some surprise.

"You look it," retorted Satin, not thinking.

"Mean I look dirty?" demanded the man.

"No," explained the girl impatiently. "Just nasty. You know how."

"How dirty is this book?" inquired the gentleman, deciding to let the point rest.

"Have we time to go into all that now?" expostulated Satin. "It's got pictures."

"All right," said the man. "Here's my card. Don't forget the book. What do you want me to do?"

"See that chap at the desk," she told him. "He seems to be having some trouble. Find out what room they give him and let me know."

The gentleman departed in the direction of the desk. Satin turned her back and stood looking out on the street.

Mr. Owen was experiencing no little difficulty with the clerk, a man of apparently the loosest morals and the most astonishing propositions. Had the escaping partner known that he was endeavoring to book accommodations at the city's most modern hotel, one which insisted on providing everything that would make for the comfort and entertainment of its guests, he would, perhaps, not have been so far at sea. As things stood, however, and in his somewhat confused mental condition, he was having a hard time in battling against the hospitable suggestions of the clerk.

"I don't want to talk to you any more," he said at

last to this puzzled individual. "You seem able to think of only one thing. Will you please send me someone else—someone with some faint conception of propriety?"

Another clerk smilingly appeared and presented himself to Mr. Owen.

"Anything I can do for you sir?" he asked in a confidential voice that gave Mr. Owen little hope.

"Yes," he answered wearily. "I want a room and a bath."

"Do you want a double room with a single woman, sir?" inquired the clerk smoothly. "Or would you prefer a nice, cozy room with two of them?"

"Two of what?" asked Owen unwisely.

"Two of women," replied the clerk.

"Haven't you any rooms without women?" Mr. Owen asked rather hopelessly.

"None for gentlemen, sir," said the clerk blandly. "It's a depression measure, you know. The hotel provides accommodations for certain members of our indigent female population while they in turn provide companionship for our male guests. We consider it an exceptionally sensible arrangement."

"I don't know how sensible it is," observed Mr. Owen, "but it certainly is good and immoral."

"Not necessarily, you know," replied the clerk. "Some men enjoy being read to, or waited on, or entertained in various other ways. It's merely a matter of individual preference."

"Well," said Mr. Owen, "from what I've been able to learn of this town, people seem to think of only one form of entertainment."

"That holds for every town," the clerk replied philosophically. "You'll always find it so. The only difference between this town and others is that here we make a virtue of what they make a vice."

"A startling conception," admitted Mr. Owen. "Doesn't anyone ever sleep alone?"

"There's no scientific basis in fact that a man should sleep alone," replied the clerk.

"Is there any that he should sleep double?" asked Mr. Owen.

"No," admitted the clerk, "but it seems more natural."

"I didn't come here to argue," said Mr. Owen. "All I want is a room and bath."

"I know," said the clerk, growing a little impatient himself. "And all I want is to get you to commit yourself to some reasonable arrangement. Do you want a single lady and a double room or two of them in one?"

"How about a double woman and a single room?" Mr. Owen shot back, spitefully giving the clerk a little something to think about.

"A double woman," murmured the clerk, running the pen through his glistening hair. "A double woman, you're wanting. We've never had one of those. Isn't it rather abnormal?"

"No more than a double Scotch and soda," Mr. Owen replied.

"Isn't it?" observed the clerk. "You must come from a rugged country. Wouldn't two single women do as well?"

"I always take my women double," retorted Mr. Owen. "It's the only way."

The clerk regarded him admiringly.

"It's a new one on me," he said at last, "but it does sound dandy. Where do you get these double women? It might be a good thing for us to know."

"We breed them," Mr. Owen replied in a hard voice. "In fact, I've got so used to double women that I don't think I could stand 'em single. I've a couple of singles already knocking about somewhere. I'm trying to give them the gate."

"Well," said the clerk, once more referring the pen to his hair. "The women go with the rooms, you know. There's no extra charge. Of course, you've got to feed them, and they don't like being left alone." He paused and looked perplexed. "I'll tell you what we'll do," he went on. "You let me talk to the women. I'll explain it to them. Trust me to handle them all right. You go on up to your room, and I'll see what can be done about it. Don't worry. And by the way——" here he paused again and leaned confidentially over to Mr. Owen——

"when you have a double woman, what do you do with the other one?"

"Chloroform her," said Mr. Owen briefly. "Or put her in a straitjacket."

Without a word, but looking many, the clerk handed a key to room 707 to the waiting page boy, and a few moments later Mr. Owen was elevated by the lift to his room on the seventh floor.

"For you, sir," said the boy, opening a door to a bathroom, then added, laconically, opening a door on the other side of the room, "This bath is for your women."

"There'll be no women," replied Mr. Owen. "What's behind those other two doors?"

"Guests, probably," replied the boy. "They belong to the rooms on either side of this one. They can easily be unlocked, sir, should you desire larger quarters."

"All I want is this room," said Mr. Owen. "Just this room and a bed and a lot of privacy."

"What about the women?" asked the boy.

"I'll ring for them," he was told.

"Sometimes they don't even wait for that," the boy remarked. "If you ask me, this place is a hotel in name only. Never saw such goings on."

Mr. Owen regarded him nervously.

"Bring me a whole, full bottle of Scotch," he said at last. "I'm going to make myself so that I won't know that there's such a thing as a woman within ten miles."

"It's the only way," approved the page boy, departing with his tip. "Sometimes we have to drag our guests out by sheer force, the women take such a fancy to them. It's hard to work with women—they don't follow any rules."

When the boy had gone, Mr. Owen walked to one of the windows and stood looking out over the city. Night had fallen now. Lights in rows and in clusters illuminated the darkness. Rivers of radiance flowed through the streets and boulevards, and occasionally splashed over their boundaries in great bursts of color in the parks and plazas. Faintly on the night air floated the strains of an orchestra embroidering the deep overtones of the city. In the park facing his window men and women were dancing while scarlet-jacketed waiters sped about between the trees with gleaming buckets of wine. A man in a velvet blouse was bending to the voice of his violin, his fingers stringing the strings along its shaft. The bare arms and shoulders of women attracted and tossed back the lights trickling through dark leaves.

Was everybody happy in this city, Mr. Owen wondered, or was this only a superficial glamour such as any city could show? He felt inclined to doubt it. As far as he had been able to discover during the short time he had been there the entire populace seemed to be much more interested in the way to enjoy life than in how to earn a living. This was how things should be, yet never were. Perhaps the encouragement of political graft and grafters was the solution. In a way it seemed logical. Political grafters usually took care of their friends. If the same benevolent attitude was extended to include the entire population, then everybody would be happy and no bad habits broken. It was a reasonable arrangement, after all, for instead of wasting a lot of time in attacking a system or a moral code as wrong, it took advantage of its wrongness and developed it to the point of perfection.

The boy, entering with the bottle and a bucket of ice, interrupted Mr. Owen's musings. He was tired and needed a drink. He took several and no longer felt tired. Without a blessed responsibility in the world, either moral or financial, and with no fear of the morrow, Mr. Owen sat down and faced the bottle. It was remarkably good whisky, he decided. What was he going to do without a lot of responsibilities to shoulder, payments to meet, obstacles to overcome? How in the world was he ever going to get through the day without a swarm of worries nagging at his mind? Would his character become weak and flaccid? Would he lose his moral standards?

To keep himself from spiritual decay, would he have to start in and endeavor to reform this world? That would be a dreadful thing to do, but no doubt that was how, or rather why, so many reformers were always cropping up to trouble the peace of mankind. They wanted to save themselves rather than to save others. Why couldn't a person be satisfied with his own ideals instead of trying to cram them down other people's throats? God, if there was one, never got a chance. Humanity was formed and reformed and fumigated and eventually embittered before He even had an opportunity to find out what all the fuss was about.

It was not a good way to go on. Mr. Owen was convinced of that. He began to worry about God and humanity. He decided that neither would suffer and that he himself would improve greatly if he had another drink. He filled his glass and rang for the boy.

"I want the largest box of the largest cigars in the house," Mr. Owen told him. "And I want some very large matches."

"Yes, sir," said the boy, apparently not surprised by such an order. "That whisky makes a body feel that way."

Perhaps the boy was right. Mr. Owen did not know. He was feeling better now about both God and humanity. They would pull through somehow. In this town they put reformers in jail, which was a good thing, yet it went to show that the only way to fight intolerance was with intolerance. And just what did that prove? There could be no such animal as complete tolerance until people learned to mind their own business. And when would that be, might he ask? He laughed aloud sarcastically and was startled by the sound of his own voice. Another drink fixed him up. He was glad to see the boy.

"Those certainly are big matches and even bigger cigars," he told the boy. "Where did you get such big matches, boy? They must be all of six inches long."

"Yes," agreed the boy. "They are very big matches, but they're not the biggest matches."

"No?" said Mr. Owen. "Have you ever seen bigger ones?"

"Sure," replied the boy. "Out in the country they make 'em so long a man has to climb a tree to strike one on the seat of his pants."

"Is that so?" replied the astonished Owen, thinking he understood, then suddenly realizing he did not.

"How does that help?" he added. "How can he strike a match on the seat of his trousers way up in a tree?"

"He doesn't," replied the boy, "but the man on the ground does."

"Oh," said Mr. Owen, then looked suddenly at the boy. "Will you please go away," he told him. "I hate stories like that. I hate even to think of the inane mind that conceives them. Imagine a man being so damned accommodating as to climb a tree—— No," he broke off, "I don't like to think about it. You'd better go."

The boy left, and Mr. Owen complacently resumed his drinking, a faint smile on his lips. He contemplated the twin beds and tried to decide which one he would choose. That double woman idea of his had been a good one. It had worked. The clerk had been greatly impressed. He, Mr. Owen, would not be troubled by a lot of loose women.

As he sat there drinking he wondered why he had run away from Satin. He suspected that she had been too bold, too sinister about her intentions. After all, he did really want her. He wanted her more than any woman he had ever known. He could not say why he did unless it was because she gave him a feeling of youth and expectancy. He wondered where she was now and what she was doing. That was too bad, too. The moment a man got interested in a woman he began to wonder where she was and what she was doing instead of just being satisfied when she happened to drop in. Still, if people did not remember each other they would get dressed in the morning, then rush out and forget to come back. Perhaps that would be a good thing, too. No lasting affiliations. Just a good time always.

He pulled his thoughts up with a start. Already his character was slipping. Depravity was setting in. He hoped a complete moral collapse was not far off. One could not arbitrarily dispose of one's inhibitions. They had to be drugged first, then knocked over the head. Still smiling faintly, he rose and ambled, glass in hand, to the bathroom. The tub looked inviting. A man could almost swim in it—a man and a woman. Once more he wondered where Satin was. Then he wondered why it was that a lovely bathroom with lots of mirrors and gadgets in it always evoked indecorous, if not indecent, thoughts.

Perhaps the human mind was so constituted that it involuntarily rebelled against the idea of absolute cleanliness. Lots of people—nice ladies and gentlemen—must look at lovely bathrooms and think bad thoughts. A woman looking at this luxurious bathroom, for instance, just could not help seeing herself in it, and as it was a well known fact that a woman cannot enjoy seeing herself alone, she would naturally have someone else along with her, and, he supposed, that was not a very nice thing, or, at least, lots of people said so. He himself had better stop wondering about so many stupid things and turn on a few of those gleaming faucets before going to bed.

What a day it had been! Now that he came to think of it, the day had almost been a life—an entire life behind which his brain refused to penetrate. There had been other things once, but at the first suggestion of them his thoughts turned and wheeled about like a drove of frightened horses. A bath would be refreshing. It might improve his character; then again, it might not. Anyway, good people bathed occasionally as well as bad. Who was he to snap his fingers at a bath? He was glad there was no eel in it. Where was that girl now that he was all ready to take a bath? He would take a bath without her. He always had in the past. Why not now? He turned on his heel and began to undress in the casual fashion of the brooding male.

What with one thing and another, Mr. Owen became so preoccupied with his undressing that for the moment he lost that awareness of his surroundings which all males, either brooding or otherwise, should exercise when performing such a delicate operation. So deeply engrossed was he in some knotty moral problem that he failed to hear the stealthy opening of the door to one of the guests' rooms.

Nor did he see the red head of a woman thrust itself through the aperture while two bright eyes studied his sparsely clad figure with frank but unladylike interest. He did see, however, just at the critical moment when he was about to attack the business of doing away with his drawers, the other door fly open and Madame Gloria, in almost as bad a fix as he was, standing resplendently in it.

"I see it all now!" cried the lady in a voice choked with emotion. "Everything is clear."

Hearing the dazzling creature for once speaking the truth, Mr. Owen became convulsed.

"My God!" he exclaimed. "What a fix! I can't stand looking even at myself, and I certainly shouldn't look at you."

"Gaze over your right shoulder," Madame Gloria commanded, "and you will see something else again—something that will cause you to swoon in your tracks."

"I need little help in that direction," he muttered, glancing over his shoulder, and at that moment the room leaped into darkness.

In this comforting concealment Mr. Owen stood, undecided as to his next move. As he listened to the strains of the orchestra drifting in from the park, he wondered how God could permit people to dance and enjoy themselves while his plight received no attention.

"Quick!" came the penetrating whisper of Madame Gloria. "Leap into my room. We can carry on there."

"A nice lady," observed Mr. Owen aloud to himself in the darkness. "If that woman doesn't go away they'll have to carry me out on a stretcher."

Whether he thought it was more impersonal or more forceful to address his remarks to Madame Gloria indirectly, Mr. Owen was not sure himself. For some strange reason it gave him the feeling of being less physically involved in the situation.

"I am still here," called Madame Gloria sweetly.

"I feared as much," said Mr. Owen. "But you shouldn't be. Can't you realize, Madame Gloria, that I am stripped to the buff?"

After this announcement there followed a long, pregnant silence which was finally broken by Madame Gloria's voice.

"Listen," she said with a trace of humility. "I've been acting all my life and I've missed a lot of words. What's your buff?"

Mr. Owen thought about this for a moment, and while doing so became convinced that he heard someone giggling softly in the room. Was this implacable woman advancing noiselessly upon him to make her kill?

"You should know that as well as I do," he exclaimed impatiently.

"Should I?" she asked. "Have I one—a buff?"

"How should I know, madam," he asked wearily, "whether you have a buff or not? I suppose you have, but is this any time to enter into an academic discussion of buffs? Maybe it's a state of being and not a thing at all."

"It would be better so," said Madame Gloria dryly. "Whenever I'm like this my audiences are in a state of frenzy."

"So am I," retorted Mr. Owen. "But you don't hear me clapping unless it's with my knees. Don't creep up on me and spring without warning."

"You looked cute with your buff," came the musing voice of Gloria.

"In my buff, madame," Mr. Owen corrected her. "It's not with. I'm sure of that."

"But you didn't seem to be in hardly anything at all," the woman protested. "Did you get them off?"

"What's off?" asked Mr. Owen.

"Your funny little drawers," replied the lady.

"Why do you want to know?" he demanded nervously.

"Who has a better right?" she asked.

"I don't know," he retorted. "I can't think clearly. I don't even know if anybody has any right to know anything about my drawers."

"That's a pitiful condition to be in," she observed sympathetically, "but cheer up. I won't leave you long in doubt."

This threat—or promise—left its hearer so unnerved that he was seized with a desire to drink. The inhibitions he had thought he was losing had flocked back to him from the past. A bathrobe would have saved his end of the situation. There was none. In the darkness he could not even find his trousers. As he reached out to grasp the bottle a shriek broke from his lips as his hand felt a bare arm. His fingers slid down it only to encounter a firm hand clutched round the object he was seeking. This time his shriek embodied a note of bitter disappointment. He had needed that drink and he still did. Was he surrounded by naked women? Was the darkness cluttered up with bodies? Abandoning his attempt to possess himself of the bottle he raced for the nearest bed, and jumping in, encountered a body in the flesh. This hotel must be used to shrieks, he thought to himself, emitting another one and reversing the direction of his jump like a diving figure in a playful newsreel. As he crawled towards the other bed the room was filled with sound. There was a scampering about in the darkness and a vigorous banging of doors. Fumbling greedily with the coverings of the second bed, he was about to crumble beneath them when the gentle voice of Madame Gloria turned him to a graven image.

"I'm here," said Madame Gloria, "if you're looking for me."

"Will you tell me where you aren't?" he chattered. "Only a second ago you were in the other bed."

"Oh, no, I wasn't," came the playful reply. "That was the other one."

"What other one?" he asked in a dazed voice.

"The other woman," the lady explained.

"Holy smokes," faltered the man, reverting to the vernacular of his youth like a person approaching the end. "Are there two of you in this room?"

"At the very least," replied Madame Gloria.

"Two women and one buff," came a voice from the other bed. "Who gets the buff?"

"From the way he's acting," complained Madame Gloria's bed, "a person would get the impression it was a blind man's buff."

"There's none so blind as will not see," observed the other voice, which he recognized now as that of Satin. "This chap won't even feel."

"Are you two going to chat there comfortably in my beds," demanded Mr. Owen, "while I crouch here in the darkness?"

"Why not transfer the scene of your crouching to my bed," inquired Satin, "and then we can all chat together?"

"If you get in bed with that women," cried Madame Gloria, "I'll damn well drag you out, buff or no buff."

"I heartily hope you do," said Mr. Owen with all sincerity.

"That works both ways, mister," Honor told him.

"You don't have to worry," said Mr. Owen, "neither of you. I'd rather crawl in bed with a couple of bears."

"No animal could be barer than I am," commented Satin thoughtfully. "Not even a billiard ball."

"For shame," reproved Mr. Owen.

"That's right," said Satin. "For shame, it is. What would a girl do if it wasn't for her shame?"

"I thoroughly enjoy mine," put in Madame Gloria. "Quite frankly, I admit it."

"Well, I can't bear mine," declared Mr. Owen. "If you all don't go away, I'm going to lock myself in one of the bathrooms."

"Who's got a match?" asked Satin. "I want to light a cigarette."

"You do yourself well, don't you?" Mr. Owen asked sarcastically. "Cigarettes and everything. I suppose you've got my bottle, too."

"I have," replied Satin. "I sip it from time to time. Crawl in and I'll give you a swig."

"If he does," grated Madame Gloria, "I'll yank him clean out of those funny little drawers."

"You'd be one yank too late," chortled Satin, and even Madame Gloria was forced to laugh softly to herself in the darkness.

"I don't see how you can laugh," Mr. Owen lamented. "Suppose the partners knew where you were, Miss Knightly."

"They'd all be right in with me," asserted Satin. "Pell-mell and topsy-turvy. They're not sexually illiterate, like you—not those boys."

"Sex! Sex! Sex!" cried Mr. Owen. "Sex morning noon and——"

"What are you shouting about?" interrupted Honor.

"You've got plenty of sex around. Aren't the two of us enough?"

"The way that man calls for his sex," put in Madame Gloria, "you'd think he wanted a harem."

"I've met men like that," commented Satin. "Never willing to start at the bottom rung."

"I have ladders in my stockings, too," observed Madame Gloria, apropos of nothing as far as Mr. Owen could see.

A match suddenly flared in the darkness.

"There he goes!" cried Honor Knightly. "It's hard to say whether it's a man running away in drawers, or a pair of drawers running away with a man."

"Looks like a running man in drawers," replied the other lady as the match went out. "Wonder where he's going?"

"Maybe he's getting ready to spring on us," suggested Honor.

"He'd have to be all spraddled out to land on us both," observed Madame Gloria. "Doubt if he could make it."

They were not long in finding out. Mr. Owen had dashed to the nearest bathroom and was clawing at the door. It flew open in his grasp, and he looked in upon a strange woman splashing busily in the bathtub.

"Come in," she said calmly. "What's your hurry?"

## CHAPTER XIV

## *The Hour Grows Late*

"I'M NOT IN A HURRY," GASPED MR. OWEN, BACKING out of the room. "I'm in a whirl."

"Come back!" called the woman as he sped in the direction of the other bathroom. "I won't look."

This invitation served only to increase Mr. Owen's speed. He reached the door, flung it open, and dashed inside, slamming it behind him. Almost immediately the two ladies in the beds were treated to a series of animal-like cries such as they had never heard before. Mingled with them were the entreating notes of a woman's voice.

"My God!" cried Honor. "A woman's got him in that one. To the rescue!"

Merging the worst features of their seemingly one and only interest in life, the two women sprang from their beds and raced to the bathroom door.

"Come out of there!" cried Honor.

"What are you doing now?" called the more imaginative Madame Gloria.

"Wrestling with a woman," came from Mr. Owen in grunts, "and she's all wet and naked."

"I'll fix her," grated Satin. "Which way are you wrestling—for or against?"

"Why don't you answer?" cried Madame Gloria nervously. "We can't see a thing. Why is the door locked? We want to know everything."

"Well, you can't be a Graham McNamee in the arms of a naked woman," Mr. Owen panted as caustically as conditions would permit. "Especially a wet one with soap all over her. I can't grab hold."

"Of what?" asked Satin.

"Of anything," called Mr. Owen.

"That's just as well," put in Madame Gloria.

"If you two molls would go away," came the voice of the woman behind the door, "I'd soon have him eating out of my hand."

"I'd rather see him starve first," said Madame Gloria in a tragic voice.

"I don't give a damn about his appetite," put in Satin. "I'm worrying about his buff, whatever that may be."

"Yes," agreed Madame Gloria. "He seemed to set a great deal of store by that buff. We have to get him out." She rattled the door furiously. "Why don't you come out?" she cried. "Unlock the door, and we'll drag you out."

"I'm trying to," Mr. Owen called back, "but my hand is trembling so I can't turn the key."

"All right," broke in the disgusted voice of his captor. "All right. Go on out. I don't want a nervous wreck."

In the meantime the lady in the other bathroom, hearing the noise, had emerged drippingly, clad strategically in a towel.

"Where'd he go?" she inquired of the other two. "I caught only a glimpse of him."

At this moment the bathroom door flew open, and she caught another. Mr. Owen found himself between two fires with the light from behind flooding down on the scene. He took one paralyzed look at all the bare flesh by which he was surrounded; then, snatching the towel from the clutches of the first bathing woman, flung it over his head.

"Back to your places!" he screamed. "Back to your beds and baths, or I'll throw you all out on your——"

"On our whats?" demanded Satin.

"On your ears," he retorted. "Make it snappy."

There was a patter of bare feet, then quiet settled down.

"You may come out from under that towel now," Satin's voice proclaimed.

"I'm going to live beneath this towel for the remainder of my life," he answered firmly.

"I think you're about to lose a button," Madame Gloria said comfortably from the pillow. "*The* button, I'd be inclined to suppose."

With great promptitude Mr. Owen snatched the towel from his head and flipped it round his waist.

"You've got four of us now," observed Satin. "What are you going to do with so many?"

"I'll show you," said Mr. Owen, striding over to the telephone. "I'm going to have you all chucked out."

"On our ears?" inquired Honor.

"I don't give a damn what they chuck you out on," he retorted into the transmitter.

"And as for me," came back a voice over the wire, "I don't give a damn if they slit your throat from ear to ear."

"I wasn't talking to you," Mr. Owen hastened to explain to the operator at the other end. "I'm sorry. Please give me the desk."

"Oh, that's all right," the girl's voice replied. "If you've no objection to my sex I'll come up there and help you to chuck them out myself, whoever they may be."

"For God's sake, don't," he cried. "I'm oversexed already. I want the room clerk."

"The room clerk!" exclaimed the girl. "What on earth does a man in your condition want with the room clerk?"

Mr. Owen emitted a howl of rage.

"Calm yourself, dearie," came the voice of the operator. "I'll give you the room clerk, though I must say—— Hold on, here he is."

"Hello!" cried Mr. Owen. "Room clerk? Good! I've got two beds and two baths, and there is a naked woman in each."

"What more do you want?" asked the room clerk. "We haven't any double women, if that's what you're after."

"I'm not," snapped Mr. Owen. "But where do you expect me to go?"

"I don't know about you," said the clerk, "but if I was fixed up as you are, I'd either go to bed or take a bath. You can't lose."

"Something has to be done about all these women," fumed Mr. Owen. "And that without further delay."

"I should say so," agreed the clerk. "The night isn't getting any shorter. By rights you're entitled to only two women. How did you manage to smuggle the others in?"

"I didn't smuggle them in," Mr. Owen protested. "They smuggled themselves in."

"Women are great hands at that," philosophically observed the clerk. "You seem to be having all the luck."

"Listen," Mr. Owen pleaded. "You don't seem to understand. There are two beds and two baths. So far I've got a woman in each."

"Let's see," broke in the clerk. "If I remember your

room rightly that leaves three chairs and one sofa un-occupied. Do you want a woman in each of those?"

"Are you mad?" thundered Mr. Owen.

"No," replied the room clerk, "but you must be, not to be satisfied with a couple of beds and bathtubs filled with women."

"I said you didn't understand," wailed Mr. Owen. "I'm more than satisfied. Much more than satisfied."

"Ah!" exclaimed the gratified clerk. "I have been stupid, haven't I? You want to compliment the hotel, don't you? Well, I'm sure the management will be delighted to hear you've had a good time. Go right to it. What a stupid ass I've been."

"You still are," groaned Mr. Owen, and hung up the telephone, a beaten man.

Suddenly he was seized by a mad idea. Springing up from the telephone, he fled across the room in the direction of Madame Gloria's door. Up from the beds and out of the baths like four naked bats out of hell the women raced after him. Across Madame Gloria's room he sped and out into the hall, his pursuers close behind. Here his flight was arrested by the sudden descent of his drawers. Yet even as he fell he had time to thank his God he was landing face forward. When he did land, the women behind him passed over his pros-trate body and became hopelessly entangled on the other side. Still in the clutch of inspiration, he sprang to his feet and, pulling up his treacherous drawers with one hand, dashed back to the room he had just quitted and locked the door behind him. Hurrying into his own room, he seized the bottle of whisky and took a deep pull. From the hall came the sounds of agitated female voices. Hands were beating on his door. Mr. Owen grinned and drank again. His telephone bell was ring-ing. Applying his ear to the receiver he listened blandly.

"Say!" came the voice of the clerk. "The floor oper-ator tells me that there are four naked women beating on your door and raising howling hell in the hall to be let in."

"Good!" cried Mr. Owen. "It's music to my ears. I was expecting them."

"But, man alive," went on the clerk, "you've already

got four naked women, and with these four it makes eight altogether. How many more do you want? People sleep in this hotel occasionally, you know."

"No," said Mr. Owen. "I didn't know that. Well, I'm going to be one of them."

He hung up the instrument and turned back with a satisfied smile to the room. Four indignantly naked women were watching him with glittering eyes.

"You forgot the other door, didn't you, dearie?" said Madame Gloria in oversweetened tones.

"And that's going to be just too bad for you," added Satin, her small white teeth gleaming.

Mr. Owen made one dive for the bed. The women made four. All landed safely, Mr. Owen on the bottom. At this moment the partners, escorted by a page boy with a passkey, entered the room with the glacial dignity of the elaborately drunk.

"Dear me!" exclaimed Mr. Larkin. "What a bevy! And where can Owen be? Ah! There he is! Underneath the bevy, of all places."

"Is he the one with the drawers?" asked Mr. Dinner.

"Yes," said Mr. Larkin. "The only one with drawers, if my eyes do not deceive me."

"He won't have them on long," Major Barney remarked placidly, "the way they're going for him."

The presence of the gentlemen spread consternation in the ranks of the ladies who, to Mr. Owen's surprise, suddenly developed scruples hitherto unsuspected. In their own strange way these women had their standards. Up to this point each one of them had believed herself to be rightfully entitled to Mr. Owen. In the face of an audience they were willing to abandon their claim. And they abandoned it as energetically as it had previously been pressed. They literally took Mr. Owen up and tossed him at his partners' feet. After that they divided the bedclothing and sat expectantly swathed.

"And now," resumed Mr. Larkin smoothly, this time addressing the highly edified page boy, "if you'll be so good as to hurry away and bring back leagues of sandwiches and oceans of strong drinks, we'll see what can be done to make this evening pleasanter—or is it morning? I forget which. Does it really matter?" As the boy hurried away, he turned to Mr. Owen. "I ask you," he resumed. "Does it? No. All that really matters is that you get some trousers on as speedily as possible. And that only matters to you, although sometimes I feel we are liberal to a fault."

Mr. Owen rose and shook each of his partners by the hand.

"Gentlemen," he said, looking vindictively at the ladies seated like so many Orientals on the beds, "you saved me from a living death."

"I cannot think of a happier one," Mr. Larkin replied, bowing to the four swathed figures. "Who are the other two? I don't seem to recall their faces."

"We go with the room," explained one of them in a husky voice.

"And he didn't want us," said the other, "but we sneaked in anyway, just in case he changed his mind."

"Conscientious to the last," observed Mr. Larkin approvingly. "You seemed even willing to change his mind for him."

"Let bygones be bygones," said Mr. Owen with a grin as he collected his scattered garments and made for the bathroom. In a moment he reappeared and picked up the bottle. "You know," he explained, "this bottle and these drawers and myself have been through so much together we can't bear to be separated."

"You almost were," said Satin grimly. "And if you keep flaunting yourself before us I'll snatch you as naked as a babe in arms."

Mr. Owen departed, this time not to return until securely as well as completely clad. His bottle was now empty, but the room was full of drinks. As usual the partners had done things on a tremendous scale. Everywhere Mr. Owen turned, a glass or bottle was ready to his hand. Nor did it take long for them to find their way to his lips. On the two beds the ladies sat in their drapery and munched sandwiches. In their eyes was that knowing expression of women awaiting developments which experience has taught them were quite inevitable even when unsolicited.

"I've literally thrown away my night," declared

Madame Gloria, adding an empty glass to two others already beside her. "Simply tossed it away."

"Why, my dear lady," protested Mr. Larkin. "All is far from lost. Instead of getting one man, you've got the four of us. Think of that."

"Yes," replied Madame Gloria. "I am. Three old faces and one new but stupid one."

"And lots of free drinks," put in the practical Mr. Dinner.

"They make up for a little," assented Madame Gloria, "but not for all—not for the new and stupid face. I'd like to slap it."

"Why can't you cultivate an attitude of indifference towards me?" asked Mr. Owen annoyingly. "My face may be new to you, but really it's an old, old story."

"But, my dear man," explained Madame Gloria. "I haven't seen the last chapter yet."

"No, but you have almost everything else," Satin lazily observed. "All of us have. Weren't his little drawers enough?"

"Those drawers were almost too much," Madame Gloria agreed reminiscently. "Especially when they tripped him."

"Can't you veer this subject, Mr. Larkin?" asked Mr. Owen, feeling that his once secret life had now become a public scandal. "Those drawers of mine are exhausted."

The senior partner daintily shot back an immaculate cuff and examined a magnificent wrist watch.

"It is," he said, "exactly three o'clock in the morning. At this hour people, if they sleep at all, are usually attempting forty winks—that is, if both parties are willing."

"Which is ideal," put in Mr. Dinner.

"It does make for party harmony," agreed Mr. Larkin. "But to continue. The halls of this hotel are infinitely long, and broad almost to a fault. For gentlemen that stagger, as what gentleman doesn't, they are occasionally discouraging. One either falls down or grows sober before hitting them. For a man who veers as much as I do, whether drunk or sober, this becomes quite a trial. It throws the responsibility for my progress on my own shoulders instead of on the walls. I mean, the walls themselves—not their shoulders. Anyway, that's not what I'm talking about."

"No?" inquired Honor Knightly. "Would it upset you greatly to veer round to what you are talking about?"

"Not at all," was the ready response. "Only, my dear lady, don't fly out at me. What I wanted to say was that I would like to have me a little foot racing done. There! I've said it."

"You have," remarked Major Barney, "but not very clearly. How do you mean, 'I would like to have me a little foot racing done?' It's not even bad English. It's worse. Something seems to be there, but one can't quite find it. Do you mean that you would like to sit in a chair and watch others run foot races for you, or that you desire to participate yourself in some damn fool sporting event, or just what intelligence are you trying to convey through the medium of human speech?"

"I would like to run a foot race on foot," said Mr. Larkin simply, but in a slightly offended voice. "But I'm getting a little exhausted about it even before it's started."

"Well, that's clear, at least," commented Major Barney. "Does anyone else feel like running a foot race on foot?"

"How?" asked Mr. Owen, who had secretly won tremendous races in the past.

"On foot," replied Major Barney.

"Oh," said Mr. Owen. "If it's on foot, I'll run one."

"On what foot?" asked Mr. Dinner, blinking.

"On one's best foot," supplied Mr. Larkin. "One puts it forward, you know."

"And drags the other behind, I suppose?" Dinner retorted with bitter sarcasm.

"No," answered Mr. Larkin. "One gives the other foot every encouragement. Although, so far as I'm concerned, one can take it or leave it, as one likes."

"I'm worried about my drawers," said Mr. Owen.

"Take 'em off, man! Take 'em off!" the Major ruggedly exclaimed. "Your face is not the only old, old story about you."

"No," decided Mr. Owen. "I think I prefer to keep my drawers on. After all, a foot race is serious business."

"Especially when it's on foot," added Mr. Dinner.

"Sure," put in Honor Knightly. "If he were running this foot race on his hands, his drawers would stay up anyway, wouldn't they?"

"How true," remarked Mr. Larkin. "And how unnecessary."

As a consequence of these elaborate preliminaries the two foot racers, Mr. Larkin and Mr. Owen, accompanied by their supporters, proceeded noisily to the hall, where they took up their positions. They were rather unsteady about this, but meticulous as to details. When they attempted to toe their marks in the conventional posture of the runner, both had to be lifted from their faces upon which they had slowly collapsed. The race itself started somewhat casually, both Mr. Owen and Mr. Larkin having to be pushed into operation. As they trotted down the magnificent hall their friends and admirers followed them at a respectful distance. As a matter of fact, they were forced to gear themselves down in order to keep from out-stripping the contestants.

"I didn't know you were a racing enthusiast," observed Mr. Larkin, veering over towards his rival. "To be quite frank I never knew that I was one before. It is jolly if one doesn't go too fast."

"Well, I'm not sure even now," replied Mr. Owen, "whether I'm a racing enthusiast or not. I've often enjoyed myself thinking I was one."

"Are you like that, too?" exclaimed Mr. Larkin, barely getting his best foot forward. "So am I. I dearly love to think of things. Oh, yes, yes. I'm a great thinker. Once I thought I was the Sultan of Turkey and, would you believe it, before I could change my mind, I had dragged seventeen strange women into my house and was eventually discovered chasing a terrified Negro porter with a huge pair of shears. It's amazing, isn't it? I mean when one thinks deeply of anything. I was thinking almost too deeply. You see, I must have wanted a harem down to the last detail."

"The Negro being the last detail," observed Mr. Owen.

"Yes," agreed Mr. Larkin. "It's a good thing for him he could run so fast. He ran even faster than we are now, if anything."

"He had something to run for," commented the other competitor.

"Didn't he, though," agreed Mr. Larkin. "Under similar circumstances I'd have run, too. I'd have fairly torn along—much faster than this."

"Has any special distance been thought of in connection with this race?" Mr. Owen inquired politely.

"None at all, so far as I know," came the cheerful reply. "I guess we'll just keep running round these halls until we get sick of it, or they get sick of us, or we think of something else to do."

"But who wins?" asked Mr. Owen.

"That's for us to decide," Mr. Larkin said with some complacency. "That's where we have the advantage. We hold the winning trick."

"How do you mean?" Mr. Owen wanted to know.

"I'll think that up, too," he was informed, "and let you know later. At the moment everything is in abeyance. We're coming to a corner."

They achieved the corner with dignity if not with speed, and continued on in amiable conversation. And as they progressed, doors opened up along the hall behind them. People in various stages of dishevelment appeared in these open doors and wanted to know things. Not receiving a satisfactory answer, they joined the ranks of the following party to find out for themselves. Presently a considerable crowd of people, ignorant both as to why they were running and where they were running, were milling quite contentedly through the corridors of the hotel. Clerks and page boys arrived on the scene to inquire into the reasons for this unusual activity. Inasmuch as no one was able to enlighten them, they too joined the ranks and started running with the best of them. Presently this impressive body of guests, clerks and attendants overtook and passed the two innocent causes of its existence. They were too busy conversing to give any coherent answers to the questions put to them. They desired to be let alone, and had entirely forgotten why they were there themselves. Looking after the hundreds of figures disappearing down the hall ahead of them, Mr. Larkin's curiosity was aroused in a refined, unobtrusive way.

"Goodness gracious," he exclaimed. "Look at all those persons running round the halls. Wonder where they can be going at this time of night?"

"I don't know about them," observed Mr. Owen, "but I'm getting pretty tired and thirsty. There should be bar-rooms along these halls for long-distance runners like us."

"Perhaps if we keep on running, we'll come at last to your room, like Magellan—or was it MacFadden?—I don't know which."

At length, barely able to distinguish the best foot from the worst, they staggered through the door of 707 and fell panting on the beds, where they lay until refreshed by a drink. The others, who had lost interest in the race, sat around with glasses in hand and waited patiently while the athletes got their breath.

"Open a bottle of champagne," gasped Mr. Larkin.

"Are you tired?" Mr. Dinner asked.

"Are we tired?" exclaimed Mr. Larkin. "My God, this hotel is endless. There's absolutely no stopping it. It goes on and on and on just as I do at times. Only I'm never tiresome. We're simply broken reeds, that's all there is to it."

"But who won?" asked Major Barney.

"Won what?" asked Mr. Owen.

"Make yourself clearer," said the senior partner. "There's not a veer left in my mind."

"Why, the race, of course," explained one of the ladies who went with the room. "Who won that?"

"Oh," said Mr. Larkin. "We were running a race, weren't we? That's so, too." He paused as if thinking deeply, then swung his feet off the bed. "From the speed the manager of the hotel was making when we last saw him," he resumed, "I'd say he was making a strong bid for supremacy. We gave our places to him because, after all is said and done, it's his hotel, and if he doesn't deserve to get a little fun out of it, I'd like to know who does."

As nobody else seemed to know, the party turned its attention to more serious matters.

## CHAPTER XV

## *Behind the Settee*

MR. OWEN WAS NEVER ABLE TO RECALL WITH ANY degree of accuracy all of the events leading up to the closing of that day. And this is, perhaps, just as well for the peace of his overworked soul. However, he was able to recall with almost too convincing vividness exactly how the next one began.

On the mezzanine floor of that splendid hotel there was a huge settce, cutting off one of the secluded corners of the balcony lounge. And this imposing example of opulent luxury had an inexplicably lofty back. It was in the corner behind this settee that the day of the debauched Mr. Owen began. He did not begin it alone. By no means. He shared it jointly with a woman who was lying in a state of appalling disorder weightily upon his chest. She was face down, and when he awoke and discovered her there he found himself wondering in a dim sort of way why she had not smothered.

Then, with less dimness, he found himself wondering whether she had smothered. Perhaps she had done that very thing and was lying there dead on his chest. To awaken with a dead woman on one's chest is not an encouraging start for a new day. Had he not been rendered unfit by all the devils of a hangover, Mr. Owen would have been subject to panic. As it was he merely lay quite still and considered things. Should he push this dead woman off? No. If she were not quite dead, such a rude act might finish her. And if she were by chance alive, it certainly would enrage her. Far better to have a dead woman on one's chest than an enraged one. It was quieter. Less disturbing. Less upsetting to a man in his delicate condition. A better thing it would be to go into the situation, to make some reasonable, tentative inquiries. He would do that. So he said in a thickly muffled voice: "Who are you?"

The woman stirred faintly. She was not dead but dying. Presently she spoke, and to the prostrate Mr. Owen it sounded as if she were using a large portion of her last breath.

"Just a nameless old moll," she said, "cast up by the river."

Having established Satin's identity, Mr. Owen now attempted to do the same thing for their somewhat sordid locality.

"Where are we?" he asked.

"Your honor," inquired Satin, "am I in the witness box?"

"No," he told her. "You're on my chest, most definitely and disastrously on my chest. I am deflated."

The girl rolled off and looked up dizzily at the high back of the settee.

"We must have fallen down the sheer face of a cliff," she observed. "What a way!"

Mr. Owen then put a third terse question.

"How did we get here?" he asked.

"Climbed over, I guess," said Satin. "Or dived."

"How pretty that must have been," reflected Mr. Owen. "We didn't even stop on the sofa proper."

"It wouldn't have been proper to stop on the sofa," was Satin's prim reply.

"With thousands of beds in this hotel at our disposal," continued Mr. Owen bitterly, "we had to pick out a corner behind a damned divan."

"At least it showed a certain amount of nimbleness and determination," she reminded him. "That's saying much for a couple in our condition."

"Did you lure me here or did I lure you?" Mr. Owen wondered.

"As to that, I cannot say," she replied. "Maybe we veered together, as Mr. Larkin would put it. Perhaps now I'm Honor in name only. A sorry business—what?"

"Let's pass over that," he suggested. "It now remains to be established, why did we get here?"

"In pursuit of privacy, I suppose. Or just in the spirit of fun. You know, romping."

It must be mentioned that all the while this unedifying dialogue was progressing a solitary gentleman whose only distinctions in life were a long beard and an inquiring mind was sitting on the other side of the settee. He had come there to pursue his paper in peace and privacy. He had found neither. At first, when these muffled sounds had begun to rise weirdly over the top of the settee, he had not been definitely convinced as to their source. In fact, he had somewhat doubted their actual existence and rather suspected his ears. But as wonder gradually changed to conviction, his amazement and apprehension increased. Abandoning his paper, he listened with a feeling akin to awe. He was a harmless soul but a persistent one. All he wanted to do was to know and to understand. Such persons should more often be discovered murdered in lonely spots. His curiosity was rapidly becoming unbearable. Also he was a little alarmed. More than a little. He was absolutely confounded. Settees did not usually talk, much less converse. As a matter of truth, they never did either. Never at all. At no time and in no place. This manifestation was positively uncanny.

At this point in the gentleman's reflections, Satin exhibited the bad taste to emit several low but penetrating groans of sheer bodily anguish. They sounded as if they had been wafted from some tortured spirit in hell. This was a little too much for the gentleman's nerves, as well as his curiosity. He must look behind this loquacious couch. He must find out. To achieve this it was necessary for him to kneel on the seat and to peer over its high back. This action gave to the bearded head the effect of having been severed. That is, this is the way the head appeared to those lying directly beneath it. There it was, beard and all, perched gruesomely on the ledge of the settee. Which way it would topple God alone knew. And only He could divine what was the intent of the head, whether it was evil or otherwise. Obviously with such a head it could hardly be otherwise. These were the distressing thoughts that trembled through Mr. Owen's mind as he gazed up for one horror-stricken moment at the apparition peering interestedly down on him. Satin failed to see it, having buried her head in her arms to suffer more privately. Mr. Owen decided to do likewise, and this with all possible speed. It was the only thing left to do, under the circumstances. Accordingly, after having satisfied the demands of his terror in one short, startled shriek, he too rolled over on his stomach and concealed his starting eyes in his arms. The head, equally startled, ducked quickly from view.

"God!" sobbed Mr. Owen. "What was that?"

"What was what?" inquired Satin.

"What I just saw," quavered Mr. Owen.

"Describe it," answered his companion. "In detail."

"Don't ask me to do that," he pleaded. "To think about the thing chills my blood. To describe it would kill me outright."

"Perhaps it will reappear," Satin hopefully observed.

"God could never be so cruel, in spite of all the things I've done," the man replied in a voice of prayer. "It was a terrible thing to see in the best of health. With a hangover, it was beyond—— Oh, let's sing or pray or talk of other things."

"Put your best foot forward," urged the girl, "and tell us what it was."

"It was a head," replied Mr. Owen, almost in a whisper. "Just that. Don't ask for more. Simply but awfully a head."

"What sort of a head?"

"I knew you would ask that," her companion whined. "Does it matter what sort? Just a head of anything is nothing to be sneezed at."

"No," came thoughtfully from Satin. "That wouldn't be nice. That wouldn't show good breeding. Nor would it damage the head greatly."

"You shouldn't jest," declared Mr. Owen. "This was a most unusual head. There was a beard to it."

"Then it must have been a man's head."

"Ha! Ha!" laughed Mr. Owen in hysterical frenzy. "Did you think I was talking of a pig's head?"

"If you had been," replied Satin, "I'd be able to see some sense in it, because I know that if I looked up and suddenly beheld a pig's head peering down it would scare the lights out of me."

"Rather the head of a pig," declared Mr. Owen, "than this devil's head I saw."

"All right," said Satin soothingly. "Now that that's settled, will you tell me what sort of a beard?"

"How do you mean what sort of a beard?" he asked wearily.

"I mean, had it any points of distinction?" explained the girl.

"I don't know the first thing about beards," he moaned back at her. "It was just a beard, you know—all hair."

"Oh," reflected Satin. "I see. All hair. Not a mixed beard. Well, approximately, how long was this beard?"

"Don't even know that, but it was quite long enough."

"Long enough for what?"

"Long enough to upset me for the day," Mr. Owen asserted. "It was a most disconcerting beard!"

"Too vague," replied the girl. "I don't quite see that beard. Now, had it been a long, strong beard you might have grabbed hold of it and pulled yourself up."

Mr. Owen shuddered from both nausea and revolted sensibilities.

"I wouldn't touch a hair of that beard," he stoutly declared. "Not a hair."

"What good would that have done?" demanded Satin. "And besides, it's very hard to touch only one hair in a beard."

"I know nothing about that," Mr. Owen retorted with a feeble show of dignity. "Have you ever tried?"

"Never actually tried, but it stands to reason."

"My reason totters when I think of that beard."

"Well, let's drop the beard," the girl suggested briskly, "and take up the mustache. I suppose there was one?"

"The way you go on," protested the huddled figure,

"you'd think I'd studied with loving eyes every line in that horror's face."

"I'd loved to have seen that head with beard attached," Satin observed regretfully, rolling over on her side. Suddenly she dug a finger into Mr. Owen's ribs. He uttered a sharp yelp. "Room mate," she whispered. "Hector! I see it. Roll over and look."

"What! Me look?" chattered her room mate. "Don't be foolish. I've seen it. You look, if you like. Feed your eyes on the ghastly object. Me—never."

Then, with surprising naturalness, the head found voice and spoke.

"What are you doing down there?" it wanted to know.

"Swimming," said Satin coolly. "Swimming. The water's great."

Mr. Owen nudged her frantically.

"Don't go on like that," he whispered. "You're virtually inviting the thing to come down."

"No," said the head. "I mean it. What can you be doing down there?"

"Just flopping about in agony," said the girl. "You know how it is."

"Then why on earth don't you get up and go to your room?" demanded the head.

"Oh, no," replied the girl hastily. "We like it here. We always reserve this space whenever we come to this hotel."

"You do?" said the head in tones of astonishment. "And they let you have it?"

"Swept and garnished," Satin assured him. "With sofa back and rug."

"Goodness gracious," reflected Mr. Owen. "What a woman! She can actually kid that atrocity, while I can't even look at it."

"But I desire very much to read my newspaper," trickled complainingly through the beard dangling above the two bodies. "It's a morning one."

"Then why not read it?" retorted Satin. "We don't want your old paper."

"But how can I do that," the head wanted to know, "with a pair of strange voices directly behind me?"

"In the customary manner," replied Satin. "Or in any way you like. Perhaps if you read aloud we might all be able to get some news."

"Nonsense," expostulated the head. "That would look silly. Suppose someone should come along? There I'd be sitting on the sofa reading aloud to apparently nobody at all. They'd think I was a little cracked."

"Well, aren't you?" inquired Satin. "Strikes me your mental hinges needed a spot of oil somewhere."

"I'll tell you this, my fine lady," snapped back the head. "You're the one who is cracked."

"You shouldn't say that," said Satin severely.

"If not, then," continued the head, "what are you doing down there and how did you get down there, may I ask?"

"You may ask," replied Satin, "but ask someone who knows. Then tell us the answer. We'd be very much interested."

At this point Mr. Owen, assured of the harmlessness of the once frightful object, raised himself feebly on an elbow.

"Will you please go away?" he coldly asked the head.

"Ah!" cried the head. "So at last your husband has the courtesy to address me."

"Am I supposed to engage in conversation with every blessed soul that comes barging into my room?" the man below demanded.

"But it isn't really a room," protested the head. "Not properly speaking. It's a public place, and you're in it. That's all."

"Well, isn't that enough?"

"It's more than enough. It's too much. I want to read my paper. I always read it here."

"Then read it here, damn it," grated Mr. Owen, "but leave us in peace. You have no idea how sick we are."

Immediately Mr. Owen realized he had said the wrong thing. The gentleman belonging to the head was easily interested in almost anything, but nothing fascinated him more than the bodily ailments of others.

"You are?" he exclaimed. "Both of you? I didn't know that. Just what is the trouble?"

"Cholera!" Mr. Owen flung at him.

"Listen, mister," said Satin. "Is there a body attached to that bearded head of yours?"

"Oh, I've body enough," the head replied. "Why?"

"I was only thinking," the girl said, "that if you want to keep it intact you'd better collect its various members and carry them speedily away. This is a plague spot, and you're right in it."

The beard wagged its indecision.

"Although I don't believe you," came through it, "I'm not going to take any chances. I'm going right away and tell the manager."

"Good!" exclaimed Mr. Owen. "He'll love you for that."

Like the sudden dropping of the moon the head slipped from view over the rim of the settee.

"Alone at last," murmured Satin, and without rhyme or reason, placed her lips against the surprised but unreluctant lips of Hector Owen.

"What do you think of that?" she asked after she had finished kissing him as it is given to few men to be kissed, that is, by Satin.

"I'd think quite a lot of it," he said slowly when breath had returned to his body, "if it meant a damn thing to you, but it doesn't."

"That doesn't matter," she said. "What do you think of it as a kiss pure and simple?"

"I think," he replied with conviction, "that it was far from pure and it certainly wasn't simple."

"As to the first, you may be right," she admitted, "but you're wrong about the last part. For me, it's child's play."

"Although you put it somewhat crudely," said Mr. Owen, "you interest me strangely. Do you mean to lie there in shocking disorder and tell me that kiss was a mere sample of your latent powers to destroy the soul of a man?"

"I do," she replied soberly. "Assuming a man has a soul."

"My good, good God," murmured Mr. Owen, brushing the moisture from his forehead. "It is obvious that this woman has no soul."

"How about the body?" asked the girl. "We'll take up the soul later."

"No, we won't," snapped Mr. Owen. "We'll take up the soul right now. As long as I'm behind this damned barricade in broad daylight the body is null and void. It ceases to exist."

"Neither time nor place makes any difference to me," observed Satin.

"Apparently," remarked Mr. Owen dryly, "but in my life they play rather an important part. I don't overstress them, but I observe, at least, a few of the less unreasonable conventions."

"If I ever went gunning for you," she assured him, "you wouldn't observe even those."

"I've no desire to argue with you on that score," he replied hastily. "I know when I've met my master."

"Mistress," corrected Satin.

"Please," protested Mr. Owen, raising an admonitory hand. "As I was saying, I know when I'm licked."

"You weren't," put in the girl. "You weren't saying that at all. And furthermore, you haven't been licked. To hear you talk, one would think I was a cat or a dog."

"I find all this very trying," continued Mr. Owen with an attempt at dignity.

"But I'm not a cat or a dog," insisted Satin. "Am I?"

"No," agreed Mr. Owen without any show of warmth. "You have the worst qualities of both. May I proceed?"

"You mean, may you crawl away somewhere on your stomach?" the girl inquired. "Certainly not. I'd crawl after you on mine."

Mr. Owen closed his eyes and shrank from the picture he saw. He was crawling snakelike through the lobby of the hotel, and behind him, even more snakelike, crawled Satin. People turned to stare after them. They remained turned, transfixed by wonderment. And wherever he crawled, still flat on his stomach, there also crawled Satin, still flat on hers. With a start he opened his eyes to free himself from the spell of this reptilian progress.

"No," he replied in a dazed voice, "I did not mean that. Most decidedly, I did not mean that. I merely wanted to do a little more talking. That's simple enough language, isn't it?"

"I seem to understand it, so it must be," said the girl. "Go ahead and talk if you like. I'll think of something else."

"And I wouldn't give the pale shadow of a bad penny for your thoughts," replied Mr. Owen with a touch of malice.

"All right," she snapped, "but that wasn't what you were going to say."

"No," said Mr. Owen uneasily. "It was merely about that gunning business. Don't go gunning after me unless you really mean it. Somewhere inside I seem to be damn well fed up with that sort of thing." He hesitated and became increasingly self-conscious. "You see," he continued, "I realize I was never cut out to play the rôle of the casual lover. At times I've assured myself that I was—yes, I've kidded myself a lot. That's the trouble with me. I've deceived myself so much I can't bear being deceived by others, especially by a creature I seem to like far more than is strictly necessary."

Once more he paused and looked hopefully at the unresponsive back of the settee as if in search of encouragement therein. Finding none, and refusing to glance at the girl beside him, he took a deep breath and continued. "Before I came here," he said like one trying to recall some lost thought, to remember some forgotten face, "life had not been looking up for me for a long, long time. I can remember that much, at any rate. I must have been living in a depressed area, and it was filled with troubles—all sorts of things. It isn't clear. There's nothing definite, but I know how I felt, how hopelessly beaten I was in all departments. Don't know why I'm talking like this unless it's because all that grog and wine are still boiling in my veins—doing things with my tongue."

He came to a full stop, and in a low voice the girl

said, "Go on." Again he started speaking, slowly and haltingly. "There's not much in life for persons like me," he said, "not much except security and sameness. There are dreams into which they escape—impossible damn dreams, dreams in which they are loved as they never have been loved and never will be. And the funny thing about it is no one ever suspects there's enough material in their beings to scrape together the raggedest stepchild of a dream. They're the steady men with unremarkable faces, the men whose wives other men take simply because the women get so damned bored they'd give themselves to the iceman for the sake of a change."

Unconsciously he had clenched his hands. He seemed to have forgotten entirely that he was saying all these things lying huddled in a corner behind a hotel settee. "They believe in loyalty, and they believe in love—some sort of an honest, sporting love—and they are as silly and as stupid as hell. They never take chances, and yet they manage to lose. They never hit the high spots, and yet they land in the low. The poor, spineless saps." The last was spoken in a whisper.

"When I came here," he resumed in an altered voice, "everything was changed. My troubles were left behind and all sense of obligation. I even felt younger, though I don't feel so young this morning. I became a different man, and yet always I must have been that man inside. I no longer want to be moral in the old sense. I no longer want to be steady, respectable, and smugly sober. And—and I no longer want to be so God damn lonely and uninspired. But I don't want to be gunned at by you, because in spite of your low character and all your bad ways, you seem to mean something, and I just won't have it. There was a woman once. That I know. I can feel it. Where the hell is she now? No more of that sort of thing for me. I'd much rather get tight with loose women and stay tight."

He broke off abruptly and turned his pale, lean face to the girl. He grinned at her crookedly. "That's the sort of chap I am, and you've helped to do it—you and my excellent partners."

Satin's eyes, as she studied the man's face, were unusually bright. And behind the brightness lay other things which Hector Owen had not the penetration to see. There were a certain tenderness and an understanding. There were emotions that surprised the girl herself, but she only smiled half mockingly when she spoke.

"Nonsense," she said, taking him in her arms. "What you need is a nice low-living, hard-drinking girl like myself, and I'm going to see that you get her."

Mr. Owen did.

# CHAPTER XVI

## Calm in a Chapel

"I NEVER KNEW I WAS LIKE THAT," MR. OWEN observed some minutes later.

"Neither did I," said Satin lazily. "Like what?"

She was sitting with her back against the wall. Between her lips was a cigarette she had borrowed from her companion. Mr. Owen was arranged in a similar posture, and he, too, was smoking.

"Why, so unremorsefully depraved," he explained. "So ready to accept all the good bad things the moment has to offer."

"I know," she said. "The other things have been forced on you too long. It isn't human to plod in harness, nor is it good for a man's soul to stand too much frustration. God doesn't like it."

"Then you do believe in God?"

"In my God, not in the usual one."

"What sort of God is yours?"

"A smiling God who can even laugh to take the edge off His sorrow. All His good intentions went by the board. He knows what failure is. Should have stuck to animals and left man uncreated. Too late now. He doesn't know what to do about it any more than we do."

"He sounds quite human," observed Mr. Owen.

"How could He be otherwise? He's supposed to deal with humanity."

"I know, but we are given the impression that God is something aloof, remote, forever veiled from the eyes of man."

"Sure. Women suffer even today from the same false rumor. Naturally, it isn't true. If you treat a woman right nine times out of ten she'll skip down from her jolly old pedestal and treat you right. The only reason a woman ever gets up on a pedestal at all is to be seen to better advantage." Satin paused and smiled across at her companion. "Like it here?" she asked.

"It's a swell place," he admitted, "but we can't just park here forever. I'm getting a little nervous about the time and the store and the state of being of my excellent partners."

"Don't worry," she told him. "Things will begin to happen soon."

They did. Hardly had Satin spoken than a sleek head appeared over the rim of the settee.

"Good-morning," said the beard.

"Thank God you haven't a beard," replied Mr. Owen.

"I beg your pardon."

"It doesn't matter. I beg yours."

"Thought at first there was a bit of a fire back here," said the head. "And that reminds me of something. The manager says I'll have to ask you to come out now."

"You'll have to do more than ask," Satin replied sweetly. "You'll have to blast us out or rig up some sort of a derrick."

"It is a problem," admitted the head.

"What's a problem?" boomed a familiar voice.

The next moment the heads of the three partners ranged themselves beside that of the sleek gentleman.

"I have been told you're enjoying the cholera," said Mr. Larkin. "Would you mind flicking us a shot? It might put us out of our misery."

"Is there such a thing as time?" asked Mr. Owen.

"It isn't late," replied the senior partner. "Not at all late for a late morning. And besides, we can always make up for a lot of lost time."

"Are you ready to emerge?" Major Barney inquired.

"Because, if you aren't," put in Mr. Dinner, "we can have some food lowered down to you in buckets."

"We emerge," declared Satin, getting up and stretching her disconcerting young body, "if we can."

"Oh, that can be speedily arranged," said Mr. Larkin. "In fact, I think it best you do come out, or up, or under, or whatever it is. The way business is at present we can't possibly spare the head of the Pornographic Department and one of our most valued partners. Come along, Major."

The heads disappeared. Mr. Larkin's voice was heard issuing commands.

"You take one end, Major," he was saying, "and this gentleman and myself will take the other. Dinner is worse than useless. Only he mustn't expect a ride. Get off the sofa, Dinner. It's heavy enough as it is, God knows. All together now. Heave!"

The edges of the settee parted company with the walls. Miss Honor Knightly stepped gracefully if a little untidily through one aperture while Mr. Owen made his exit through the other. Both joined the partners in front of the settee and received their morning salutations.

"Where's Madame Gloria?" demanded Satin.

"Still sleeping, my dear, still sleeping," said the senior partner. "Such a woman for sleep. She plays hard and rests hard, poor soul. What's a stronger word than veer? I'd like to apply it to my head."

"Swirl," suggested Satin, "twirl, or spin."

"Splendid!" cried Mr. Larkin. "It's doing all three."

"Once more on the road," said Major Barney. "Time is tearing along. These people must wash and we all must eat. Then to the store. It can't get along without us."

"Exactly," agreed Mr. Larkin. "I always like to be present whenever the place is robbed. Things seem to go better then. There's less excitement and scurrying about."

"I hope we're not robbed today," said Mr. Dinner in a bleak voice. "My nerves are jumpy enough as they are, without the added stimulant of thieves."

"Spoken for us all," declared Mr. Larkin. "Let us fly. This gentleman will push the settee back. He's new on the managerial staff. It will be good experience. Good-morning, sir. Forward."

With a slightly dazed expression in his eyes the sleek-headed young gentleman, so beautifully attired, gazed after the departing partners, gallantly ushering that stunning creature down the quiet reaches of the balcony lounge.

Half an hour later the partners and Satin, now spick and span, arrived at the store through the cool fragrance of a glorious morning. At the private entrance to Mr. Larkin's office they paused and turned to look at it—the morning. In the eyes of each was a touch of wistfulness and rebellion.

"What a day!" sighed the senior partner.

"What a night!" said Mr. Owen.

"It's too bad to know how to play," remarked Satin.

"It would be worse to know how to work," observed Mr. Dinner. "I mean, only how to work."

"Don't worry, my children," consoled Mr. Larkin. "A plan is forming. Don't ask me now. It is not quite ready. In the meantime, to your places, but don't overdo it. Don't strain yourselves. We are not in the best condition. And remember, there is always lunch. A cheerful thought."

The Book Department itself was not an uncheerful place in which to spend a hangover, and the Pornographic Section was almost deserted, except for a clean little man in clerical garb who was approaching the counter. There was something about his clean neatness and his mild yet eager expression that made Mr. Owen wish he had lived a better life. Satin gazed on the little preacher with her usual cynical tolerance.

"I'm going to the Holy Land," the preacher informed her happily, "and——"

"My dear sir," cut in Satin, "you were never farther away from that region than you are at this minute."

"Perhaps a book with maps might bring me a little nearer," suggested the little fellow with a disarming smile.

"Do you see that volume upon which your hand is resting?" said Satin. "Well, that's called *Strumpets at Dawn*."

"How beautiful!" cried the small, clean preacher. "It fascinates me."

"What!" exclaimed Mr. Owen involuntarily, and glanced at Satin.

Even that imperturbable young lady appeared to be momentarily stunned.

"But the Holy Land first," the preacher continued agreeably. "Have you such a book?"

"You will find no end of them," replied the girl, "about three aisles farther down—in the Travel Section, sir."

"How nice of you," said the little chap, the eager light in his eyes increasing at the mention of travel. "I think I'll take this one, too, before I go."

"No!" broke from Mr. Owen's lips as Satin selected the book and calmly wrapped it up. "You can't do such a thing."

"Nonsense," retorted Satin. "It will do him a world of good."

The little preacher accepted the package and turned away.

*"Trumpets at Dawn,"* they heard him murmur. "How beautiful! How deeply religious!"

Satin and Mr. Owen inspected each other.

"You shouldn't have done that," said the man.

"Why not give the little chap a break for once in his life?" replied Satin. "After he's finished that book, he'll need to go to the Holy Land. Now, there's no particular reason."

"After he's read that book," said Mr. Owen, "he may never go to the Holy Land but spend his savings in riotous living."

"There's no such thing as riotous living," Satin retorted. "It's merely a frame of mind. He was a nice little preacher."

"I hope he stays nice," Mr. Owen remarked skeptically. "I wouldn't read that book myself."

"If you did," she told him, "you would find more beauty and tenderness in it than in a six-foot bookshelf of inspirational works. That's the truth. Come along now. I want to show you a place."

By way of a spacious lift she took Mr. Owen to the top floor of the building. They stepped out into the subdued, mellow atmosphere of the Music Department.

"It's tranquil here, isn't it?" said Satin, a new note in her rather husky voice.

"After life's fitful fever," murmured Mr. Owen.

Silently gleaming beneath artfully shaded lamps the pianos stood about on the heavy carpet. Between them lay shadowed spaces so that each instrument was isolated in its own pool of radiance. Looking at them Mr. Owen thought of lovely rooms in quiet homes.

"It's awful to think," observed Satin, cutting into his thoughts, "that many of these pianos are doomed to the grubby hands of rebellious little boys and girls. Instruments of torture instead of beauty."

"You would have to say something like that," Mr. Owen told her. "Always throwing flies."

She smiled at him almost sympathetically.

"I must toughen you spiritually," she said, "as well as physically. Come along with me."

Noiselessly they made their way between the pianos until they came to a small stout door that looked as if it should have been set into the ivy-clad wall of a church. Satin opened the door and, passing through, they entered a chamber of utter quietness and peace. It was a long apartment with a high, raftered roof rather than a ceiling. The entire end of the room was occupied by an organ. The windows on either side were of richly stained glass. But for the absence of pews Mr. Owen would have thought himself in a church. The windows were partly open. There was a feeling of wings in the sky. Somewhere outside a band of small birds was chirping. The little chirps sounded speculative and decently modulated in this quiet place. The hum and drone of the city far below only added to Mr. Owen's feeling of remoteness. Here they were entirely detached from life. It was as if this room might rise at any moment and float away through the blue.

Satin was moving slowly towards the organ. She turned back and smiled at the man behind her. He decided there was a quality exceedingly lovely in that smile.

"Bring your hangover down here," she said, "and rest it comfortably by the organ. Whenever my breast becomes too savage I come to this place and play to it."

In a deep chair near the organ Mr. Owen sat down and rested his head. It no longer seemed so hot and tired. Within him there was a sense of peace. Gradually little liquid notes began to splatter round him like refreshing drops of rain. Satin played. Time swept by unheeded on a tide of low, throbbing harmony. Thoughts strayed idly through Mr. Owen's mind. They were vague, these thoughts, for he was unable to place himself. More like sensations they were—remembrance of things too remote to name. Far-away days and far-away feeling. Time when it was young, before it had grown a fretting beard. As the velocity of the notes increased from a shower to a flood of melody, Mr. Owen changed the position of his head the better to observe the figure at the organ.

"She might be a priestess," he reflected, a little thrilled, "instead of a hard-boiled purveyor of indecent literature."

There was an expression on Satin's face he had never seen there before. Emotions seemed to be straining within her, crying to be released. As he looked at the girl he felt that one barrier had been removed only to be replaced by another. To him she was still as enigmatic and as baffling as before. There was beauty here unquestionably, but now it was beauty in pain, in conflict with itself. Through the medium of the organ her fingers were searching for something, for a completeness, it seemed, beyond life, beyond her days as she lived them. Suddenly she stopped. The sobbing notes fled through the stained-glass windows, but little wraiths of harmony still lingered in the hushed air of the room. She swung round on the bench and sat for a moment contemplating Mr. Owen. Her eyes were large and dark and touched with the spell of her playing. But her lips were disturbingly mocking.

"Suppose," she said quite distinctly, "I should tell you I loved you. Would that do any good?"

"It would be better than a quart of aspirins," he replied.

"Would it? Then consider it said."

"Why?" asked Mr. Owen.

"Because I do," said Satin.

"Still why?"

"Don't ask me that. There is no special reason."

"I can think of none myself," Mr. Owen replied. "No good and sufficient ones. You can't play away the years, you know. I own to a number of them."

"Let me worry about your years," the girl told him. "They're none of your business so far as I'm concerned." She hesitated, and for the first time Mr. Owen detected a suggestion of timidity in her bearing. "Think I'm a pretty hard girl, don't you?" she advanced. "All sexed up and everything—an easy make?"

"Not all of that," said Mr. Owen, "but I wouldn't go so far as to call you sexless."

"You'd better not," the girl replied. "I'd consider that an insult. What's all this noise about sex, anyway? Why make it a vice and keep it in the dark? It's an amiable gesture, after all. Why not make nerves a vice, or egotistical talking, or patriotic speeches, or spying on one's neighbors, or interfering with one's personal liberty, attempting to supervise a person's conduct, or any number of things beside which sex is a mere flash in the pan. As a matter of fact, sex is swell. I thoroughly enjoy it."

"That makes us even," admitted Mr. Owen, "but my greater wisdom tells me it can be misused. I mean, a man so often slips round the corner on his woman or vice versa. You know, not playing the game, and getting emotions all mucked up."

"That's just rotten," said the girl slowly. "And it's

worse because it's so unnecessary. People who cheat like that want two things at once. They lack in guts."

"Forcefully if not nicely put," observed Mr. Owen.

"Come over here," said the girl.

He sat on a stool at her feet. She leaned over him and taking his head in her arms, held it against her breast. The moments passed and neither of them spoke. A still room. Only the notes of birds.

"Well, Mr. Man," she said at last, "I'm not so sexy as you think. I've had only a few moments—never a real lover."

"That, also, is none of my business," replied Mr. Owen. "I suspect your good judgment far more than your morals."

"Why?"

"For various reasons. I'm one of them."

She pushed his head up from her and looked into his eyes.

"How long have you been lonely?" she asked irrelevantly.

"How do you know I have?"

"The look's there. I found a lost dog once."

"Thanks," said Mr. Owen. "Aren't we all?"

She was holding his head now rather carelessly in her lap, much as if she were holding a cantaloupe or a grapefruit. Above his head she was gazing dreamily through one of the windows at a small white cloud drifting past.

"Perhaps," she admitted. "Yes. I've been, but I'm not going to be any more. I have you now."

"Right," said Mr. Owen. "But what about the head? Have you finished using it? I'm afraid it will roll off."

"No," she replied with determination. "I want the head. I feel like hugging it."

"All right, but just don't forget it. After all, it's a head."

Once more he felt his face pressed against the firm young breast of the girl. He cleverly contrived to breathe without thwarting her purpose. He liked it that way. He had a feeling of having come home at last. Peace entered into his so long troubled soul, or whatever it was that served for one.

"I can't remember," he told her. "And I don't want to."

"Good," she said. "Do you love me?"

The head nodded vigorously.

"I guess that will have to do," remarked the girl. "Then we're sweethearts, you and I?"

This time the head nodded rather bashfully.

"Yes," he said. "I guess that's what we are."

"How nice," mused Satin. "Never had a sweetheart proper. Not a regular one. Are you glad?"

Then it was that Mr. Owen abandoned his passive rôle and took the girl in his arms with surprising zest and vigor.

"You must be glad," she managed to get out at last. "Thanks. That was very nice. We just find a little place and begin to live very busily together. I have no ties."

"My bridges are down," replied Mr. Owen with a shrug. "Thank God they led to you. Don't let me ever remember—only you, Satin."

"That's the decentest thing you've said. I guess that's why you found me, or rather, why I found you."

They were standing now, facing one of the windows. Below them throbbed the city and around them swam the sky. It was one of those moments. Both seemed to feel it. Mr. Owen did not know what it was, but it was there—all that his heart could carry.

"Of course," he heard the girl saying, "you'll have to be careful about beds—whose you get in. But I won't be strict. Running around with those partners, God knows what might not happen."

As if the mere mention of them was sufficient to call them into being, the little door opened, and the three gentlemen came swinging down the room. Mr. Owen grinned. They looked for all the world like God-fearing, sober-sided vestrymen. They should have held plates in their hands.

"At last!" exclaimed Mr. Larkin. "At last! Although, I must say, this is a far cry to the Pornographic Department. Can you imagine what I've done?"

"I don't like to think about it," said Mr. Owen.

"Well, you will," proudly retorted the senior partner. "I've declared a holiday."

"Go on," said Satin. "For everybody?"

Mr. Larkin nodded.

"Even for Horrid and Blue Mould," he assured her.

"Sweet man," said Satin.

## CHAPTER XVII

## *Lascivious Dancing*

"AM I NOT?" REPLIED MR. LARKIN. "ALL THE GIRLS are saying that today, at any rate. What a time we had getting our customers out of the store."

"Never saw the place so full," observed Mr. Dinner.

"One large lady came charging back at me three times," declared Major Barney, "before I successfully repulsed her. Said she wanted to buy a bird cage."

"The poor thing," remarked Mr. Larkin sadly. "And the bird. I suffer for the bird, too. But still, all work and no play would simply be too bad. Besides, people buy too many things, anyway. Everybody wants to own something. Would you believe it? Frequently I haven't a shirt to my back, and we have a counter devoted entirely to shirts—lovely ones. I rebel. I refuse to participate. I feel like giving my possessions away and running naked through the streets. Of course, I should wear shoes. Light ones."

"Are we to spend our holiday mentally watching you run naked through the streets?" Mr. Dinner inquired.

"Naked save for shoes," corrected the senior partner. "I have the most amazingly sensitive feet. They fairly shriek at the approach of a pebble."

"I must confess," observed the Major, "that your thoughts are veering today as they have never veered before."

"But people do grab and snatch," Mr. Larkin protested. "You'll have to admit that. They do grab and snatch. Makes me so ashamed, I'm frequently reluctant to approach one of my own counters on some slight personal mission. Therefore, my back sometimes finds itself without a shirt." He turned to Mr. Owen as if in search of an understanding heart. "You see how it is," he resumed. "Our partners are too degenerate to care about backs and shirts. Drawers are a joke to them, if they ever think of them at all."

"I thoroughly understand," said Mr. Owen, "and sympathize deeply. Do you like to drink?"

The senior partner's face brightened visibly. He clasped his hands.

"Immensely!" he exclaimed. "Copiously! How did you ever know? Why, you removed the very words from my mouth. I was going to suggest that we all go out and get ourselves rotten drunk, if you'll pardon the expression."

"God, yes!" cried the Major. "It's the only intelligent thing you have said."

"And then we'll dance lasciviously with lewd women," continued Mr. Larkin. "Oh, life, life, life and a whole lot of lust."

"He's outdoing himself today," said Mr. Dinner in a low voice. "These poetic raptures of his will get us all into trouble."

"Where shall we go?" asked Mr. Dinner.

"I suggest the Woods," said the senior partner. "There'll be a large, open taxi, and we'll all get in it."

"What's the Woods?" Mr. Owen wanted to know.

"Oh, a jolly place," replied Mr. Larkin. "There are woods, you know."

"I know," said Mr. Owen. "Just woods?"

"Heavens, no!" exclaimed Mr. Larkin. "What would we do with a lot of woods? There are other things— acrobats, for example. I know a couple of artists. They contort. We'll have them to lunch with us."

"I know the man who handles the bears," announced the Major. "A sterling character."

"It would be safer if he were of iron," observed the senior partner, "or brass, if he associates with those bears. They're a hard lot. I know them."

"May I suggest," put in Mr. Owen, "that we begin actively to enjoy these rare delights instead of merely discussing them?"

"You may and you shall," Mr. Larkin declared. "Let us hurl ourselves into a lift and then debauch into the boulevards. Holidays come to us too rarely. We must take advantage of everything and everybody. Hats and sticks are in my office."

As they left the little chapel, as Mr. Owen had come to regard it, he glanced back almost regretfully. It had been a pleasant retreat. He still saw in fancy Satin seated at the organ, playing away his hangover.

"It was quiet here, wasn't it?" he said to her in a low voice.

"Yes," she answered, "and eventful, but now the battle is on. These men are entirely mad, and we are not much better."

"It isn't such a thin way to be," observed Mr. Owen philosophically. "There's plenty of room in my system for a lot of madness."

Satin made no reply but pressed his thin hand as the door closed behind them. A few minutes later they were debauching into the street.

"On such a morning as this," declared Mr. Larkin, "an employer would be a criminal not to declare a holiday."

"Especially when he wanted one himself," remarked Satin.

"Exactly, my dear, exactly," said Mr. Larkin. "The Major might know a sterling bear tamer, but he overlooks the fact that my heart is entirely of gold. I love to share my pleasures. Ah, yes, indeed, to share and let share. Taxi! I hope he stops. That's just the kind."

He did stop, and the party with much dignity and seemliness distributed its members upon the seats of the open taxicab. Soon they were speeding along the handsome boulevard in the direction of the Woods. Suddenly Mr. Larkin spied a café and became highly excited.

"We must stop there for a rest," he proclaimed. "It's simply filthy with lewd women—the lewdest and lowest in town. Also the most beautiful. Stop at the Wild House, taxi. We will break our journey there."

The Wild House was doing good business for so early in the day. Already the tables were well filled, and the floor was sprinkled with dancers. Mr. Owen regarded the couples a little nervously in an effort to ascertain how lasciviously they were dancing. He did not know the first thing about it and was not at all sure whether he wanted to learn.

"Captain," Mr. Larkin commanded, "we want something just a trifle better than the best table in the house."

"Certainly, Mr. Larkin," replied the captain. "Be seated right here at this one. It's a new table."

"How nice!" exclaimed the senior partner as the party arranged itself round the table. "I am greatly pleased. New tables affect me that way. Now, captain, we intend to get very drunk and perhaps disorderly. You know, the strain. It has been great. It has been terrific. One must relax with a crash. Bring us lewd women. We wish to dance lasciviously while we're still on our feet."

The captain understood perfectly. He was almost sympathetic about it. He glided away, as captains do. Presently the party was reinforced by four girls. Mr. Owen could not remember ever having seen such evil-looking faces. At the same time he had to admit that these women were not without an element of fascination.

"Don't mind me," Satin whispered to him. "You have to go through with it now. Dance with one of these molls when the time comes. I'll stay here and pick up the pieces."

"All this is very upsetting," Mr. Owen complained. "I can hardly dance decently, much less the other way—lasciviously, as he keeps calling it in a very nasty manner."

The drinks came thick and fast. Everyone began to feel better. The dark eyes of the senior partner were gleaming with infantile happiness. He rose abruptly from his chair. The orchestra had burst into a frenzy of syncopation.

"Now, ladies," he said, "you must take us out there

on that floor and make us dance lasciviously whether we want to or not. We are on a bit of a holiday, you know. The strain has been great. We must relax all over the floor."

Before Mr. Owen knew what was happening, he felt himself seized, dragged from his chair, and whirled out upon the slippery dance floor.

"Darling!" breathed his woman, and, swirling suddenly, bent forward seductively and dealt him a terrific blow with the most prominent part of her body. Mr. Owen was entirely unprepared for this particular manifestation of lasciviousness. He was literally shot through space and would have fallen had he not slid into the senior partner, who seemed to be performing the same maneuver. In mutual protection they clasped each other round the neck.

"We seem to be alone," remarked the senior partner. "God! My woman's lascivious. She's nearly killed me already."

"What do they wear in their pants?" gasped Mr. Owen. "Horseshoes?"

"No, my boy, it's training. They're in perfect condition, these girls."

"Must we go back?" asked Mr. Owen. "I feel shattered."

"We can't very well stand here embracing one another," said Mr. Larkin.

With a wrench they were torn apart. Mr. Owen found himself once more in the arms of his lewd woman.

"Slow down," he pleaded.

"Not with you in my arms," she panted.

"Well, why the hell don't you keep me there," he managed to get out as they spun, "instead of buffeting me about?"

"This is the double rumba," the woman told him, and thrust a powerful leg between his.

Once more they parted company. Mr. Owen's legs were as tangled as human legs can well get. For a brief moment he gave the appearance of a man giving a solo performance; then as nature sought to readjust itself, he involuntarily spun about and dived on top of Mr.

Dinner, who, very white in the face, was sliding on his back stiffly across the floor.

"Sorry," said Mr. Owen. "Couldn't help it."

"How's your woman?" asked Mr. Dinner exhaustedly.

"I don't know how lascivious she is," Mr. Owen replied, "but I do know she's as tricky as hell."

"Mine pulled a fast one on me with her stomach," explained Dinner. "I fairly bounced off like a rubber ball."

"Shall we get up?" suggested Mr. Owen. "Or relax all over the floor?"

"I suppose we better had," sighed Mr. Dinner, "though we're a great deal safer here."

The two gentlemen arose painfully only to find their partners cutting various capers round them while snapping their fingers in the air. Mr. Owen regarded his woman broodingly. His manhood was stirred, but hardly lasciviously. Awaiting his opportunity, he made a sudden wicked lunge. He caught the woman about her revolving stomach and carried her halfway across the room. There, encountering an entangling foot, she went over backward with Mr. Owen on top.

"That's the half Nelson," he grated, glaring down in her face.

"Not here," said the woman, game to the last.

"Do you think I did that for pleasure?" he indignantly demanded.

"*Chéri,*" she whispered.

"*Chéri,* hell!" exclaimed Mr. Owen. "I'm sick of this double rumble and the whole brutal business."

He climbed to his feet and helped the woman to hers. With a crash the music fell silent. They made their way back to the table.

"Waiter!" cried Mr. Larkin, "bring me two collar buttons and one safety pin. What a dance! What a dance! So stirring. I fear I'll never stop drinking."

Satin was busy getting Mr. Owen back into some sort of condition. He was still eyeing his lewd partner with a dangerously hostile light in his usually mild blue eyes. It looked as if at any moment he might hurl himself upon her and pitch her across the floor. He felt very much like doing it if only to ease his injured dignity.

"Want a rub-down?" suggested Satin.

"General overhauling," he muttered. "Lay me up in drydock like a battered old hulk. That little affair was worse than a bullfight."

"Do you gentlemen wish to take further advantage of this splendid opportunity to dance lasciviously?" Mr. Larkin inquired.

Mr. Dinner laughed a shade hysterically.

"How beautifully you put it," he said. "The answer is, no. I don't intend to let any more lascivious dancing take advantage of me."

"How about you, Major?"

"I managed to keep my feet," that gentleman explained, "but I think I'm internally injured. I'm quite willing to declare the battle a draw."

"Not today, thank you so much," said Mr. Owen politely. "I didn't manage to keep my feet, and I know I'm internally injured."

"Then the lewd women may withdraw," announced the senior partner. "I'm sure you did your best, and we're all very grateful. The captain will give you your fee."

As the girls filed away, Mr. Larkin looked fondly after them.

"Such nice, willing girls," he murmured, "and so very, very lewd."

"Hell hath no fury like the double rumble," quoth Mr. Owen.

"Rumba, dear," said Satin.

Beneath the table Mr. Larkin's hands were doing things with the safety pin. On his face was an expression of profound concentration mixed with a shade of alarm.

"There!" he exclaimed at length in accents of relief. "They're fixed. Shall we skip along to the next stop?"

The party rose and departed. Soon it was speeding merrily along in the direction of the Woods. Arrived at that gracious park they rushed to the nearest café, where they drank like men but recently rescued from the desert.

"A thirsty dance, the rumba," breathed the senior partner, gulping down a champagne cocktail.

"Especially when it's double," put in Mr. Owen.

"Let's all go swimming," suggested Satin.

For a moment the partners paused and seemed to consider. Fresh cocktails arrived and were hastily dispatched. After this there was no more hesitation. They were enthusiastic about going swimming. Nothing could restrain them.

A short walk brought them to the pool. It gleamed beneath the sunlight, blue water caught in marble. To-day the large pool contained a frolicsome rout of bathers. Mr. Owen looked at the women, and his heart went out to them. Never had he seen such lovely figures so satisfyingly unadorned. What little covering they wore literally hung on a thread. Many of them seemed to have clad themselves on a shoe string. At the sight of so much beauty the partners, like old war horses, threw back their shoulders and put their best foot forward. Satin remained undisturbed. She knew she had little to fear where figures were concerned. God had been gracious to her. She departed to the bath houses and bought a ravishing outfit, feeling the occasion justified the expense.

Mr. Owen, who seemed to possess an instinctive knowledge of bath-house technique, found the partners no end of a bother. The first thing they succeeded in doing was to lock themselves in their bath houses. The din they raised was deafening. Attendants came running from all directions, while Mr. Owen vainly strove to appeal to the imprisoned gentlemen's reason. Apparently at that moment they did not intend to exercise any reason.

"God Almighty by the score!" exclaimed the senior partner as he emerged. "What are they trying to do to us—give us claustrophobia?"

The attendants blinked.

"Wot's that?" asked one of them.

"Don't worry," Mr. Larkin assured the man. "You'll never get it. It has to do with the mind. Hurry away like a good fellow and bring us a swarm of drinks— champagne cocktails. I must and will relax."

The next contretemps arose over the showers. The partners strongly objected to being forced to immerse themselves. Mr. Owen, who had returned to his bath house to get his cigarettes, heard their voices raised in indignant protest.

"If I got under that shower," Mr. Larkin was saying, "it would be tantamount to a public declaration that I was an unclean man. I'll not do it."

"And if I stepped under that shower," rumbled the Major, "I would feel myself demeaned. I'm too big and too old to be forced to take a bath."

"It's an outrage, that's what it is, an outrage," vociferated Mr. Dinner. "I lost ten pounds I could ill afford to spare under a shower this morning. I'm as clean as a whistle."

"Or a hound's tooth," added Mr. Larkin.

"I don't care what the lot of you say," put in the flint-hearted attendant. "You don't go in the pool unless you take a shower."

"We will and we won't," Mr. Larkin declared.

Mr. Owen decided it was high time to take a hand in the affair of the showers. He presented himself to the group. His partners were well crocked. He could see that at a glance. He himself was feeling a trifle giddy, but some sixth sense still held him to the rails.

"What do you mean, you will and you won't?" demanded the attendant. "That don't make sense."

"I've forgotten," replied Mr. Larkin. "It was just a thing to say."

The situation seemed to be at an impasse, but suddenly Mr. Owen was seized by an inspiration. Without a word to his colleagues he deposited his cigarettes in a dry place, and hurrying to the nearest shower, began to splash water about with every indication of enjoyment. The partners looked at him in astonishment which gradually changed to simple-minded interest. They grouped themselves before him.

"Why are you doing that thing?" Mr. Larkin wanted to know.

"For no particular reason," Mr. Owen replied in a careless voice. "I always do it before entering a pool. It takes the edge off of the first plunge."

For a moment the three gentlemen eyed one another speculatively, then as if moved by a common impulse they dashed to the showers under which they furiously sprayed themselves.

"We always do it too," shouted Major Barney, "but we don't like to be told."

"Oh, dear me, yes," called Mr. Larkin. "Nothing like a shower before taking a swim. I'd simply be lost without one."

"Tact is what they need, these attendants," proclaimed Mr. Dinner. "Tact and a deeper understanding of the human soul."

Eventually Mr. Owen succeeded in herding them to the deep end of the pool, where Satin, looking shockingly shapely, was waiting.

"My word!" exclaimed the senior partner. "Just to look at you makes me believe in God. You never simply evolved. Oh, no. You were most carefully planned."

"Did they make you take a shower?" asked Mr. Dinner.

"No," replied Satin. "I always take a shower."

"Isn't that splendid!" cried Mr. Larkin. "So do we, my dear girl, so do we. In fact, we're seldom without one."

Without a word of warning the Major threw himself away. For a moment he was seen scrambling hugely through the air, then the pool received his great body and concealed it. Mr. Owen watched with interest. The Major should be a powerful swimmer, but why was he not swimming? Why did he not come up? Presently his head did emerge. There was a frantic thrashing about. His face wore a surprised expression.

"I forgot——" he gurgled, but the water once more claimed him.

"Now, what could he have forgotten?" queried Mr. Larkin.

"Perhaps he forgot he couldn't swim," Mr. Dinner suggested.

"Can't he swim?" Mr. Owen demanded.

"Not a stroke," replied Mr. Dinner.

"Then what did he jump in for?" Mr. Owen asked incredulously.

"Well, you see," explained the senior partner, "just because he couldn't swim the last time doesn't mean that he couldn't swim this time. People change, you know."

"Then the man is actually drowning," said Mr. Owen.

"That's it exactly," Mr. Larkin assured him. "You've sized up the situation nicely. The poor dear Major is drowning all by himself."

Looking disgustedly at his associates, Mr. Owen, without a word, dived into the pool. As he did so the Major's head reappeared and he finished his sentence in a great watery gasp.

"—I couldn't swim," he got out, and then he went down again.

Realizing the hopelessness of attempting to drag the Major ashore, Mr. Owen resorted to desperate measures. He took the drifting body on his shoulders and thrust himself upward and forward. Twice he emerged for air and left the Major to his own devices. Finally, after a series of plunges and pushes, he succeeded in bringing his cargo to shallow water, where he abandoned it. The Major clung to the side of the pool and made horrid noises. Mr. Owen did likewise, only his noises were not as bad as the Major's. Finally, the big man quieted down.

"Thanks for the lift," he said. "It's so difficult to find out whether one knows how to swim or not."

Mr. Owen had no decent answer to this. He pulled himself from the pool and rejoined Satin and Mr. Larkin. In the midst of their congratulations he remarked the absence of Mr. Dinner.

"Where's Dinner?" he demanded.

"Dinner?" inquired Mr. Larkin as if hearing the name for the first time. "Ah, yes, Dinner. Why, the little fellow must have stepped off into the pool somewhere."

"Does he know how to swim?"

"Even less than the poor dear Major," said the senior partner, "but you know how he is—hopeful, always hopeful."

"Has he been gone long?" asked Mr. Owen.

The senior partner considered this.

"Not quite long enough," he said at last. "He should have a few moments left."

"What do you mean?" cried Mr. Owen.

"Before he is dead, you know," was Mr. Larkin's bland reply.

"My God," muttered Mr. Owen, desperately scanning the pool, "what utter irresponsibility!"

Suddenly he saw a foot thrust up through the water—a small, thin foot that was wiggling appealingly. As winded as he was, he dived back into the pool and made for the foot. Dinner climbed all over him. He was an exceedingly active small man. He appeared to be bent on drowning his would-be rescuer. Mr. Owen saw little hope as he fought with the man in the water. Just as he was about to pass out himself he succeeded in stunning Dinner and dragging him to the side of the pool. Mr. Larkin was bending over in an effort to be helpful. To his own surprise and horror he fell in with a protesting splash. Cursing as bitterly as his strength would permit, Mr. Owen passed the limp body of Mr. Dinner up to the strong arms of Satin and turned wearily to look for Mr. Larkin. That gentleman was just emerging.

"I'm an awful ass in the water," he cried. "You'll have to do——"

Down went Mr. Larkin, for once unable to have his say.

Under ordinary circumstances the rescue of the senior partner would have presented little difficulty. In his present condition of exhaustion Mr. Owen was taxed up to and beyond his capacity. Nevertheless, he went for Mr. Larkin and seized him by his hair.

The space separating them from the side of the pool was not great, but to the spent Owen it seemed leagues long. At last, with the assistance of Satin, he got his burden out of the water.

"Any more?" he croaked, grinning ironically up at the girl.

Instead of answering, she reached down and pulled him over the side of the pool. He collapsed by Mr.

Larkin, who had collapsed by Mr. Dinner. Several yards away the Major had collapsed by himself.

"Can you swim?" Mr. Owen asked Satin wearily.

The girl nodded.

"Well, will you please dive in there," he went on, "and swim about a bit? Sort of represent the firm. I'm *hors de combat.*"

While Satin sported in the water the partners lay crumpled grotesquely round the edge of the pool. "A hell of a way to go swimming," Mr. Owen kept saying to himself. He was bitter about it. Presently the senior partner weakly raised his head.

"The only way," he said, "to rid ourselves of the memory of this horrid debacle is to have an excellent luncheon. At least we know how to eat."

"And drink," added Dinner faintly.

CHAPTER XVIII

## The Partners Purchase a Whale

THE PARTY HAD NOW BEEN AUGMENTED BY THE presence of two contortionists and one snake charmer. The contortionists were man and wife. The snake charmer was just man and snake, but that was enough. By his side was an old potato sack which Mr. Owen regarded with the deepest mistrust. He could not help wondering how the senior partner ever managed to meet such odd characters. Then he thought of the senior partner and ceased to wonder. The man himself was an odd character. They did not come any odder.

They were gathered round a large table in a large café. This festive establishment was situated in an amusement resort contiguous to the park. Merry-go-round music droned and shrieked through the air. The energetic voices of barkers, proclaiming the allurements of their respective attractions, could be heard. Occasionally the shattering sound of a scenic railway broke in upon them as the cars hurtled round the sharp curves. Everyone was apparently having a good time in a vigorous sort of way, but no one was having a better time than the partners themselves. Mr. Owen marveled at their recuperative powers. He was exhausted beyond measure, while they seemed as fresh as the dawn.

"See over there?" said the Major to Mr. Owen, pointing to a high wall in the distance. "Well, that's where the bears live."

"In happy amity with their trainer of sterling character," Mr. Owen replied with a grin.

The Major thought this over.

"No," he said at last. "They hate him. They even hate themselves, those bears."

Mr. Larkin got up from his chair and raised his glass.

"To our savior!" he cried, indicating Mr. Owen. "Without him we would have been full of pool water instead of champagne."

Everyone at the table save Mr. Owen arose and drank the toast. He regarded them with a caustic smile.

"I wonder," he said when they had reseated themselves, "just what is going to happen next. This is supposed to be a holiday, and yet all we do is to punish ourselves almost beyond endurance. That lascivious dancing was a dangerous riot. The pool was a downright disaster. Are we going to settle down now and have a nice quiet time?"

As he spoke he glanced about the table, then became rigid in his chair. A six-foot snake was peering deeply into his eyes. Honor Knightly gave a small shriek and put her napkin over her head. Mr. Owen, considering it a wise idea, falteringly did likewise. The snake charmer was laughing heartily and with truly disgusting oiliness.

"Kim is hungry," he gurgled. "Poor Kim."

"Tell Kim he can have my steak," replied Mr. Owen in tremulous tones, "if he'll only go away."

"But, my dear sir, Kim is quite harmless," explained its owner. "He merely wants to play."

"He isn't harmless to me," Mr. Owen assured the

man, "and I'm far from feeling playful. I've been unhappy before in my life, but never quite as unhappy as I am at this moment."

In a burst of affection Kim curled himself gently round Mr. Owen's neck. The snake charmer roared his approval. Mr. Owen sat very still in his chair.

"Listen," he said in a low voice, "I believe I'm going to die."

"What's it doing to you?" came Satin's muffled voice.

"More than flesh can bear," Mr. Owen answered, then laughed crazily. "Luncheon!" he said in a bitter voice. "A nice quiet luncheon."

Kim, disturbed by the laughter, slowly uncoiled himself and returned to his master, who dropped him carelessly back in the sack.

"Has Kim gone away yet?" asked Satin in a hushed voice.

"Entirely," Mr. Larkin assured her. "To the last inch. You may come out from under your napkin."

Pale and wan, Mr. Owen's face reappeared. He regarded the table feverishly, then gulped down a glass of wine.

"I hope that exhibition failed to amuse you," he said to his partners. "You weren't convulsed with mirth?"

"Not with mirth," put in Mr. Dinner. "Kim did me little good."

"I agree," said the senior partner. "A mere fraction of Kim goes a long, long way."

Mr. Owen returned to his plate and manfully endeavored to eat. He felt that he owed his stomach a little solid food. As he raised his fork to his mouth he chanced to glance across the table at the lady contortionist. His mouth remained open, but the fork refused to enter. In some weird manner the woman had contrived to dislocate her neck so that her head was hanging down between her side and her left arm. In this inverted position she was daintily sipping champagne while gazing unwinkingly at Mr.Owen. That gentleman was fit for the madhouse. His eyes bulged in his head. Never in all his life had he been so shockingly revolted.

He tried to speak, but no words came. At last his tongue obeyed the dictates of his tortured mind.

"Is she going to be like that," he quavered, "throughout the rest of the meal?"

"Why not?" inquired her husband.

"Can't you see that for yourself?" muttered Mr. Owen. "Do you expect me to swallow food with that head dangling there before my eyes?"

"They feel that they owe us something for their luncheon," soothingly explained Mr. Larkin.

"Her debt is paid with interest," Mr. Owen replied. "Tell her she's too kind. Tell her I'd be more than satisfied if she'd stick to cracking her knuckles or dislocating her thumbs. It takes so little to amuse me."

The contortionist spoke to his wife in a low voice. The lady angrily shook her head. This gesture of negation had a devastating effect on Mr. Owen. He closed his eyes and clung to the table.

"She says," came the voice of the contortionist, "that she intends to stay that way. She gets double the effect from the champagne with her head hanging down."

"So do I," muttered Mr. Owen. "In fact, I don't have to drink at all."

"Perhaps this will take your mind off the head," suggested the contortionist. "It's one of my favorite stunts."

"What is?" asked Mr. Owen, clinging to a straw.

He opened his eyes, then almost fell from his chair. With unhurried efficiency the contortionist was feeding himself with his feet. The daintiness with which he did this only added to Mr. Owen's feeling of horror and revulsion.

"My word!" Mr. Larkin exclaimed in a voice of awe. "That's enough to take one's mind off everything. I'm actually rotating in my chair."

"If they'll only stop what they're doing," said Mr. Owen, "I'll let that snake sit on my lap."

"Why, this is a cinch to do," the contortionist proclaimed. "I can keep it up all day."

"It must be easier to do than to look at," Mr. Owen

told him. "If you enjoy your food that way, won't you eat it at another table?—at some table far back of me."

"Nonsense," scoffed the contortionist, deftly spearing a piece of steak with a fork held in his left foot.

With fascinated eyes Mr. Owen watched the leg as it conveyed the fork to its owner's mouth. Then he looked at Mr. Larkin, who was feeling no little disturbed himself.

"Did I understand you to say," asked Mr. Owen distinctly, "that we must all relax, that the strain has been terrific, and that we needed a bit of a holiday?"

Mr. Larkin met his partner's cold eyes apologetically.

"Well, you see," he began lamely, "I'm always hoping things will turn out for the best. It's my nature."

"If this keeps up much longer," announced Mr. Dinner, "I'm going to put my plate on the floor and gnash my food like a beast."

"The trouble is," said Major Barney, "they get me all mixed up. I can no longer coördinate my movements. Only a moment ago I was deliberately trying to sip champagne with my ear."

"I was searching for my mouth," put in Satin, "and I jabbed myself an awful crack in the stomach. Bet you it left marks. Shall I look?" Here she glanced at Mr. Owen.

"Don't begin!" he admonished her. "Don't begin! We'll take those marks for granted. There are enough public exhibitions going on as it is."

At this moment Kim's malevolent head slid stealthily between Mr. Owen's frozen limbs and appeared at the table. For a long minute, during which the man was too petrified to breathe, the snake examined the contents of his plate. At length, having come to a decision, Kim selected the steak, snapped it up with a hiss of pleasure, and started to withdraw. Mr. Owen sucked in his stomach as the snake slid down the front of him. His eyes were tightly shut, and there was a prayer in his heart.

"Ah, what a pity," came the solicitous voice of the

snake charmer. "He has taken the gentleman's steak. He must put it right back."

"Oh, no, he mustn't," cried Mr. Owen with all possible haste. "Kim can have the steak. He's entirely welcome to it. In fact, I'd buy Kim a cow if he'd keep away from me."

A sudden burst of clapping startled his eyes wide open. Satin and the partners were also looking about with expressions of consternation. Mistaking the events taking place at the table for a public exhibition, the public had responded as only the public can. The party was surrounded by a wall of peering faces. Mr. Owen felt sorely tempted to hide his head once more beneath his napkin.

"Honor," he said to the girl, "will you hold a glass of wine to my lips? My hand is shaking like a shuttle."

As Mr. Owen was drinking his wine, a little boy pointed an unclean finger at him.

"Mom," shrilled the little boy, "that must be the Bloodless Man. Take a look at his face. There ain't nothing in it."

"Guess you're right," agreed Mom. "And look at the other little feller." Here Mom indicated Mr. Dinner. "He's what they call a midget," Mom explained, "and I guess the other one's a jint. They always look so stupid, them jints."

The Major looked at Mr. Dinner, and Mr. Dinner looked at the Major, then both of them looked at Mr. Owen. Across the table Mr. Larkin sat convulsed. Tears were streaming down his face.

"Oh, God," he howled, "to think I have such peculiar partners."

His voice broke on a high contralto note.

"What's wrong with that guy?" a spectator wanted to know.

"I guess he's what they call a half-and-half," somebody suggested. "A weird sort of freak, he is."

"What's a half-and-half?" Mr. Larkin quickly asked Satin, his laughter stricken mute on his lips.

"I don't know," she told him, "but it must be pretty awful. Whatever it is, you're it."

Mr. Larkin looked dismayed, and for the first time

in years, it seemed to him, Mr. Owen grinned maliciously.

"Go on, lady," a coarse voice called out. "Give us a bit of the kooch."

All four partners raised their heads at this insulting request. Without a word they rose from the table, singled out the speaker—a large, bull-faced individual—and knocked a hole through the crowd with him. Through this hole passed Satin. When the man was ready to rise she kicked him with brutal directness. The gross object doubled up in pain.

"I owed that to my sex," she explained to the partners as they walked towards the place where the bears lived, "as well as to my self-esteem." Then she added irrelevantly, "I can do the kooch."

"A highly successful luncheon," said Mr. Owen tonelessly. "Not a scrap of food passed my lips."

"The contortionists and the charmer seemed to enjoy it," remarked the senior partner, making an effort to glean comfort from something.

This unfortunate remark almost did for the Bloodless Man. Raising his clenched hands to heaven he confronted the senior partner, who stood regarding him with innocent interest. Sighing deeply, Mr. Owen let his hands fall to his sides. What was the use? He might as well strike an idiot child. The man knew no better.

"Holiday," he muttered. "A good time was had by all."

"Show him some bears," said Mr. Larkin to Major Barney. "He's all unstrung. Bears go very well when one is all unstrung."

They found the bear trainer of sterling character, and they found him exceedingly drunk. He too seemed to be unstrung. He declared himself to be bored to tears by bears.

"It's bears, bears, bears," wailed the man, "morning, noon, and night. Great shaggy beasts. Loafers. They get treated better than I do."

"May we look at some of your better class of bears?" asked the senior partner humbly.

"You may look at the whole damn lot," the trainer replied, fumbling with a locked gate. "Not out there where all those people are, but in here where you can get a better view."

With childlike confidence the partners followed the trainer and Satin through the barred gate, which locked itself behind them. The keeper, apparently losing interest, wandered off somewhere on his own affairs. The partners looked at a huge rock and beheld more bears than they had ever seen before or cared to see again. The bears in turn looked disagreeably down on Satin and the partners. Thus matters stood for a moment; then suddenly the air became charged with electricity.

"There's nothing," said Mr. Larkin vaguely. "Just nothing—nothing at all between us and all those bears."

"What!" cried Major Barney. "Has that drunken sot locked us in with his vile beasts?"

Mr. Dinner tried the gate. It stoutly refused to open.

"He has," he announced with the utmost simplicity. "They won't get much off me. What little there was left I've lost during this day of giddy pleasure."

"Dear considerate God," murmured Mr. Larkin piously. "He might as well have let us drown if we're going to be consumed by those shaggy monsters."

"It's a holiday," observed Mr. Owen. "A feast day for the bears."

"Didn't the early martyrs do something in the line of song?" Satin asked coolly. "Who can dig up a snatch of a hymn? My business is pornography."

"You can't very well tell an infuriated bear a dirty story," observed Mr. Larkin. "And as for those early martyrs, I don't know how they did it. Why, I can't even shout for that drunken trainer, much less sing a hymn."

Apparently the bears had grown weary of watching this huddled conference. Behind their mighty leader they came lumbering down from the rocks. On the outside of the enclosure women were screaming frantically above the hoarse shouts of men. Looking decidedly sloppy, the bears lurched forward.

"Aren't they untidy in their appearance?" observed Mr. Larkin.

"All except their teeth," replied Mr. Owen. "They seem to be in perfect order."

Major Barney lighted a cigarette, then tossed the match aside.

"We should all stick closer to business," he remarked. "All this gadding about doesn't get us anywhere."

"It has now," replied Mr. Larkin. "Don't be silly, my dear chap. It's got us in a terrible place, and it's going to get us into a worse one—inside those bears, you know."

Satin pressed Mr. Owen's arm as the bears came on. When she looked up at his thin, unremarkable face she did not feel afraid. She could see no sign of fear written on his features. He looked like a man who had been annoyed beyond endurance. And that was exactly how Mr. Owen felt as he stood there eyeing the bears with cynical animosity. To him they were not so much bears as fresh sources of irritation. And then an amazing thing happened—something that made the spectators gasp and the partners rub their eyes. Mr. Owen completely lost his temper, also his poise.

"I'm sick and tired of all this," he exclaimed. "You all wait here. I'll be back in half a moment."

He took a few rapid strides forward, filling the air with sizzling obscenities, and with the heavy end of his walking stick struck the horrified leader a vicious blow across his nose. The great beast uttered a gasp of dismay and sat down stupidly. His followers did likewise. They had never heard of such a thing. Were they not bears? Certainly. This madman did not seem to realize it. Blow after blow from the heavy stick descended upon the unfortunate beast. Mr. Owen's temper was far out of control.

"Heavens!" exclaimed Mr. Larkin. "My heart actually bleeds for that poor animal I disliked so greatly only a few minutes ago."

"I hope he gets his temper back," said Mr. Dinner, "after he polishes off that bear. If he doesn't, he'll disjoint us on our feet."

With squeals of pain and anguish the stricken leader turned and lumbered off in the direction of his less enterprising associates. It was at this point that Mr. Owen really outdid himself. In the bitterness of his heart he made a dive after the retreating animal and seized him by one of his hind legs. This he proceeded to bite with the utmost ferocity. It is difficult to say whether the bear was more pained than surprised. He cast one frightened glance over his shoulder, made a pitiful noise deep in his throat, then fell swooning to the rock, his paws pressed against his eyes. At this stage of the game the drunken keeper came staggering up to Mr. Owen.

"You've got to stop knocking my bear about," said the man of sterling character, smelling heavily of gin. "No more of this. Come away from that bear's leg."

Mr. Owen came away and attached himself to the trainer's ear. Picking up his discarded stick, he dragged the drunkard to the gate.

"Open it," said Mr. Owen, and the man obeyed as well as his fumbling hands would permit.

The partners, following Satin, passed through the gate with dignity and aplomb—as usual. Mr. Owen came last. The gate closed behind him. People were cheering on all sides, running from all directions. Mr. Owen, his good temper completely restored, turned to Mr. Larkin.

"Do you drink?" he asked the senior partner.

"Well, if I didn't I'd be afraid to say no to you," said Mr. Larkin, "but it just so happens I do."

"How did that bear taste?" asked Satin, slipping her arm through Mr. Owen's.

"Execrable," he told her. "Far, far from pungent."

"You should gargle with champagne," suggested the Major.

"We all should," put in the senior partner. "Facing a flock of infuriated bears is no way to spend a holiday. No way at all. I suggest we find comfortable chairs and refuse to be lured out of them. I'm veering more than that scenic railway. We'd have been dead twice over had not the lionhearted Owen been along to save our lives. Too bad about that bear, though. The old boy actually fainted. Fancy that—a bear."

The senior partner's sudden burst of loquacity expressed the depth of his relief at having escaped from the place of the bears. Mr. Owen regarded him with mild affection. Perhaps after so much sound and fury the party might settle down now in some relatively quiet spot and keep itself out of trouble. And seemingly this is exactly what the party did for some few hours, but it could not be expected to keep out of trouble forever. Late in the evening, more or less wall-eyed from overindulgence, its members found themselves ranged before nothing less than a preserved whale lying at full length on a huge six-wheeled trailer. The owner of this preserved whale was sitting by it on a box. His attitude was one of listlessness and dejection.

"Dear, dear me," observed Mr. Larkin, balancing himself on his stick. "Yards and yards of sheer fish. My eyes swirl in their sockets."

"It's a whale," muttered Mr. Dinner. "A whale in the flesh."

"Is it, now?" exclaimed Mr. Larkin; then, addressing himself to the dejected-looking owner, "That's a very nice whale you have there, my friend."

The man looked up with a spark of hope in his eyes.

"Thank you," he said politely in behalf of his whale, "but you people are the only ones who have looked at her today. Something's wrong with this town. It doesn't seem to be whale-minded. I'm actually starving here alongside of my whale."

"Can't you eat a bit of the whale?" suggested Mr. Owen. "With so much whale about, no one would ever miss a bite here and there."

"I couldn't touch Minnie," retorted the owner. "We've been together for years."

"Under the circumstances," observed Satin, "I wouldn't eat a morsel of Minnie myself."

"Minnie," murmured the fascinated senior partner. "How chic. How very, very chic. It takes a man of vast daring to call a whale Minnie."

"She's a good whale, Minnie," said the man with morbid pride.

"Do you mean, a virtuous whale?" inquired Mr. Larkin.

"She hasn't had a chance," replied the owner of the whale. "She's preserved."

"Poor, poor Minnie," contributed Miss Honor Knightly with sincere emotion.

The partners turned and seriously considered that young lady. She met their gaze with large, innocent eyes. Mr. Owen looked at his partners, then shrugged eloquently. They turned back to the whale.

"She's a sperm," the man told them.

"Huh?" said Mr. Dinner. "I thought she was a whale."

"She's a sperm whale," wearily replied the man.

"I see, I see," said the senior partner. "How exceptionally nice." He turned to his companions. "She's a sperm, is Minnie," he told them. "A sperm whale, no less."

"And to think that she once sported in the ocean round her mammy," murmured Mr. Dinner with a surprising burst of sentiment.

Mr. Larkin turned and looked deep into the eyes of his small partner.

"Mammy?" said Mr. Larkin with a rising inflection.

"Yes," answered Mr. Dinner innocently. "Mother, you know."

"Yes, I know," pursued Mr. Larkin. "But this isn't a negroid whale. From the way you talk you'd think she had been born and bred in the cotton belt. Don't get silly about her. You must have been thinking of a black fish."

"All right," said Mr. Dinner. "Don't go on about it. I was merely thinking."

"Don't," the senior partner warned him. "It might throw you off entirely. Just be yourself." He turned back to the owner. "Now, about this whale," continued Mr. Larkin. "You were saying?"

"I was saying she was a good whale," the man replied. "One of the best in the country."

"Have whales taken up living in the country?" broke in the irrepressible Mr. Dinner. "I thought they lived in the sea."

"This sort of whales don't," said the man. "This is a preserved whale."

"Odd they don't come in tins," remarked Mr. Larkin. "Or in jars. However――"

"My heart is fair breaking," interrupted the man. "I'm afraid they're going to attach Minnie. Nobody pays to look at her, and I can't meet my bills."

"It would be awful to let a whale fall into the hands of strangers," observed Mr. Larkin in a serious voice. "Nothing less than a tragedy."

"How much would you want for this whale?" asked Major Barney. "We would give her a good home. She'd be among friends—people of education and refinement."

"You don't know any such yourself," put in Mr. Dinner.

"And I suppose you do," snapped the Major.

"No, thank God," the little man replied.

The owner of Minnie pondered several minutes, then mentioned a price.

"That's a lot of money for a mere fish," said Mr. Larkin.

"That's a lot of fish," the man replied, measuring the huge body with his eye.

"Come over here to this table and sit down," suggested the Major, indicating a near-by refreshment hall. "One doesn't purchase a whale every day in the week. The occasion demands a little thoughtful drinking."

Eventually, after much give and take, the ownership of Minnie passed from the dejected man—now no longer dejected—to the partners. It was a joint enterprise. A truck was attached to the huge trailer and a sleepy driver provided. The partners and Satin swarmed somewhat unsteadily into the body of the truck. After taking an affectionate farewell of the whale's erstwhile owner, the truck and trailer moved majestically through the broad gates of the amusement park. They had hardly proceeded a block before they were stopped by an outraged policeman.

"What are you doing with that great fish all over our streets?" he demanded.

"Nothing at all, officer," Mr. Larkin called out cheerily. "Nothing at all. Merely taking Minnie home to bed. It's a late hour for whales. Proceed, driver, proceed."

The policeman was baffled. He had no precedent for the regulation of whales. The last thing the partners saw of him he was standing in the middle of the avenue, diligently scratching his head as it has been ordained that men should scratch when subjected to intolerable mental strain.

## CHAPTER XIX

## *Dawn Breaks on Minnie*

"WHAT ON EARTH ARE WE EVER GOING TO DO WITH this whale?" Mr. Larkin asked a shade nervously as the truck rolled along through the streets of the slumbering city.

"Search me," replied Mr. Dinner. "What on earth does one do with whales? I never had a whale."

"I never owned even part of a whale," put in Major Barney. "I'm too astonished to think."

"Imagine," said Mr. Larkin. "Just imagine. Here we've gone and saddled ourselves with a whale—life is difficult enough as it is, without the added complications of a whale."

"If," observed Mr. Owen thoughtfully, "if forty-eight hours ago my closest friend should have assured me I was going to own one fourth of a preserved whale, I would have laughed at him tolerantly and invented a pretext to shamble away."

"Life is so full of queer little twists," said the senior partner, gazing moodily back at the partly opened mouth of Minnie. "Our whale," he murmured. "Think of it. All that fish."

"I never owned so much of anything before," commented Mr. Owen. "Too bad it has to be whale."

"The question still remains," quoth Mr. Larkin. "What disposition are we going to make of the body and person of this female sperm whale, Minnie? We can't dedicate our lives to her."

"No," agreed Mr. Dinner. "A flock of merchant princes can't very well serve as nursemaids to a whale."

"Why not put her in dead storage?" suggested Honor Knightly.

"How?" asked the senior partner.

"Why not take Minnie to a garage," explained the girl, "and put her in dead storage."

"She belongs in dead storage," Mr. Owen contributed. "Properly speaking, the whale should be buried."

"With full honors," said Major Barney.

"Couldn't we give Minnie to someone?" asked Mr. Dinner. "Someone wanting a whale."

"Who wants a whale?" demanded Mr. Larkin. "One can't walk up to any Tom, Dick, and Harry and say, 'Drop round to my house this evening and I'll give you a preserved whale.' People would veer off. They wouldn't come. They'd try to be polite about it, but they'd invent some excuse. 'You're so generous,' they'd probably say, 'but we're not quite fixed for a preserved whale. We have no shut-off room.'"

"I hate to admit it," declared the Major, "but already I'm sick of the very sight of Minnie."

"So am I," agreed Mr. Dinner.

"Driver!" cried the senior partner. "We're sick of this sperm whale. Drive to the nearest garage."

The driver obeyed, and Mr. Larkin descended from the truck. He approached the garage, hesitated, and came back. He wanted Miss Honor Knightly to accompany him. A woman, especially a pretty woman, might succeed in obtaining a haven for the whale where a mere man would fail. They found the garage in darkness, its doors closed. Mr. Larkin applied a finger to the night bell until a man appeared who looked upon the late callers with no show of favor.

"Good-evening," began Honor Knightly winningly. "Will you take our whale into your garage?"

"No, I won't take your whale into my garage," the man snapped back in a disagreeable imitation of Satin's dulcet tones.

Mr. Larkin laughed as if he knew perfectly well the man did not mean a word he said.

"We have the whale with us," he told the man. "Perhaps if you looked her over you might take a fancy to the poor beast. Name of Minnie."

"Mean ter say," grated the man, "you want me to turn my garage into a bloomin' aquarium?"

"Not at all," replied Mr. Larkin. "This whale is quite dead. It's preserved, or embalmed, or something."

"I see," said the man nastily. "You want me to make my place a mortuary for dead fish."

Satin felt that she had listened to just about enough of this sort of thing.

"Do you want that whale or don't you?" she demanded. "Answer yes or no."

"Don't fly out at the man," interposed Mr. Larkin. "After all, it's his privilege not to want a whale."

"How do I know whether I want a whale or not?" the man asked petulantly. "It's not a thing you can decide offhand. I've never thought about whales, and it's no time of night to begin thinking about them now." The man turned on his heel and walked back to the door of the garage. "Besides," he said surprisingly, "you've been drinking. Like father like son."

He disappeared.

"Now what did he mean by that?" asked Satin. "I can't be a father."

"I can," admitted Mr. Larkin. "Most disastrously, I can. But I don't quite see where his remark fits in. The man must have been somewhat mad from the loss of sleep."

Once more they climbed into the truck and started off down the boulevard.

"Wouldn't the man take the whale?" asked the Major.

"No," replied Mr. Larkin. "The man didn't want a whale."

"Isn't there any place in our great social organization for a preserved whale?" Mr. Dinner demanded. "Surely one would think it would fit in somewhere."

"A whale out of water is a square peg," observed Mr. Owen. "It's not unlike a bull in a china shop."

At this moment an individual came staggering out of the shadows. Unsteadily he attached himself to the rear of the truck and wobbled along after it. With his free hand he made mysterious gestures over his shoulder. Obviously the man had been drinking. Mr. Larkin bent down to hear him.

"You're being followed," whispered the man, pointing over his shoulder. "Pursued."

"What?" demanded the senior partner.

"You're being followed," whispered the man once more. "A great beast is stalking you on no legs at all."

"Oh," said Mr. Larkin, "I see. That isn't a beast. That's a whale."

"Worse and worse," the drunkard hurried on in a low voice. "It might be Moby Dick, and you wouldn't like that."

"Don't worry, old chap," replied Mr. Larkin, patting the man on the shoulder. "That whale's name is Minnie. You wouldn't like to take her home by any chance?"

The man looked bleakly over his shoulder into the half-open mouth of the whale.

"God, no!" he muttered. "I don't think I'll take up whales, but I've tried everything else. Forgive me if I stop off to catch a drink. The sight of that monster is driving me sober."

The man veered off and disappeared into a near-by café. The truck and trailer with its amazing burden continued their stately progress down the street. When they came abreast of Mr. Owen's hotel they were once more halted, this time by another policeman.

"What you got there?" the policeman demanded.

"Only a bit of a fish, officer," Mr. Larkin told him. "A whale, you know. It's a sperm."

"Is it stuffed?" demanded the officer.

"What bearing has that on the question?" inquired the senior partner. "As a matter of fact, it is stuffed, or preserved, or pickled. You know how whales are."

The officer's eyes were popping out of his head. He

had removed his hat and was diligently mopping his brow.

"This is the damnedest thing I ever saw," he declared at last. "You should have better sense than to go knocking about the streets with a mighty creature like that at this time of night. I've a good mind to run you in."

"Whale and all, officer?" Satin sweetly inquired.

The officer was stumped.

"No," he reflected. "The chief would never be the same. He's a nervous wreck as it is. The sight of that horrid creature would drive him mad. But, just the same, you've got to do something about that whale."

"What do you do with whales?" asked Mr. Owen, thrusting his head from the truck.

"Damned if I know," replied the officer. "I never had to do with a whale before, but if you don't get this one off the streets I'll have to run you in."

"Listen, officer," said Satin persuasively. "Can't a lady buy a bit of fish in this town? You can't eat meat all the time."

An expression of revulsion took possession of the officer's face.

"You're not going to eat that thing?" he got out in a strained voice. "God, lady, don't tell me that!"

"Why not?" replied Honor Knightly. "It's merely an overgrown bloater."

"Then, will you go away somewhere else," the policeman pleaded, "and eat it by yourself? I can't bear the thought."

"Very well," the girl replied. "An occasional chunk of whale never did anyone any harm. Drive on, driver."

The policeman gulped as the truck got under way. For half an hour or more they drove undecidedly through the streets, the whale following after. Honor and her companions had seated themselves on the floor of the truck. They were weary and discouraged. Life to them seemed to consist entirely of whale. Far away in the east the sun was beginning to do things about a new day. Five pairs of moody eyes were fixed on the flanks of Minnie. They tried to avoid the mouth as much as possible.

"I can't imagine whatever possessed us to purchase that whale," observed the senior partner. "Had it been a goldfish it would have been different. But of all things, a whale."

"I know a red-headed man who bought a circus once," contributed Mr. Dinner. "He was drunk, too."

"Don't tell us about it," said the Major. "Haven't we enough troubles of our own?"

Suddenly Mr. Larkin rose with an air of determination and called to the driver to stop. Bidding Mr. Owen to accompany him, he descended from the truck.

"What are you going to do?" asked Satin.

"I'm going up to that house," replied Mr. Larkin, pointing to a modest dwelling set back on a lawn, "and ask if they want a whale."

"Nobody wants a whale at this hour of the night, or rather, morning," declared Mr. Dinner.

"Nevertheless, I'm going to ask," replied the senior partner. "Some people will say yes to anything if you let them go back to bed."

Followed by Mr. Owen, the senior partner approached the house and rang the bell resoundingly. Presently a man appeared to them with an expression of great annoyance on his face.

"Good-evening," said Mr. Owen easily. "We thought that perhaps you might like a whale."

"It's a sperm," added Mr. Larkin.

"What would I want a whale for?" asked the man in a harsh voice.

"We don't know," came the hopeless voice of the senior partner. "What do people want whales for, anyway? They must be good for something."

"A whale is good for nothing," growled the man.

"Hen!" called a woman's voice from the darkness of the hall. "What do those men want?"

"I can't make out," replied Hen over his shoulder. "One of them seems to want to give me a whale."

"Tell them we don't want a whale," came the woman's voice meditatively. "We already have a canary."

"Madam," called Mr. Larkin. "Why not have a whale and a canary, too? They don't clash, you know."

"What do you say, Father?" said the slow voice of the hidden speaker. "Do you think we should have a whale?"

"It would make an imposing lawn decoration," put in Mr. Owen.

"Say, mister," called the woman. "Do whales eat grass?"

"She wants to know if whales eat grass," said Mr. Larkin to his partner in a low, nervous voice. "I haven't the vaguest idea what the horrible creatures eat. You tell her something, like a good fellow."

"Not this one, madam," replied Mr. Owen. "This whale has been preserved."

"I do very well with peaches," the voice of the woman informed them, "but I'd hate to try a whale. I don't think we would like a preserved whale, Father, do you?"

"I'd hate one," he replied. "I'm dead set against that whale, Mother. You've enough things to dust off already."

"Guess you're right, Hen," replied the woman. "Dusting all day long. Just tell the gentlemen we're not fixed for whales and shut the door. It's draughty in the hall."

"We're not fixed for whales," said Hen, and slammed the door in the partners' faces.

"Who is?" asked Mr. Owen bluntly, scanning the closed door.

"We're not," said Mr. Larkin. "Offhand, I can't think of anyone who is fixed for whales. That's just the trouble. Whales are so unexpected."

They returned to the truck and bade the driver to move on. In one corner Mr. Dinner, his small body curled like a dog's, was sleeping gently. The Major was nodding, his back against the side of the truck. Mr. Owen sat down, and Satin put her head on his knee. She looked up at him dreamily out of her great, deep eyes; then lashes slowly fringed them.

"I don't care where I am," she murmured, "as long as I'm with you."

After that effort she slept. Mr. Owen gazed down at the girl's face and felt himself compensated for the presence of the whale. Then he raised his eyes and gazed at the whale's face. It was remarkable, he reflected, how different faces could be. He wondered who thought them up. He glanced at Mr. Larkin. That gentleman was standing with his arms folded across his chest. About him hung the brooding dignity of Napoleon.

"If I don't get rid of that whale soon," he said, "I think I'll go mad and fling myself upon it the way you did to that bear."

"That's an idea, too," remarked Mr. Owen. "We might have to dismantle Minnie. Take her apart rib by rib."

"It would be better to blow her up," commented Mr. Larkin. "More fun."

The truck was now rolling along through the spreading dawn. They were in open country with the sea only a mile or so away. Through the fresh morning air, birds flew down to look at Minnie. Some of the more daring perched upon the whale and made up songs about her. The road was steadily winding upward. An unusually enterprising farmer, his small truck laden with vegetables, tried to pass, then thought better of it. Throwing his gears into reverse he backed through a fence with the utmost expedition. With his eyes still riveted to the great fish on the trailer, he continued on backward down the field. The last glimpse they caught of him he was crashing through a corn field in the direction of a small forest.

"Probably," observed Mr. Owen, "that man will never get up early again for the remainder of his days."

"He certainly didn't want a whale," replied the senior partner. "I can understand that, though. It must be frightfully discouraging to see so much of anything at this time of day."

A man with a hoe hailed them from the roadside.

"Hi, mister," he called, "what you got there?"

"A very nice whale," Mr. Larkin told him, a spark of hope in his voice. "Would you like it?"

"Nope," replied the man. "I don't hold with whales, but it sure is a dandy. It's a big whale, ain't it?"

"Whales are big," said Mr. Larkin wearily.

"Yes," agreed the farmer cheerfully. "Seems like they run to flesh. Well, so long. I've got some pertaters to hoe for Mrs. Mumpford. This is her farm. I only work here."

"It's amazing how much personal information one can pick up," observed the senior partner, "when one really doesn't want it."

"You know," replied Mr. Owen, "if we didn't want to give this whale away, if we had our hearts set on this whale, people would beg us for it with tears in their eyes."

"Perhaps you're right," commented Mr. Larkin, "but I'm so fed up with that whale I'd cross the street to avoid her."

Gradually they approached the sea. The road was now sloping steeply. Less than a quarter of a mile away a white beach lay gleaming beneath the slanting sun. Suddenly Mr. Larkin clutched his partner's arm.

"I have it!" he cried. "I have it! We'll launch this infernal whale back into the deep."

He shouted to the driver to stop. Everyone woke up and swarmed out of the truck. Stones were placed under the wheels of the trailer until the truck could draw out of the way. Ahead of them the road ran straight to the sea. A small wooden house was the only dwelling in sight. It stood by the roadside. There was a feeling of tenseness in the air as the partners rolled the stones away from the wheels of the trailer.

"Good-bye, Minnie," murmured Satin, and waved a crumpled handkerchief.

The trailer gathered headway and rumbled down the road. Straight to its course it held, until it came to the house. Here it swerved horrifyingly from the road and bounded forward. There was the crash of snapping timber, and Minnie's great head disappeared from view through the walls of the frail structure.

"It veered, my God, it veered!" sobbed the senior partner on Mr. Owen's chest. "Oh, what a whale! I'd like to take a stick and beat it within an inch of its life."

"What's that?" asked the voice of a sleepy woman within the wooden house.

Her husband opened his eyes, then snapped them shut with a click.

"Don't say a word," he whispered. "Perhaps it hasn't seen us."

"What hasn't?" asked the woman.

"The whale," replied the man, his head buried under his pillow.

"The whale," replied the woman. "Since when have whales taken to prowling round the countryside? Something's got to be done about all this."

"Well, don't ask me to do it," came the muffled voice of the man. "One look at that face and all ambition fades."

"Just to think of it," continued the woman. "Whales bounding about on land and visiting decent people in their beds. It's an outrage."

"It wouldn't be any less surprising," replied her husband, "if they bounded about the country and visited indecent people in their beds."

The woman opened her eyes and looked reprovingly at Minnie.

"It's a whale all right," she said at last. "A great huge whale, but the blow must have killed it. There's a glassy look in its eyes."

"That whale has nothing on me," replied her husband. "My eyes are burned out like a couple of bulbs, and it took only one good look to do it."

"To be awakened at dawn by a whale," mused the woman. "Who says that all the novelty has gone out of life?"

"You seem to take that whale with the utmost equanimity," remarked the man, nerving himself to withdraw from his place of concealment beneath the pillow. "What are we going to do with the brute? Is it going to become a member of the household? Is it going to remain in our bedroom, watching our lyings down and gettings up? I'd hate like hell to undress myself before the critical gaze of those glazed eyes."

"If we remove the whale," said the woman, "we remove one side of our little home. Our bedroom stands disclosed to the world. The general public will be able to bear witness to our habits."

"That would be almost preferable to the scrutiny of that monster of the deep," observed the man.

"We could hang a sheet over its face," suggested his wife.

"Two sheets," amplified the husband. "One on either side."

"There's another thing to be said in favor of that whale," went on the lady on the bed. "It will effectively keep from the house our old and rare relations."

"I wish we could have Uncle Alfred down here and show him to that horrible head," the man advanced suggestively. "One look, I think, would do the trick. His heart isn't strong. We'd be on easy street then."

"And it wouldn't quite be murder," added the woman. "Not quite."

"Exactly," agreed the husband. "All the old boy needs is a bit of a shove. That whale would do the trick."

"One man's whale is another man's poison," observed the woman, yawning daintily. "The wonder of it all, if not the beauty."

"I fear we won't sleep very soundly under the prow of that monster," remarked the husband. "Our dreams won't be so fragrant."

"No," replied the woman. "I must confess I hardly admire the perfume it is using."

"I dare say," her husband remarked, turning over on his side, "that one grows accustomed to almost anything in time."

From the crest of a distant hill came the chanting of several voices. It was the triumphal song of the partners, reinforced by Satin. Farmers in the field paused at their honest labors as the truck rolled along in the direction of the town.

"You must all dine at my house tonight," Mr. Larkin was saying in his great-hearted manner. "We want you to meet our wives."

"Didn't know you had wives," replied Mr. Owen. "You act less married than any men I ever knew."

"Isn't it awful?" agreed the senior partner in a voice touched with sorrow. "From one excess to another— bounding always. The truth is, we're miserable with our wives. How glad we would be to change them. You see, they don't understand us, especially when we relax."

"With a crash," added Mr. Owen.

The senior partner endeavored to look pained.

## CHAPTER XX

## *Too Many Wives in a Bed*

THAT SAME EVENING AT NINE SATIN AND HECTOR Owen had the somewhat dubious pleasure of meeting the wives of the partners. Mr. Larkin's town house stood in a side street only a few yards removed from one of the main thoroughfares of the city. It was difficult to distinguish it from the neighborhood cafés, the senior partner having conceived the quaint idea of placing tables before his front door and shielding them from the sun with parasols of startling floridity. A waiter stood in attendance. The same festive atmosphere was maintained within the house itself, the dining room having all the earmarks of a first-class barroom.

In the hall a check girl was waiting to relieve the callers of anything with which they cared to part. She gave Mr. Owen a check and an after-hours smile. He felt at home immediately.

The reception room was wildly luxurious. It gave the impression of veering like its owner. In it awaited the wives. The introductions were almost touchingly simple.

"This is Nana," said Mr. Larkin, indicating a small,

dark woman of middle years with youthfully wicked eyes.

"Shall I kiss him on the lips," asked Nana, removing a cocktail glass from hers, "or shake him by the hand?"

"Why not bite him on the ear?" suggested Mr. Larkin.

Nana looked for a moment into Satin's glittering eyes. One look was sufficient. She shook Mr. Owen's hand.

Dinner's wife was tall and rawboned in a good-looking way. Although no longer in her first blooming, she was still in full possession of her sex and wore her blonde dye recklessly. She was referred to as the Kitten, for no reasonable reason at all. The Major's source of dissatisfaction was undeniably plump. Snow-white hair fell round a pink, youthful face. There were dimples in the face. Her name was Aggie, and like Nana and the Kitten, she too, was a little drunk. The partners were surprisingly sober, a social error they made haste to rectify.

The party came to rest against the bar in the dining room. It occupied one entire wall. Behind it were two redfaced, benevolent individuals with the most meticulously brushed and parted hair Mr. Owen had ever seen.

"We've been running these poor men ragged," the Kitten explained, "all day long. They're exhausted mentally as well as physically. Can't think up any more drinks. We've tried them all."

"You know," put in Nana, trying to look naïve and failing most lamentably, "we get so lonely when our husbands are away—"

"As they always are," put in Aggie.

"—that the only thing left to do is to drink like fish," Nana concluded.

"Please don't, my dear," said the senior partner hastily. "Don't mention fish in my presence. We had such an unfortunate time with a whale only last night. Stayed up with the monster till dawn. You can't imagine how troublesome a whale can be until you've actually met one."

"Good!" exclaimed Nana. "I like that better and better. One can hardly go to bed with a whale."

"But if anyone could go to bed with a whale," quoth Aggie, "those three men would be the ones."

The partners looked distressed.

"Would it be possible to veer this conversation into more savory channels?" suggested the senior partner with a delicate lift of his eyebrows. "The mere idea of going to bed with a whale makes my reason totter. Harry, a triple Martini, if you please. Serve it in a stein."

"And what do you do at the store, my dear?" asked Nana, turning to Satin. "Are you a model?"

"I sell dirty books," said Satin, and Mr. Owen thanked his God she did not add, "lady."

"Marvelous," cried the Kitten. "Simply marvelous. And you go around with a lot of dirty men—our husbands."

"Come, come," put in Major Barney. "Take us off the pan for a while. There are worse husbands than we are knocking about this town."

"A depressing thought," said Aggie.

"Incredible," added Nana. "Say something, Mr. Owen. We've hardly heard your voice. Do you lech, too?"

"Do I what?" asked Mr. Owen, shrinking a little at the very sound of the word.

"What I meant was," explained Nana, "are you a lecherous man?"

"May heaven turn my toe nails blue," exploded the senior partner. "What a question to ask a guest! Do you lech? Hold me before I begin to careen all over the room."

"I wouldn't call him overly lecherous," answered Satin for the stunned Mr. Owen.

"Then you know, my dear. You've found out," said the Kitten in tones of delight. "I do hope he's promiscuous, at least. There are so few fresh faces. His is not unattractive."

The three wives looked closely into Mr. Owen's face, then nodded significantly at each other. Mr.

Owen drank steadily and endeavored to appear at ease. Presently he succeeded far better than he had intended.

By the time they had finished with the bar the dinner was in even a worse condition than the diners, yet no one seemed to mind, as the courses were snapped through and set aside in favor of wine.

"He bit a bear yesterday," Mr. Larkin announced, pointing at the guest of honor, "and the bear swooned."

"If he bit me," retorted Aggie, "I think I'd swoon, too—right in his arms. Will you bite me sometime, Mr. Owen?"

"Try not to be so mollish," interposed the Major.

"And he saved our three lives," put in the small Dinner from behind a large glass. "We were drowning and he saved our lives. All three of them."

The wives looked reproachfully at Mr. Owen.

"Why did you do that?" demanded Nana. "Have you no consideration for us?"

"But my dear lady," protested Mr. Owen, "I couldn't let my partners drown right before my eyes."

"We could," said the Kitten. "We could even go so far as to help them to drown."

"Pay no attention to them, my boy," Mr. Larkin called out from the end of the table. "Our wives have a sense of horror instead of humor. If you want to make a hit with them, although I can't understand why you should, just take them to the morgue for an outing. They'd love it dearly." He glanced at his watch, and uttered an exclamation. "What do we do with time?" he said. "It's eleven o'clock already."

"We tossed time over the bar in great handfuls," his wife told him, "and besides, we didn't begin operations until well after nine o'clock."

"I must get in touch with the Mayor," continued Mr. Larkin. "Something has just occurred to me. Owen, I loathe policemen. They're always under one's feet. I feel so splendidly now I'd like to assault a cop."

"It's been a dream of mine," replied Mr. Owen, "a beautiful dream unfulfilled."

"Well," said the senior partner, "it's become a mania with me. Therefore, I suggest that by way of entertainment we indulge in a little concentrated cop baiting. The Mayor is my brother-in-law. He is putty in my hands as well as in those of his bosses. I must make some arrangements with him for the protection of our various bodies and persons."

"It would do me a lot of good to bash a cop in the eye," Mr. Dinner declared as the senior partner left the room to arrange things with the Mayor.

"It would do the cop no harm," his wife replied. "You're such a little man."

"And it would do me even more good," the little man went on dispassionately, "to bash you in the eye."

"Is that so," replied Mrs. Dinner. "I'd have to sit on the floor, my midget, to give you a chance."

Mr. Dinner's bitter retort was interrupted by the slightly swaying entrance of the senior partner.

"It's all arranged," he announced. "Larry, the Mayor's secretary, is going to sit by the wire. We will be permanently connected."

"What did you tell his honor?" inquired Major Barney.

"Merely that we were going to have a bit of a lark," replied Mr. Larkin, "and we didn't want any police interference. Larry has been instructed to take care of that side of the business. All we have to do is to assault or insult an officer, then run like hell to this house. You see, we must lure them in." He paused and thought deeply for a moment, then addressed himself to his wife. "Nana," he said, "as I remember it, you have somewhere about the house a sort of a heavily stuffed leather bar we foisted off on the women of this city under the guise of a flesh-reducing device. Will you get it? While not being exactly lethal, it will make a decidedly effective weapon."

The senior partner, with all the solemnity of a chief of staff giving instructions for an approaching engagement, turned to Major Barney. "Major Britt-Britt," he began, "on our first sortie from the house you are to remain behind and close to the door. When we lure a policeman in, you whack him with the leather bar with the object in view of reducing his flesh to atoms."

Nana, who had left the room, returned with a long,

felt-packed leather bar. The Major took it and swished it through the air. Then he smiled a trifle grimly and sat down, looking infinitely pleased. It was going to be a good evening.

Then began one of the maddest and most undignified adventures in which either Mr. Owen or his partners had yet taken part. It was reprehensible in every detail, in conception as well as in execution, and yet like so many reprehensible exploits it was entirely and most satisfyingly successful. It was not that these thuggish gentlemen had any personal score to settle with the minions of the law, but merely that as private citizens they felt it only fair that they should get their innings once. And in extenuation of their conduct it must be borne in mind they were still suffering from the effects of the previous night as well as from an overdose of Minnie, the female sperm whale.

Leaving the Major at the front door, Mr. Larkin led his two partners from the house. They looked about at once for a policeman. Unfortunately for him one was standing on the corner. As Mr. Larkin approached the officer he, the senior partner, thought of the lowest and most objectionable word he could fling in the man's face. When he found this word Mr. Larkin shivered a little himself and wondered if he could get it out.

"Can you pretend to laugh?" asked Mr. Larkin of his partners in a low voice. "Irritatingly. You know—tauntingly?"

"I'll be able to make some sort of offensive noise," replied Mr. Owen, "although I still find myself a trifle awed by the majesty of the law."

"You must both wait until I've done my stuff," continued the senior partner, "then, like a Greek chorus, you're to come in with peals of taunting laughter. After that we must run like hell."

"That part I will play to perfection," Mr. Dinner muttered.

Walking snappily and with every indication of purpose, the three men swung up to the unsuspecting policeman and confronted him.

"Officer," said Mr. Larkin in a businesslike voice, "are you listening?"

"No," snapped the officer. "Whatta you want?"

"Officer," continued the senior partner quite distinctly, "listen well. Officer, you're a punk, and I'm going to tweak your repellent nose."

Before the policeman could recover his stunned faculties Mr. Larkin's hand shot out and affixed itself to the man's nose which he proceeded to tweak with both skill and vigor.

"Laugh," murmured Mr. Larkin to his partners. "Tauntingly."

Weird noises issued from the throats of Messrs. Owen and Dinner. They sounded more terrified than taunting, yet they served one purpose. They brought the assaulted policeman back to life and fury with a snap.

"You're a low punk, officer," Mr. Larkin assured the appalled policeman in his rather precious accents. "Try to paddle those great flat feet."

It is needless to say that the policeman did try. He tried his level best. Down the street he pounded after the flying heels of the partners. At the door of the house they paused and looked back. The officer was close at hand.

"Here we are, low punk of a policeman," called the senior partner, then ducked into the house, his companions close behind him.

"Be ready, Major!" Mr. Larkin cried, darting for the telephone. "The blow is intended to outrage more than it is to maim."

The officer did not hesitate until the resounding whack from the stuffed leather bar brought him to a full stop. As the weapon struck him across the stomach he exhaled vastly great quantities of air, then sat down on the floor. His face was working furiously, while inarticulate sounds issued from between his lips. Presently, as he pulled himself together, these sounds formed themselves into words.

"A punk, am I?" he was heard to mutter. "Holy Saint Patrick preserve us, they'll never get over this. Never. I'll tear them all to pieces. I'll torture them for years."

Mr. Dinner glanced at Mr. Owen and discovered

that he too was taking the policeman's words very much to heart. By the telephone Mr. Larkin was calmly sitting, the receiver in his hand. Slowly the officer rose from the floor and advanced into the room, his eyes alight with the fires of madness. Before he could bellow his rage, the senior partner addressed him in a voice of authority.

"Officer," he said, "you're wanted on the telephone. The Mayor's office speaking."

The officer paused and glared at the speaker.

"If this is some more monkey business," he muttered, "I'm goinna drag your insides out by their roots."

With this dire threat he seized the telephone and applied the receiver to his ear. And as he listened the red flush of his face changed to a light green.

"Donovan speaking," he began. "I've just——"

"It doesn't matter what you've just done," came the voice at the other end of the wire. "I'm speaking for the Mayor. This is Larry. The boss says you're not to lay a finger on the four gentlemen in 33 Harvest Street. There's no harm in them."

"What!" almost screamed Donovan. "No harm in them. They're dangerous maniacs, I tell you. Do you know what they did?"

"What did they do?" asked Larry, who liked to be entertained.

"They called me a punk," Donovan whispered into the telephone. "A low punk of a policeman. That's what they did."

"Well, aren't you?" asked Larry easily.

The officer gasped and strangled. Finally he collected his voice.

"And—and," he continued, "one of them tweaked my nose right in front of everybody. A mighty tweak, it was. And his accomplices laughed at me, very nastily they laughed. And that's not all. For Gord's sake, Larry, can't I do a thing? I'm that upset—all aquiver."

"What would you like to do?" inquired the voice at the other end of the line.

"Shoot 'em," replied Donovan without a moment's hesitation. "Shoot 'em in painful places."

"You can't do a thing," said Larry, "except to go back to your post. Hurry away now, Donovan, and don't keep me here all night."

With an expression of incredulity in his strained eyes the policeman put down the receiver, and regarded the occupants of the room. Coolly the partners returned his stare. The women looked sympathetic. Suddenly he uttered a wild scream and, springing from the chair, seized Mr. Dinner by the nose.

"Mayor or no Mayor," he grated, "you're going to stand for this."

Mr. Dinner stood for it with fortitude and calm.

"It didn't hurt at all," he announced to the interested gathering. "This punk cop hasn't the strength of a flea."

Donovan's lips were mumbling as he looked hatefully at the telephone. Then with a sound like a sob he staggered from the house and arrested the first citizen he saw on a charge of criminal loitering. From this point on Mr. Owen was scarcely in a condition to remember the remainder of the evening with any degree of clarity. The assault of Officer Donovan had moved him very deeply. It had addled his brain and doubled the potency of the drinks he had already consumed. The fact that an officer of the law could be so treated with impunity filled him with a sense of loss. It was like some great upheaval in nature—a fundamental change in the structure of the universe. His amazement temporarily outstripped his satisfaction.

After the crazed departure of the policeman the air was filled with the sounds of popping corks and general jubilation. Some time later he became hazily aware of a terrific battle taking place between the partners and their respective wives. He was impressed by the extreme bitterness and vitriolic quality of this brawl. They were reviling one another with recriminations of the most shocking nature, in the midst of which he fell asleep, his head on Satin's shoulder.

When he awoke the following morning, he was not in bed with one woman as he had expected, but with three, his partners' wives in the fullness of their rage having left their husbands more or less flat. On a day bed by the French windows through which the sun was streaming, Satin was sleeping with the confidence and grace of youth.

There are men who, upon finding themselves so well placed, grow both elated and grateful over their great good fortune—three women in bed and one in reserve. Mr. Owen was not one of these men. He was panic stricken and fearful. For one awful moment his heart stopped beating, then frantically leaped into action. He himself was unable to move, being wedged in between Nana and the plump person of Aggie. And while he was considering the situation with all its shocking implications, his consternation was further intensified by the inquiring scrutiny of three pairs of eyes.

"Look!" exclaimed Aggie. "There's a man in bed between us."

"I know it," was Nana's gloomy reply. "I don't have to be told when a man is in bed with me. He's the new partner."

"First drunkenness," came the sleepy voice of the Kitten, "and then dishonor. It always works out that way. Sordid, I call it."

"It's lucky," resumed Nana, "that this is an oversized bed. Otherwise we would have had no sleep at all."

"I don't even remember the name of this threefold seducer," the Kitten observed.

"It's Owen," replied Aggie. "Hector Owen."

"Mr. Owen," inquired Nana, "would you mind giving us a brief résumé of what has gone on in this bed?"

"I can't tell you," said Mr. Owen, a weary groan escaping his lips. "All I can say, ladies, is I'm shocked to the quick."

"To the what?" exclaimed the Kitten, her head popping up.

"Don't ask," replied Nana. "We don't care to know."

"Do you all remember anything?" asked Mr. Owen timidly. "No details, of course."

"I don't, worse luck," replied Aggie, "but I can draw my own conclusions."

"Oh-h!" exhaled Mr. Owen. "What have I done?"

"Use your imagination, my dear sir," said the Kitten from her side of the tremendous bed. "It is only too clear to me."

"But couldn't I have slept steadily through the night?" pleadingly asked the man.

"That would have been an insulting thing to do," observed Nana, "as well as foolhardy."

"Rather dishonor," said Aggie, "than such gross neglect."

The Kitten laughed shortly.

"No fear of that," she told them. "A man might neglect one woman, but he could hardly keep out of the way of the three of us, especially a man who bites bears and saves lives and deals in pornographic literature."

"And to think," murmured Nana, "I wanted to know if he leched."

Once More Mr. Owen groaned.

"Don't use that word," he pleaded. "It isn't a verb, anyway. People can't lech."

"Then how would you put it?" snapped Nana.

"I wouldn't even bring up the subject," Mr. Owen replied.

"He must have started over here," the Kitten reflected aloud, "and grimly worked his way across. I've just found one of his socks."

"Have you anything on, Mr. Owen?" asked Aggie, fumbling with the bedclothes.

"Don't!" cried Mr. Owen. "Don't look underneath. I'll find out for myself."

He ducked his head under the bedclothes, then immediately popped it out.

"Little," he said in a hoarse voice. "Very little."

"I'm amazed you made that concession," declared Nana. "How are we fixed for garments?"

"Not at all," replied Mr. Owen. "My God, ladies, this is terrible. I kept one of mine, at least."

"Meaning, we didn't?" inquired Nana.

"I'm very much afraid not," said Mr. Owen in a low voice. "There seems to be nothing as far as the eye can reach."

"What did you do with our clothes?" demanded Aggie.

"I don't know," replied Mr. Owen hopelessly. "I can't remember."

"That will sound good to the judge," put in the Kitten.

"What a man!" observed Nana. "What thoroughness and determination!"

"Come out of that bed at once," commanded Satin from across the room. "What are you doing in there with all those women?"

"Nothing, dear," replied Mr. Owen placatingly. "I'm doing nothing at all."

"Not now, he isn't," sarcastically commented Nana.

"Satin," called Mr. Owen nervously. "All I have left are my drawers."

"They're poor protection against the attack of three full grown women," said Satin with a dry laugh. "I'm surprised they left you with those."

"Don't blame us," the Kitten protested. "He didn't leave us a scrap—not a blessed shred."

A smothered ejaculation turned Mr. Owen's eyes to the door. The partners were standing in it, their eyes fixed on the bed.

"Heavens!" exclaimed Mr. Larkin. "He's slept with all our wives."

"Our partner," said Mr. Dinner. "Our dear brother in arms—in our dear wives' arms."

"But I don't understand it at all," protested the senior partner. "I asked him only to dinner, and here I find him in bed with every wife we have. Isn't that going too far?"

"Owen," said the Major sternly, "what are you doing in bed with our wives?"

"Not a thing, Major," answered Mr. Owen. "Just lying here talking."

"The chat after the storm," observed Satin.

"That's not the way to ask it," Mr. Larkin said to the Major. "Ask him what he has been doing in bed with our wives."

"That would make good listening," Satin commented lazily. "I like droll stories."

"Listen," said Mr. Owen earnestly. "This is God's own truth. I don't know how I got here, why I got here, or what I did when I did get here."

"I never thought a man could cram so many unchivalrous statements into one short, compact sentence," remarked the Kitten indignantly.

"Three fair names dishonored at one fell swoop," mused the senior partner. "It's almost like magic. You know, I wouldn't be a bit surprised if he had the cook and the check girl under the bed and the maid tucked in the closet."

"A new broom sweeps clean," Honor Knightly tossed in. "I'm actually proud of the man."

"I admire him a little myself," admitted Mr. Larkin. "Such industry. Such enterprise. Such dogged perseverance. I'd like to exhibit him in a show case."

"Madam," thundered the Major, "have you dishonored my name?"

"Search me," Aggie answered. "I don't believe your name was mentioned."

"It would hardly have been in good taste under the circumstances, Major," put in Mr. Larkin. "I think she was right about that."

"Mrs. Dinner," demanded the small partner, "what have you been doing all night long?"

"Trying to get some sleep," the Kitten answered sulkily.

"My God!" exclaimed Mr. Larkin. "Was he as bad as all that?"

"Ask him," said the Kitten.

"I shrink from the very suggestion of such pell-mell activity," the senior partner declared. "This room must have been a bedlam. I'd actually wring my hands if I thought it would do any good."

"We can't stand here discussing this triple adultery all day," the Major broke in. "You three women are as good as divorced already."

"Of course," agreed Mr. Larkin. "A divorce is most necessary. We can't afford to be dishonored *en masse*, especially by the same man. Owen, my boy, do hurry up and dress yourself and you, too, Miss Knightly. People buy pornography at the most amazing hours."

"Divorce and be damned," snapped Nana. "To live with you is about the same as staying single. If your face wasn't so silly I'd forget what it looks like half the time."

"It looks just the same during the other half," Mr. Larkin assured her. "We'll wait for you downstairs, Owen. Your night's work should earn a day's repose and all that, but we can't spare a man of your unflagging energy from the store. Hurry down."

As the door closed on the partners Mr. Owen, casting modesty to the wind, lunged out of the bed and wearily began to dress. Satin did likewise. The three wives watched them with interest, and then calmly went back to sleep.

## CHAPTER XXI

## *The Triple Co-respondent*

THE PARTNERS SAT AT ONE TABLE, THEIR WIVES AT ANother. Mr. Owen, the co-respondent, and Miss Knightly, the chief witness, occupied a smaller table between the two. Looking down on them from behind his elevated desk sat Judge Hampton, who knew nothing at all about the why and wherefores of divorce procedure. He had been appointed to handle the case in the absence of the official referee. The wives did not like his looks. Neither did the partners and, from the expression on Judge Hampton's face, he failed to like anyone's looks. Disgust with mankind ran eloquently through all the wrinkles of his rage-punished face. The iron-gray hair on his head seemed to bristle forward in a gesture of contempt for humanity. So light blue were his eyes that they gave the impression of being sightless. This peculiarity made the good Judge all the more disconcerting. One was never quite certain upon whom those eyes were fixed.

Never had Mr. Owen been so popular with the partners. From their table they gazed across at him with eyes overflowing with gratitude and affection. Not only had he twice saved them from extinction, but also he was now about to liberate them from their wives. In celebration of the auspicious occasion they had succeeded in getting themselves comfortably yet still competently inebriated. The pitcher on the table, supposed to contain fresh water, had been cleverly filled with gin by the crafty Mr. Dinner. In the folly of their childish confidence they had dispensed with the services of lawyers. They would conduct their own case.

Satin, motivated by some misguided impulse, had dressed herself so deeply in mourning one could only conclude she had lost an entire family. It made Mr. Owen feel partly buried merely to sit beside her.

The courtroom was packed to the rails, moral turpitude still being the greatest show on earth. Judge Hampton's head was turning in the direction of the partners. His misty eyes seemed to be weaving a curse around them.

"The air from the plaintiff's table," he said, "has an unpleasant suggestion of a barroom. It makes me blink. Charlie, turn on the fan before I begin to dance and sing." Charlie, an aged court attendant, directed the full power of an electric fan against the indignant partners. "That's better," continued the Judge, "but not, I fear, for those sitting behind them. Did not this paper tell me differently"—here the Judge raised an official looking sheet—"I would come to the conclusion that these ladies here were quite rightly endeavoring to divorce themselves from a trio of alcoholics instead of serving as defendants."

"Your honor," Mr. Larkin politely replied, "the ladies, as you inaccurately called them, have the capacity to drink this trio under the table."

"They should add another bottle," his honor retorted in a cruel voice, "and drink you under the sod."

Mr. Black, attorney for the wives, rose to his feet.

"In denying the plaintiffs' implications, your honor," said the suave Mr. Black, "my clients wish me to remind you that no fan was needed to be turned against them."

"Back in your chair," snapped Judge Hampton sharply. "The torrents of so-called perfume deluging me from your clients' table suggests another resort of vicious amusement the name of which I will leave to your imagination. Between these two tables I find myself leading a life of vicarious depravity. Such tactics will have no effect on me save an unpleasant one."

Upon the reception of this remark, derogatory to their wives, the partners broke into a volley of spontaneous clapping.

"You will either be quiet where you are," the Judge told them, "or raving in your cells. Take your choice." He paused and frowned down at the paper on his desk, then he both shook and raised his head as if suddenly coming back to life. "I did not come here," he said, "to discuss the various odors of those before me. Suffice it to say both are thoroughly obnoxious. As I understand it, Messrs. Larkin, Dinner, and Britt-Britt charge their wives with excessive adultery and on those unsavory grounds submit a plea for a divorce."

"Quite correct, your honor," replied the senior partner. "Those three women do nothing else but."

"But what?" demanded his honor.

"You know," Mr. Larkin answered significantly. "That word you used. It began with an 'a'."

"Do they now," murmured the Judge, a small spark of interest faintly illuminating his eyes as he fixed them on the wives. "Aren't they getting a little old for that sort of thing?"

"Your honor!" cried the Kitten, stung to a disregard of the good offices of Mr. Black. "We look ten years older with our clothes on."

"Madam," replied Judge Hampton, "are you arguing for or against yourself and your companions? As I interpret your remark you are deliberately attempting to convey to me the disgraceful information that when your clothes are off you look ten years younger. Just where does that lead?"

"Well, your honor," faltered the Kitten, "you know how women are."

"You mean with their clothes off?" interrupted the Judge.

"I mean," the Kitten struggled on, "no lady likes to be told she's too old to be otherwise, if you get what I mean."

"I do," put in the Judge. "You have just told me, and it hasn't done any of you a bit of good. Please sit down and cease from disgracing yourself." Again the Judge paused and passed a hand across his eyes. "Owing to the sudden calling of the case and the suspicious circumstances surrounding the whole sordid affair, it has been deemed expedient to have the three co-respondents in court. Will they now come forward?"

"Your honor," announced Mr. Larkin, "there is only one co-respondent."

"What!" exclaimed the Judge, his blue eyes swimming in his face. "Only one man for these three women? My word, has he no other occupation?"

"He's our partner," Mr. Larkin answered, a little proudly.

"Do you mean to say this frantic adulterer is still your partner?" the Judge demanded incredulously.

"We never confuse business with pleasure," was the senior partner's hypocritical retort. "The gentleman's name is Hector Owen, and he is one of the busiest and most progressive men in town."

"He must be," commented the Judge. "Will Mr. Owen please stand up? I can scarcely wait to see him."

The entire courtroom rose as Mr. Owen got to his feet to confront the Judge. Here was a man worth looking at—a man of solid achievement.

"Mr. Owen," began the Judge, "if what I hear about you is true you must be a very horrid man indeed. Who is that woman beside you? She's all in black. Did you happen to murder her husband?"

Before Mr. Owen could reply to these questions Satin's voice was heard.

"No, your honor," she announced devastatingly. "I'm only his mistress. I was there and saw it all."

"I had hoped not to veer," muttered the senior partner to his companions, "but that girl's candor is simply muscle binding."

Upon the reception of Satin's information the Judge's eyes seemed to die in his face. For a brief moment he gave the impression of a man withdrawn from life.

"Good God," he was heard to remark to the courtroom at large. "What an amazing character. What an unregenerate soul. He wrecks three homes, then drags his mistress into court. And although she saw it all they are still as thick as thieves."

At this point Judge Hampton clasped his hands and leaned across his desk. Mr. Owen received the uneasy impression he was being most disagreeably scrutinized. "Hector Owen," resumed his honor in a meditative voice, "you're not an especially powerful man and most certainly not a handsome one. I must confess, I don't understand how you get away with it. If this were a criminal court I'd greatly enjoy putting you away for life. As it is I can only ask you to confirm the charges, but, for God's sake, don't tell the story in what I can well imagine would be your own words. A few of us present still have a shred of decency left."

"Your honor," replied Mr. Owen, "I am happy to say I don't remember a thing."

"You are happy to say that, are you?" observed the Judge with biting sarcasm. "Well, I'd be ashamed to say it. Do you mean to tell me that you've grown so accustomed to your misconduct that it leaves no impression on your mind?"

"No, your honor," put in the helpful Mr. Larkin, "he doesn't mean that. Our partner was drunk at the time. You must forgive him. Also, he's been extremely busy selling pornographic literature."

Judge Hampton was seen to sway a little in his chair. His mouth opened and closed, but for a few moments no words issued therefrom.

"I have never," he got out with an effort, "I have never in my life encountered so disreputable a character in human form. He gets himself drunk, ruins a lot of women, and then pops off and sells dirty books to the general public. I'd prefer to deal with a poisoner. Owen," he suddenly thundered, "tell me when and where these several incidents took place. What period of time did they cover?"

Satin was on her feet now, standing loyally by the wretched Mr. Owen.

"Your honor," she answered for him, "it all happened at the same time and at the same place. You see, the three wives were occupying the same bed and——"

"Have you by any chance mistaken this courtroom for a stag party?" interrupted the Judge. "We don't care to hear any vile stories, if you please."

"But it's true, your honor," Satin insisted. "I was there at the time."

"Cheering him on to further endeavors, I suppose," observed the Judge icily. "Why didn't you intervene? Why didn't you raise a protesting hand?"

"I couldn't even lift a finger, your honor," the girl replied, with an engaging smile. "I was as drunk as a lord myself."

Judge Hampton closed his eyes and sat like a man frozen inanimate with pain. Presently he spoke as if from a great distance.

"Merciful heavens," he told all who cared to listen, "I'll have to go into a retreat after this case is ended. Never have I been forced to hear such demoralizing testimony. There isn't a scrap of fragrance anywhere. The indecency of it all is quite unrelieved. What were all those women doing in that one bed?"

"Well, you see," replied Satin, "the ladies were drunk too—petrified."

"It only remains now for you to tell me," said the Judge in a dead voice, "that the husbands were smoking opium in a waterfront dive, and the whole vicious circle will be complete." Here he looked scornfully upon the partners. "What I want to know is, how could so many persons and so much activity be confined to a single bed?"

"It wasn't a single bed, your honor," Mr. Larkin put in. "As a matter of fact, I had that bed especially made. It's about twice the size of a double bed."

"It must be a huge bed," his honor reflected aloud, as if picturing the object in his mind's eye.

"It's a tremendous bed, your honor," enthusiastically agreed the senior partner. "There would have been ample room for you."

The Judge started in his chair as if suddenly and mortally stung.

"What would I be doing in that bed?" he gasped.

"Seeing life," quoth Mr. Dinner with startling clarity.

At this his honor seemed to be deciding whether to burst a blood vessel or to faint dead away on his desk. Finally, after a desperate mental effort, he succeeded in pulling himself together into a compact mass of venom.

"Dinner," he said, "if I had my way you'd be warmed over in hell. As it is, if you make any more remarks you'll grow cold and stale in jail." Here the Judge turned sharply upon the three wives. "Do you or do you not deny the charges of your husbands?"

"My clients cannot answer that question, your honor," replied Mr. Black, rising. "They say they do not remember."

"This," commented the Judge bitterly, "is by all odds the most forgetful series of adulteries on record."

"If you'd been in our place," said Nana defensively, "you wouldn't have remembered either, your honor."

"Madam," rasped the Judge, "you will kindly refrain from putting me in your place. I am a judge, you must remember, of long standing."

"All the more reason for lying down in bed," Nana retorted, "and getting a little rest."

"Under the circumstances," said his honor tartly, "I'm afraid there would have been little rest for me."

"Oh, your honor!" exclaimed Nana coyly. "What a thing to say!"

The Judge looked shocked.

"I didn't mean that at all," he told her.

"Mean what, your honor?" she asked sweetly.

"Never mind," retorted the Judge. "We will drop the bed and take up other things." He turned back to the partners who, for the sake of verisimilitude, had been drinking gin like water. Mr. Dinner was now snoring gently with his head resting against the pitcher. "You gentlemen," observed the Judge, "appear to be in worse condition than when this case started. Are these divorce proceedings making you drunker? Wake that little chap up. His noises make me nervous."

Major Barney reached out and shook Mr. Dinner vigorously. The small man woke up and started to his feet.

"Are we divorced yet?" he inquired.

"No," snapped the Judge. "You're lucky you're not hung. As far as I can see, we haven't got anywhere except deeper and deeper into a morass of immorality."

"Would you like me to tell you about it, your honor?" asked the senior partner.

"Go ahead," retorted the Judge.

"Well," began Mr. Larkin, "it was this way. When we came into the room, there they were in the bed—all three of our wives, and would you believe it, your honor, I don't think they had a stitch between them. And there he was, too, plump in the same bed. Well, your honor, I almost screamed. You should have seen me veer. I had to be held to keep from spinning like a windmill. And he had on a pair of drawers—I didn't actually see the drawers, your honor, and I don't understand how he could have possibly kept them on when you come to consider everything, but he claimed he was wearing his drawers and so I let it go at that. And he was lying all squeezed up between my wife and Mr. Dinner's wife——"

"One moment," interrupted the Judge. "You seem to be enjoying this so much, perhaps you'd like to draw a picture of it."

"I could never do that, your honor," said Mr. Larkin delicately. "It wouldn't be at all nice."

"I appreciate your scruples," heavily observed Judge Hampton. "Sit down and keep quiet."

"Your honor," said Mr. Black, "one of my clients, Mrs. Larkin, to be specific, wishes me to state that her husband is not without blemish."

"I should say not," commented the Judge.

"Three weeks ago," continued Mr. Black, "he, Mr. Larkin, spent the week-end with the wife of another one of my clients, Mrs. Dinner, to be specific, at a near-by watering resort."

Mr. Dinner looked reproachfully at Mr. Larkin.

"What a thing to do," he said, then fell asleep once more against the pitcher.

The Kitten, furiously angry, sprang to her feet.

"Your honor," she cried, "the reason Nana Larkin is so sure of her ground is that she herself was stopping at the next hotel with no less a person than my shrimp of a husband, and I hope that's specific enough to suit everybody concerned."

It was difficult to judge whether the senior partner looked more surprised than amused. He aroused the slumbering Dinner and shook his limp hand.

"That makes us even," Mr. Larkin said.

Aggie, the wife of the Major, was now confronting the shocked and astounded Judge.

"Your honor," she proclaimed, "as you can easily see for yourself, I am not exactly a cripple. I don't intend to be left out in the cold. I, myself, have spent some pleasant week-ends with both Mr. Larkin and Mr. Dinner. They are altogether different when they're not with their wives. And as for my own husband—my word! He and Nana Larkin have been just like that for years."

Before the shrinking eyes of the Judge she held up two fingers, eloquently pressed together. Even the spectators in the courtroom were too stunned by this unedifying exposé of these extra-marital activities to create the usual buzz of satisfaction and surprise. Many of them were either too afraid or too well bred to look at the Judge.

"Tell that woman to sit down," he croaked. "I don't want to hear any more. Who was it mentioned veering? Well, I'm doing a lot of that myself. Of all the licentious groups this one wins the palm!"

Judge Hampton's voice drifted away. He sank back in his chair and mopped his brow with a large tan handkerchief. The partners were exchanging apologetic glances. Satin and Mr. Owen smiled at them encouragingly. Mr. Larkin waved a debonair hand and raised his glass. When he had finished drinking he passed the glass to the Major, who in turn quaffed deeply, then passed it on to Mr. Dinner. Apparently it would take something far more serious than mutual infidelity to break up the *entente cordiale*. Suddenly Judge Hampton sat forward in his chair. The attorney for the wives received the chilly impression that he was under the observation of those faint blue eyes.

"Go on, Mr. Black," came the spiteful voice of the Judge. "Why don't you say it?"

"Say what, your honor?"

"That at one time or another you have spent week-ends with all these ladies," replied the Judge. "That would bring in everyone involved in this disreputable case except myself. How those women must look forward to Saturdays."

"Unfortunately, your honor," said Mr. Black with a smooth smile, "my relations with my clients have been purely professional."

At the introduction of the word purely Judge Hampton laughed shortly. To some of the spectators the jurist sounded common; to others, merely crazed.

"The criminal immorality of this case almost frightens me," he said. "Here we have three husbands suing their respective wives for divorce. What do we find? A round robin of infidelity—a frantic scramble of corruption. No sooner have they unpacked their bags after one vicious week-end, than they begin repacking them again to pop off on another one with the wife of one of their dearest friends. They're partners, no less. Look at them. They look like a glee club. Probably comparing notes. And why, may I ask, why did they deem it necessary to drag the man Owen and his mistress into court? Each one of those husbands can serve as a co-respondent for the other two. Each one of the wives can act in the same disgusting capacity."

Mr. Larkin was on his feet. His face was flushed from gin, and his eyes were glittering.

"Judge," he said, "we thought you would like to see him. You know, it is rather unusual. My other two partners and myself may have been a trifle informal as regards each other's wives, but Mr. Owen was simply epic. He got all three of them. Imagine! All three. At the same time and in the same place, at that. And with his avowed mistress present. I wouldn't have believed it possible if I hadn't seen him with my own two eyes. The man should run for office. I'd vote for——"

"Will you please stop going on like that," interrupted Judge Hampton. "Someone might get the impression you knew me personally. I feel slightly tainted to be found in the same courtroom with you and your wives and your partners. Pass that pitcher up here."

Mr. Larkin obediently gave the pitcher to the Judge together with the glass. His honor poured and drank, coughed and drank again.

"Even the water you drink is different," he commented. "Is my face flushed?"

"It's just beginning," replied Mr. Larkin. "That's powerful water, your honor."

"The strongest I ever drank," agreed the Judge. "Hope I don't fall in the pitcher. Would you mind telling me how long you and your partners have been married to these women?"

"Well, your honor," replied Mr. Larkin somewhat uneasily, "properly speaking, we never exactly married them—not legally, we didn't. We forgot to tell you that. But they've been sticking round for a long time now. Nearly ten years."

"Do you mean to say," cried the Judge, leaning incredulously over the desk, "that the three of you are trying to get a divorce from women you haven't even married?"

"Judge Hampton," called Major Barney, "if you can't exactly give us a divorce, couldn't you help us to get rid of them? These women are awful. We want some more."

As the Judge was collapsing in his chair another interruption called him back to life. No less a person than Madame Gloria had burst through the rails.

"Your honor," she cried, pointing at the startled Mr. Owen, "I want to sue that man for breach of promise. I gave myself to him for life and he hasn't even called to get me."

"Do you mean," asked the Judge in a weak voice, "he actually promised to marry you?"

"Oh, no!" exclaimed Madame Gloria as if shocked

at the suggestion. "Nothing as stupid as that. I never marry, your honor, I just get kept."

A wild scream rang through the court as the Judge tottered towards his chambers.

"I want to be alone," he mumbled. "Send everybody away and tell them never to come back, especially those partners."

In a compact and not unfriendly mass, wives, husbands, the co-respondent, Owen, with his publicly acknowledged mistress, and even Madame Gloria made their way to the street. As if by common consent they continued across the broad thoroughfare to the nearest café. Here, after much confusion, tables were arranged to accommodate the large party.

"What are we celebrating?" asked Mr. Owen as the senior partner ordered wine in lavish quantities.

"Our reunion," replied Mr. Larkin, smiling across at Nana.

"If we want to get rid of these women," observed Mr. Dinner, "I guess we'll have to marry them first."

"Oh, shucks," said the Major indulgently. "Let them stick around. They're not such bad women."

## CHAPTER XXII

### Fire and Farewell

MR. OWEN WAS AWAKENED AT MIDNIGHT BY THE dream-shattering jangle of the telephone. He was just as well pleased, for in his current dream the unclad wives of his partners had been chasing him down the aisles of the courtroom into the arms of Madame Gloria, hiding coyly behind a whale. Reaching across a protesting Satin, he hauled the instrument to him.

"I've a big surprise for you," came the casual voice of the senior partner. "The store is burning up, or down, or whichever way stores burn. It really doesn't matter—the shop and all that's in it are heavily overinsured."

"Are you going down?" asked Mr. Owen.

"I thought I would," replied Mr. Larkin. "People might think it unnatural not to watch one's own store burn down. There's a lot of good grog in my office I'd like to get out."

"Are you veering any?" Mr. Owen inquired, knowing it would please his partner.

"Stupendously," cried Mr. Larkin. "I'm simply a dance of flames."

"Then I'll meet you at the store."

Mr. Owen had hardly hung up the receiver when the bell rang again.

"What do you know?" came the voice of Mr. Dinner. "The store is on fire. Isn't that a laugh?"

"Are you going?" asked Mr. Owen.

"Sure," said the voice of the little man. "Have to carry bottles. They belong to his nibs. He'd never stop veering if the fire got them. You know, Owen, I sometimes think he's mad."

"No!" exclaimed Mr. Owen. "You surprise me. See you at the fire."

He hung up, then once more lifted the receiver as the bell gave tongue.

"This is Major Barney Britt-Britt speaking," came the heavy voice of the Major. "Is this Mr. Owen? It is? Fine! Do you want to see a good fire, Owen?"

Mr. Owen did.

"Well, come on down to the store," continued the Major, "and you'll see a top-notch fire. Of course, inasmuch as we own the store, we'd get first-rate places."

"I'll be right down," said Mr. Owen.

"Excellent," replied the Major. "Thought you might like to see it. Don't get a good fire often. Then there's some liquor in the senior's office that might bear looking into. The rest doesn't matter. The whole damn place is criminally overinsured."

"The store is going up in smoke," Mr. Owen announced to Satin, who was flinging on her clothes, "and all those three maniacs care about is their private supply of grog."

"That proves to me," quoth Miss Honor Knightly, snapping on her garters with a businesslike click, "that their minds are in the right place. More people should be like them. Why not salvage the gay things of life instead of casting about for gloom? There's plenty of that as it is."

Leaving the hotel they hurried to the store and succeeded in gaining entrance through Mr. Larkin's private office. Standing before a huge locker the senior partner and Major Barney were frantically extracting bottles.

"Good-evening," called Mr. Larkin. "The fire is all inside. Flames no end. An inspiring sight." He turned back to the locker. "Major, should we drink this liquor now or carry it away? It might be easier to drink it."

Opening the door to the huge emporium, Satin and Mr. Owen hastened through. Immediately a curtain of flames rolled down and cut off their retreat. Columns of fire and smoke were rising and writhing down the full length of the vast hall. The galleries were filled with heavy clouds. The crackling was so intense that the place seemed full of machine guns. And above the sound of crackling roared the voice of fire rampant.

Glancing back into the senior partner's private office they caught a glimpse of the three charming gentlemen in the act of removing bottles from their lips.

"We'll build a bigger and better store," cried Mr. Larkin, "on the money we'll make from this jolly old conflagration."

A low, ragged wall of flame ran swiftly across the floor, driving Satin and Mr. Owen before it. At the far end of the hall they were stopped by a partition.

"Doesn't look so good," panted Mr. Owen. "I might bite bears and all that, but I can't swallow flames."

"I feel sorry as hell for the devil," she said, "if he has to stand for much of this sort of stuff."

Mr. Owen put a hand behind him, then thrilled as it touched a knob.

"Quick!" he called to Satin. "Come with me."

For a moment the girl hesitated, and Mr. Owen was

surprised to see a look of unsuspected tenderness creep into her eyes. Then he opened the door and followed Satin back into the rain. And as an "L" train thundered overhead all that lay behind him seemed to flicker and die out. Dimly, but with desperate eagerness, he tried to recapture something, if only a little, of the past—the past behind the door. The other past was now his present. Once more he was plunged back into it. Raindrops splattered his hot face as he gazed down the glittering reaches of Sixth Avenue. Then he turned to the girl in the doorway, and, like a man still in a dream, he looked deep into her eyes as his lips tried to form a word.

"Don't you even remember my name?" she asked in a low, strained voice.

"Satin," he muttered, taking her face between his hands. "Satin. I remember. Is it all over now—everything? What has ended?"

Honor Knightly nodded.

"Everything," she answered. "We're through, the pair of us."

He dropped his hands from her smooth, fresh face and fumbled in his pockets. His left hand encountered a key. He drew it out and looked at it, the key to his house. Then he looked down at the quiet figure beside him.

"Somehow I know you've been wonderful to me," he said haltingly. "I don't know how to tell you about it all. I'll remember when I begin again—when I get back home." He paused and repeated the word. "Home," he muttered. "All married and everything. I'll be using the 'L' in the morning—just like old times."

Satin held out her hand.

"If you're okay now," she told him. "I'll have to let you go."

"I'm all okay," he said in a flat voice. "Much too okay."

"It's good-bye, then," said Satin, the torturing words scarcely audible. "Don't ever grow too respectable again. I can't help feeling you're still partly mine."

As Mr. Owen stepped out of the doorway back into the rain he was wondering to himself if her lips had brushed his cheek. His old inhibitions had conventionalized his own farewell.

Slowly he moved down the street, his shoulders gradually drooping as he walked. Everything was back with him now—every grim little detail of his days—Lulu, Mal Summers, the office, the threat of business extinction. Satin. Who was Satin? Satin was far behind. New York had swallowed her as soon it would swallow him. He himself swallowed several times. It was no easy matter. How familiar everything was. He wanted to get away. He stopped and gazed into the window of a florist shop. He tried to ease his mind by concentrating on the flowers. Slowly he lowered his head. The flowers grew dim, their color draining out.

From behind came the quick tattoo of flying heels. Small firm hands took hold of him and turned him roughly about. Then arms were around his neck.

"You poor lost soul," he heard her saying. "You poor lost soul. Did you think I'd let you go? God, what a man, what a nice, clean little man! And just because he's married he shakes hands and says good-bye."

"What happened to me?" asked Hector Owen some moments later as they crossed Washington Square in the direction of his house.

"You've been on a mental binge," said Satin. "I'll give you the details later. I picked you up in a department store. You were dazed among a lot of books. Ever since then you've been mine to take care of—and you still are. Keep that before your eyes."

"There seem to have been so many things," he replied, "but a curtain lies between. I can't get them back. Were they all batty, Satin."

"Not all," the girl told him. "Some of them were disrepeatably real—the best ones. At other times I didn't know where your mind was straying. People get like that, then come back with a snap. There's some sort of a name for it, I believe."

"I came back with you," he said; then, self-consciously, "Do you think I'm so old, Satin?"

"If you must get personal," said Miss Knightly primly, "there were times when you acted so young I wouldn't like to mention them. You were a mere babe in my arms."

"Don't," replied Mr. Owen.

He opened the door to his apartment. The place lay in darkness. He must go and inform Lulu he was going away for good. She would probably wake the neighbors with her cheering. At the door of the bedroom he paused. Out of the darkness a man spoke to him. Mr Owen shuddered.

"Is that you, honey-bunch?" asked the man.

Mr. Owen felt himself mortally insulted.

"Who the hell are you calling honey-bunch?" he growled snapping on the lights. "I'm honey-bunch's husband."

As the lights flooded the room Lulu, clad in a kimono, came in through another door. There was a song on her lips and a bottle of gin in her hand. When she saw Mr. Owen the song fell flat and she almost dropped the gin.

"I—I thought you were dead or something," said the startled lady.

"It turned out to be something," Mr Owen informed her. "Is this gentleman the chief mourner?"

The gentleman might have liked that bed once, but now he was looking as if he never wanted to see it again.

"No," faltered Lulu. "When he arrived from Europe he came here looking for you."

"I see," murmured Mr. Owen. "Did he think I was lost in the sheets, perhaps?"

Before Lulu could come back at this Satin popped her head into the room.

"Good God!" cried the man in bed. "That girl is my sister."

"Two good Gods to your one," replied Mr. Owen. "That woman is my wife. Also, I own the bed."

"There's something almost incestuous about all this talk," Satin observed coolly.

"I've been looking all over for you," continued the man in an injured voice. "You shouldn't run off like that, Honor, and let the estate go hang. We wanted to change its management."

"Over my dead body," said Satin. "I'm very fond of its management. And so for you, Tom Knightly, isn't it bad enough to ruin a man's home without wrecking his business?"

Tom Knightly grinned.

"Forget it," he said lazily. "Forget it. You fix things up, kid. I mean no harm. Just a good time Daddy."

But Hector Owen heard none of this. He was in another room, cramming some clothes into a bag. This finished, he walked to the window and looked out across the park. So many things happened, he thought, and when they did happen you really were not as shocked as you had thought you were going to be. Satin came up behind him and slipped her hand into his.

"Isn't it disgraceful?" he asked her.

"What is?" she asked him.

"All of us," he exclaimed.

"Nonsense!" exclaimed the girl. "It merely goes to show that after all two wrongs can make it right."

A few minutes later, when Mr. Owen carried his bag away from his home, everyone felt good about it.

At the curb he called to a taxi. The cab drew up.

"Where to?" asked the driver.

Mr. Owen was much too busy to answer. He had never been clever with taxicab doors. He suspected a conspiracy.

"Just start in driving," the girl sang out. "And keep on going. We might hire you for life."

"I hate taxi doors," Mr. Owen explained in an aggrieved voice. "Cabs should be built without any. They deliberately pick me out not to open for. They always stick, these doors."

"And so do I," said Satin, her bad eyes glowing with all sorts of uncensored enticements.

Mr. Owen, to say the least, was most pleasantly impressed. Scarcely a moment later so was Satin. Had she been a nicer girl, a wee bit more conventional and a little less impulsive, she might even have been shocked.

For Hector Owen's inhibitions had passed beyond recall.

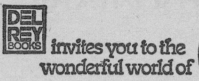

DEL REY BOOKS invites you to the wonderful world of Oz